About the author

From as early as I can remember the fascination of the written word ran through my veins.

I do not remember how I came by a copy of Kitty Hart's, *I am alive*, a book I read many times. Then later, I encountered the brilliance of Khaled Hosseini.

Many years passed until life finally slowed and allowed me to write my own book. I do not compare it in any way to my literary heroes' work, but I am pleased to have finished it and hope that in some way you enjoy it.

ETERNAL VICTIM

Ed Adams

ETERNAL VICTIM

Vanguard Press

VANGUARD PAPERBACK

© Copyright 2021
Ed Adams

A CIP catalogue record for this title is
available from the British Library.

ISBN 978 1 78465 926 4

*Vanguard Press is an imprint of
Pegasus Elliot MacKenzie Publishers Ltd.*
www.pegasuspublishers.com

First Published in 2021

**Vanguard Press
Sheraton House Castle Park
Cambridge England**

Printed & Bound in Great Britain

Dedication

To Michael, Chris, David, Grace and Logan. The best things in my life.

Acknowledgements

Michael Adams. For his ideas and imagination.

Prologue
December 31st, 1999

A private ground floor elevator activated by palm print was the only access to the suite of offices and the apartment Jason Warren called home. The Bell 430, permanently stationed on the helipad would get him away fast, should the need arise. The photo-reactive glass overlooking the river was bulletproof and the antique bookshelves concealed a reinforced panic room.

It was 6.30 p.m. on New Year's Eve, the beginning of a new millennium. Jason was dressed in a Dormeuil suit, crisp starched white shirt, bowtie and two-thousand-pound Italian leather shoes. He glanced up and caught his reflection in the solid-gold-framed mirror.

Jason Warren didn't believe in luck. To him it was simply a short-term variable which evened out with time. Walking across a motorway with a blindfold on and getting hit by a truck wasn't bad luck, it was stupid. Being in the right place at the right time wasn't good luck, it was good planning. That was his philosophy, and following that thought, he'd decided he wouldn't be flying anywhere tonight. Tonight, December 31st at midnight, was the moment the computer whizz-kids were predicting total computer apocalypse, nuclear power stations in meltdown and planes tumbling from the sky. He laughed at the hysteria, the panic, the threat of computer Armageddon. He was sure a simple change in two digits would not have a substantial impact on him. This wasn't his bank account, after all.

He walked to the desk and picked up a small gold embossed envelope, opened it and took out two tickets you couldn't buy to the place everyone wanted to be. Life could not be better. This was his home now, far away from the streets of London's East End. It was different here, life was cheaper, the stakes higher. This was the new frontier. Here you didn't talk hundreds of thousands of pounds, you talked millions.

He placed the tickets in his inside breast pocket and looked through the window. Watching the cars speed by brought back memories of his father and the car showroom on Barking Road. What a playground it had been for a kid of four! On the top floor, a long wooden table sat in the middle of an immense oblong room. His chair, the biggest of the dark, heavy chairs, loomed at one end, and there he would sit, like the king of an enormous empire. Important people came and went, waiting in line for his advice and commands. A click of his fingers summoned imaginary servants who appeared from nowhere, eager to please their lord and master.

The lessons learnt then would go on to sculpt his character and personality, subtle suggestions growing like embryos as the years passed. No normal concepts, just the darker seeds of life's shadowlands, where money distorts, power corrupts, friends can be bought and enemies converted, but where, ultimately, money rules and only the strongest rise to the top.

This was all true, but time had twisted the memory. It was his father, Mickey Warren, who sat in the big chair, and by Mickey's side a man who made the impossible seem likely, a man who would teach him as much, if not more than his father. That man was Harry Fleet.

For a moment, Jason was back in the big room, looking up at his father and tugging his trouser leg. "Dad, why do these people come here all the time?"

Harry Fleet stepped forward and picked him up. The smell of his aftershave and the warmth of his body always made him feel good. "Jason, your dad and I are two of the musketeers, and you are the third. These people work for us."

That was his cue to wriggle out of Harry's arms and run over to the heavy metal safe. On top, never there long enough to gather dust, sat the first story he ever heard. He grabbed the worn copy of Dumas' famous novel. "Can you read to me, please, Uncle Harry?" No matter what Harry was doing, he would stop, open the book at the bookmark and read a few pages, recharging Jason's fertile young mind for his next adventure.

He smiled at the thought of those innocent childhood days, although looking back, years later, with the cynical perspective of an adult, he saw clearly that he was being groomed to one day join the family business.

He looked out through the tinted glass, powdered with a light covering of fresh snow, to the murky river beyond. He did not see the twinkling lights of the riverboat. In his mind he was still a small child dancing around the dark oak table with his sword in hand as he vanquished the evildoers.

PART ONE
1961

Canning Town, London

The three-storey red-brick building rose above the grimy terraced houses lapping at its feet, dominating the landscape. It was lunchtime, and Mickey Warren stood on the elegant curve of the time-worn Victorian stairs of Star Lane School. He was distracted by the sight of a large brown rat, which momentarily looked at him before scurrying into a broken drain.

Mickey loved school. Not because he wanted to learn, but because it was giving him his first opportunity to make some money. Like a praying mantis, he was strategically placed, ready to accept the next offering. His victim would not see him until it turned the corner, by which time it would be too late.

Mickey grinned as Tommy Bednar, his favourite plaything, came into view. Tommy's head was down; it was always down, as though by not looking ahead he would not have to face what was in front of him. Mickey had trained him well and made his walk from the classroom to the dinner hall, a walk of fear. Mickey knew if Tommy Bednar could wish for one thing, it would be an invisibility cloak, but until that day came, Mickey would continue with the daily enjoyment of humiliating him.

Tommy Bednar's big mistake, and the reason for his daily persecution, was giving the answer to a question Mickey could not. He'd made him look stupid in front of the whole class and that was a crime, a big one in Mickey's eyes, and he was determined the clever little bastard would pay for his moment of cheek.

The colour drained from the boy's face as he turned the corner and saw the smirking face of Mickey Warren.

"Watch out, Bednar, you clumsy little bastard. You almost touched me."

"Sorry Mickey, I didn't see you there."

Tommy tried to carry on walking. He should have known better. Mickey grabbed his arm. "Where do you think you're going, scum? What have you got for me?"

He had hoped to avoid Mickey today, but had failed, again. Mickey took pride in the dark circles beneath the other boy's eyes, knowing fear invaded his sleep and plagued his day.

"I haven't got anything, Mickey, honest."

Mickey smirked, seeing the rising panic turn into abject fear on the trembling face in front of him. "I know you're lying Bednar, give me what's mine you cockroach. I'm getting sick of this game of yours, where you don't give me what's mine." He grinned, watching the other boy's tear-filled eyes sink in a show of submission. Tommy Bednar reached into his pocket and held out his hand. Mickey snatched the coins and looked at them, then dropped a coin on the floor.

"Pick it up."

Mickey was aware of the other classmates passing them, seeing the pleading eyes of the broken boy in front of them. None would stop and intervene. They knew better. If it was not Tommy Bednar being terrorised, it could be them, so, quickened their pace as they walked by.

"Hurry up, Bednar, I haven't got all day," said Mickey.

As he bent down to pick up the coin, the thought of kicking him entered Mickey's head. He drew his foot back, but Tommy Bednar had learned to move swiftly and today would avoid the sharp end of Mickey's boot. Quivering fingers placed the coin into the waiting hand.

"This is a lot more than normal, Bednar. Have you been holding out on me? Because now I'm going to want the same every day."

"It's my mum's birthday, I was going to get her a present in the shop after school."

Mickey sneered at him. "Come here, Bednar, I want to tell you something." He grabbed his shirt and moved his mouth close to Tommy's ear, thinking for a moment to take a chunk out of it with his teeth. He felt him trembling in his hands and it gave him the feeling he loved most, power. "Do you know why you don't have a dad, Bednar? It's because he looked at you when you were born and you were so fucking ugly, he left. They should have kept the afterbirth and thrown you away, because you're a freak, Bednar, a freak."

Mickey watched the boy close his eyes and keep them shut tight. Then pulled back his fist and hit him hard in the stomach. "Look me in the eye, Bednar," he hissed.

Tommy lifted his head, unable to hold back the tears. Mickey gathered the spit in his mouth and spat at the ashen face in front of him, the saliva ran down Tommy's forehead and into his eyes. "You piece of shit, Bednar, go on, fuck off, and not a word." He watched his victim walk away, wiping the mixture of tears and phlegm from his face with his shirt sleeve. Mickey knew Tommy hated him, but like everyone else, was too scared to do anything about it.

Mickey had learned early, the easiest way to make money, was to take it from someone. Work was for mugs.

A few years later

Mickey closed the front door of the two-up two down terraced house in Ordnance Road and began the short walk to Rathbone Market. He had some business to sort out with a liberty taker who was not getting the message, and that was annoying him. He'd lain awake waiting for the sun to come up and the wait had further annoyed him. A spot of terror was in the offing, and he was in the mood for some fun.

"Who is this cheeky little bastard not to pay me?" he muttered to himself, walking past Caters', the supermarket, and headed straight for Bert Broadman's market stall. The old man's posture changed, realising Mickey was approaching. It had been a bad week. Business was quiet, mainly due to Mickey, warning people off from getting their meat from him.

"I hear you've been having a bit more trouble, Bert. You know I can sort it for you, don't you? I don't understand why you don't give me what's mine. The problem is, you're making me look like a mug. Do you think I'm a mug? You're running out of chances. Have you read that advertising shit above your head, 'Ask today, here tomorrow'? Well, I'm not asking, I'm telling. You're finished old man, unless you pay me."

Mickey had been developing a new menacing stare, one you could only get by practising in front of a mirror for hours. It amused him to see the sudden look of terror on people's faces when he gave them 'the look'. Bert Broadman was the only trader in the market not to have signed up for Mickey's 'peace of mind' protection scheme. He had done his homework on Broadman, a man known to be a hard worker, a family man, who cared about his customers. There was also a rumour he was ill and did not have long left. All the more important, Mickey thought, to get what he could out of the old man before he kicked the bucket.

He watched him gather his courage, and then struggle to speak.

"I fought the Germans in the war, they didn't beat me, and you won't either."

"Really, Bert, you are funny. I heard you ran away at the first sign of trouble. I've been looking forward to seeing you today, and I think you're forgetting whose market this is. I don't give a fuck about those Germans and your boring war hero stories. I'll be back tomorrow, have a good sleep."

Mickey picked up a few joints of meat. "This will do for today." He laughed, dragged some phlegm from his throat and spat into Bert's face. The old man wiped the spit from his eyes but said nothing.

Mickey laughed again. "You old bastard, you're running out of chances, in fact maybe you already have." He turned and left, knowing, it would not be long before the stubborn old man would break, one way or another.

The next morning the sun finally won its battle to break through the mist and haze, as Bert Broadman drove through the near empty streets from Smithfield Market. It was Friday and usually a good day for business, but he had the look of a man with a heavy heart and an uneasy feeling about what the day would bring. He looked across at his son sitting in the passenger seat.

"What's that smoke, Dad?" asked Bernie.

Bert looked across to see a tall plume of smoke rising into the air, playing in the light morning breeze. The dark shadow curled higher and higher, growing ever larger, now dancing with the clouds. He tasted bile in his throat. The thought in his head had turned into a thin layer of sweat on his forehead. Turning into the market, he saw a fire-fighter dousing the last of the charred wooden slats that had been his market stall.

Bert looked into his son's eyes, eyes that did not understand what they were seeing. "I'm sorry you had to see this, son. That was all we had."

He tried to find some words to comfort his son and ease the forlorn look on his face, but no words came. He coughed, a long racking cough. The cancer eating away at his lungs reminded him of the futility of his life. He hadn't found the strength to tell his wife about the cancer. How could he now, what was left in life for them?

Bernie Broadman looked at his father. "We'll think of something, Dad."

Bert Broadman fought against the tightness in his chest, a crushing tightness that these days never seemed to go away, not sure if it was the cancer, or the omnipresent Mickey Warren.

"Come on, son, let's go home." He looked across to see Mickey Warren smiling at them.

"Well, there's a bit of luck Bert, you don't have to pay me now, keep your money."

Bernie Broadman woke early, and after helping himself to some cereal, wandered into the living room to put the radio on. The sight in front of him stopped him in his tracks, the cereal bowl crashed to the floor. His father hung suspended a foot above the carpet, swaying very gently back and forth, a rope tight against his neck. His eyes were bulging and looking upwards, as though pleading to the God in heaven who had deserted him. Something was dripping onto a sodden patch on the carpet — urine.

His father looked as though he'd prepared for a normal day. A half-eaten breakfast lay on the table, and he was dressed in his normal butcher's overalls, freshly laundered as always. On the table lay a single sheet of paper. He recognised his father's handwriting.

Mickey sat in the Jubilee Cafe eating his 'free' breakfast. 'Smiley' Rinker bounced into the cafe, not smiling for once. "Mickey, have you heard? Old man Broadman's topped himself, hung himself in his living room, poor man. His boy found him."

"That selfish old bastard owed me money, Smiley, so I'm out of pocket. Don't be worrying about an old war criminal like him. Anyone who kills himself is a coward. Only thinking about their own miserable lives, never thinking about the people they leave behind, and of course the people they owe money to. You don't think the old git, left anything for me in his will, do you? Anyway, it's my birthday today, so stop annoying me with your hard luck stories. Go on, fuck off before you put me in a bad mood."

Smiley Rinker's face turned three shades lighter. "Sorry, Mickey, I didn't mean to upset you, mate. I'll be going then. Happy birthday." He turned to leave, knocking over a chair as he rushed by it. Mickey smiled, luxuriating in his power.

Mickey was pleased with his handiwork. That will teach any cheeky fuckers to mess with me, maybe someone should die on all my birthdays. The thought appealed to him. Mickey's tentacles of evil were spreading, people were looking at him with a growing respect and fear. He was on the up, and like everyone else, knew it. He decided to put in an extra-long session at the gym.

Mickey Warren wasn't a lost soul, or a victim of the East End's grinding poverty. He was Mickey Warren, serial offender, all round prize bastard, scary as, and hard as nails. The only way to beat him was to kill him. He was in the fear business and wanted to be the King. Mickey's scams worked because he knew. You only had to hurt a few. Fear would do the rest.

As a child, Harry Fleet had no idea that one day he would become a pioneer in the importation of medicinal herbs into England, the distributor of barbiturates for recreational use, and the purveyor of mind-altering LSD to cheer the dull lives of the masses. He would also be responsible for covering the streets of London with a fine layer of snow, blow, Charlie or whatever the street name was for it at the time. At the same time, evolving into a libertine, devoid of moral constraints, not seeking out pleasure, but becoming its epicentre. His body, the vehicle to carry him to his chosen pleasure zones. "Create the environment," he would say, and that's exactly what he did. But that perhaps is jumping slightly ahead.

Poplar in the East End of London, or the Manor of Popelar as it was called in earlier times, started as a small hamlet linking the villages of Limehouse and Blackwell. That sounds quite pleasant, but by 1935, when Harry Fleet was born, things had changed. He was the third eldest in a family of ten children. The family patriarch, a docker, stood six foot four, his drinking had become local legend, taking half the Poplar cops to restrain him, which, unfortunately for the Fleet family, was most days. Harry had a slim, elegant figure and the finer features of his Romany Gypsy mother. His face was attractively androgynous.

A fireman held Harry's small hand and led him down the smoke-filled stairs. Minute specks formed clouds of pungent smoke, his face and hands covered in small smudges made by his futile efforts to snuff out the latest in a long line of experiments. Just above his left eye, a fast-forming lump marked the fall from the table he'd clambered up to set fire to the curtains. Harry wasn't malicious, he was just curious.

Three days later, with one foot on the memorial on the corner of the High Street, Harry was looking at the drab, grimy, red-bricked Poplar buildings. The rain had begun to fall in heavy sheets as he felt the tugging of his mother's hand. "Come on Harry, this rain will be the death of us."

"Mum, these buildings are so ugly. They could do with knocking down and starting again."

She looked at her young son. "Come on, Harry, and don't you be getting any ideas."

A week later, German bombs began to fall. He wondered if it was somehow all his fault and promised to be more careful about the things he wished for, especially on seeing what was left of the body of his neighbour, Mrs Gunter. He picked up an arm and thought how strange it looked. A gnarly stub of bone protruded where her elbow used to be.

It wasn't long before a new word was being heard around the breakfast table, "evacuation", or as his mother had begun to call it, the great adventure. If that was so, he thought, why had she cried on giving him the news, the day had finally arrived?

The steam from the train rushed past, high above his window as he waved goodbye to his mother, who was crying again. He looked down at the battered brown leather suitcase, full of sandwiches, apples and even some chocolate, a few clothes, and the most interesting thing of all, a gas mask. The label pinned to his coat had his name, address and a word he didn't understand, 'Cricklade'.

As the small, rickety horse-drawn cart reached the brow of Blunsdon Hill, the tower of St Sampson's Church came into view, and over the next hour, grew in size, until finally it towered above him. Jumping off, rewarded him with a painful ankle as he landed. Hobbling over to a huge door, and standing on top of his suitcase, he reached up to a heavy iron knocker, lifted it and let it fall on the thick wood. The loudness of the metal on wood surprised him.

The door opened, creaking as it moved, and a giant slowly appeared before him. The thunderous voice seemed to shake the leaves on the trees. "Harry Fleet! Come in, you must be hungry."

The promise of food instantly endeared the rather scary, loud giant to him. It seemed this giant was a gentle one, which pleased Harry no end.

The next morning, they set off on an adventure to the small river at the end of the High Street. Harry jumped into the river and fished for sticklebacks with a small net. He threw stones, watching them skate along, before disappearing to the bottom of the gently flowing water.

"What's that river called?" he asked the housekeeper and vicar later at dinner.

"It's called the Thames, Harry."

Harry looked puzzled. "We've got a river called the Thames where I live, but it's a lot bigger." They burst out laughing, he didn't know why. They were strange people here, and they didn't speak right either. It was a land of gentle, happy giants, but more important in Harry's mind was the abundance of food.

The day arrived when the last of the bombs had fallen on London and it was time to return to the rubble that was now Poplar and back to Russell Road School. Harry worked hard and a decade later became the first East Ender to go to Oxford University. Well, that was his story, and was sticking to it.

Experiments don't always go according to plan, and the board of governors were now being strangely rewarded for their generosity in giving Harry Fleet a fully funded bursary. There was a problem, and the Dean decided something must be done about it.

"Now, Fleet, I have arranged some elocution lessons for you," he said. "We really need to get you speaking English." He wiped some crumbs from his mouth with a starched white monogrammed napkin. "The problem is, Fleet, we are finding it rather difficult to understand a single word you say, and you will get nowhere in this world speaking in what is as good as a foreign language. How you got through the interviews I shall never know."

The elocution lessons were not to be a solitary affair. He was joined by Howard, a tall rakish lad from the Welsh Valleys. Harry had just met the man who would start him on the path of his future career.

"Harry, I saw you smoking some hash yesterday. Could you get me some?"

"Of course. How much would you like?" he replied.

"Harry, bach, I will have as much as you can get for me, as long as the price is right. I can sell whatever you can get."

"OK, Howard, leave it with me."

The next morning Harry boarded the train to London, thinking, if there was a market for drugs, then why wouldn't he also get in on the game. After spending a few hours by the river, he walked into the Drum and Whistle on the Kings Road. Lenny 'Bagels' Bernstein sat at the bar, finishing his drink, then pouring himself another from his own personal bottle of Dimple Whisky. Lenny was the Brick Lane bagel king, and business was booming. Everyone loved bagels, but not so many as would account for the four-storey house in Cheyne Walk with its uninterrupted view of the river.

"My boy, what is so urgent you come and see me so soon? Have they kicked you out already? I will be very disappointed if that's the case?"

Harry looked at the man who, three years before, had given him his first job selling bagels.

"Actually, Mr Bernstein, I would like some more bagels."

"Bagels?" Lenny looked at him. "How many bagels, Harry?"

Harry looked down at the suitcase at his feet and pointed to it. Lenny smiled. "I guess you haven't got the money to pay for them?"

"Not at the moment, Mr Bernstein."

"OK, I know you won't let me down."

Harry sat by the window on the train back to Oxford, his head turned towards the rolling countryside, but saw none of it. He was thinking about all the ways to spend his new income stream.

A headquarters for his new business enterprise was needed, and what better than the student union bar. Sitting at the bar, swaying gently in a non-existent breeze, was the man Harry would choose to be his quartermaster, Jules Danby. He was a bright sitar-playing extrovert, with an odd view of his place in the universe. In Harry's mind therefore, ideal for the key position of storing and distributing Harry's hash. Jules would provide a layer of protection between him and a very uncomfortable meeting with the Dean. Harry knew, one small mistake could bring his world crashing down.

Within a year, Harry had moved half a ton of the finest hash and a shedload of other desirables. Firmly believing, not just in the theory of pharmacology but also the practice. What was the point of having a sports car if you didn't drive it? He was a blend of history and the future, a man never quite content with the period, trying the latest drug between hits of snuff and drags on cigarettes. Very early on, deciding his mouth was for breathing, freeing up his nose for the sole purpose of snorting his favourite drug — cocaine.

Chapter 1
July 1988
Puerto Banus, Marbella

Puerto Banus, once a sleepy little fishing village, had evolved into the Monte Carlo of Spain. Luxury yachts floated in the harbour and Louis Vuitton, Christian Dior and Versace boutiques fringed the marina and the crystal-clear water of the Mediterranean. Maseratis and Bentleys circled like a convoy of peacocks, doing their best to avoid running over the toes of the *turistas* along the Calle Ribera. Lurking one street behind, dimly lit bars, clubs, drug dealers, prostitutes, the occasional murder and mucho mayhem, represented the darker side of the port. It was the go-to place for the faces of London's underworld. Once their feet touched the tarmac at Malaga Airport, those fleeing from the law were untouchable by the not-so-long arms of British justice. It was also the gateway to Morocco, and its supply lines of hashish and cocaine.

The Jungle stood out from its rivals. It was owned by the 'Pink Prince of Stratford', one of the two Great Train Robbers never caught. He'd invested a sizeable chunk of his share of the proceeds into the club. Large stone Buddhas, cascading waterfalls, pole dancers and platinum-painted waitresses made it the most popular club in the port.

Mickey Warren was having a ball, the drink and cocaine working in harmony to deliver him to his own version of the Promised Land. He sat in one of the roped-off private areas and as usual looked the part, wearing Versace jeans, a white embossed Ralph Lauren shirt and a cobalt blue Hugo Boss jacket. He was surrounded by some newmade friends, who hadn't the slightest idea they were partying with one of the most dangerous men in London.

He looked over at his handsome son. "Jason, come here boy."

Jason looked at his father and smiled. Mickey was on good form, which was a relief, because it wasn't always that way. Mickey in a bad mood was not someone you wanted to be around. Jason walked over and Mickey ran his hand through his son's hair just as he had when he was a small boy. Now nineteen, he still found it reassuring, a vestigial comfort blanket from darker times.

"Boy, let me tell you something about hookers," said Mickey.

This should be interesting, thought Jason. His dad should know, he was an expert on the subject.

"On the first day at hooker school, they learn the most important lesson. It's not about fifty men a week for fifty quid a time. It's about finding the mug that's gonna give you everything."

Mickey paused. Jason wasn't sure why, effect maybe.

He continued. "Here's the question. How do you get laid for nothing? You, convince her, you're falling for her bullshit. Splash the cash. Tell her you suddenly have to leave, and as you're going, invite her for lunch the next day. She'll think she's landed the golden passport to Hooker Heaven. The night after you will be screwing her for free. Works every time unless she's Russian. They're far too fucking clever to fall for that."

He paused again, and this time Jason saw why. Mickey's eyes were transfixed on a pair of glistening breasts in front of him, the silk blouse made translucent by the ultra-violet revolving spotlight.

Mickey turned towards him. "Think you can handle that little task, son?"

Jason wondered for a moment whether he meant the gorgeous tits two feet away. "Yes, I get it, Dad."

"Don't call me dad, it's Mickey, how many times do I have to tell you?" He turned to his new friends, "I ask you; do I look old enough to be his dad?"

"No, Mickey, no," they replied in unison, beginning to catch on to the slight menace in his voice.

Jason knew this was another lesson Mickey thought would be invaluable in building his character. In reality, it was just another little game for Mickey Warren. Yes, some of the lessons Mickey had taught him were useful, like opening a bottle of wine with a wet towel if you didn't have a bottle opener but couldn't see the value in this. Why would you go to all the bother instead of just paying?

He decided, as always, to play along. "Why don't I just pay, Mickey, like you?"

Mickey lifted his eyes, released from the hypnotic pull of the woman's see through mini-skirt and her lack of panties. He looked at Jason, who recognised the playful look Mickey gave to people, just before they got their skull cracked or received one of his special 'manicures'. "Very funny, son. Go on, off you go, and don't come back till you've finished the job."

Jason walked out of the bar reflecting on what an unusual role model Mickey was. Not a normal father, no one could describe him as that. He'd seen his father do many things over the years; dark, violent things. Worse, the look in his eyes of enjoyment at the pain he inflicted on other people. He struggled with this view of his father. Sometimes wanting to be like him, other times sickened by what he'd seen and heard.

The lights of Cubanga bar broke his thoughts. The staff could wear anything as long as it was no bigger than a tea towel, and you didn't get to work there unless you'd walked straight off the catwalk. Free shots were poured a dozen at a time, you could get pissed just licking the bar. Naked dancers clung to the poles suspended from the ceiling. In a cage high in the heavens, a body contorted into shapes he didn't think possible.

Money was everywhere and so were the brasses; one always followed the other. He scanned the bar, wondering when he would finally graduate from Mickeys' school of life. Always he'd tried to please him. Even now at nineteen, there was a part of him that wanted to impress, and show he was a worthy son. It was a new challenge, and sure as hell would end successfully, as always. Failure was never an option.

Anna stood at the foot of the stairs talking to two older women. Blonde hair reached her waist. There was nothing about her he didn't like. She moved, elegantly, almost floating, like gravity didn't affect her.

She saw him looking at her and smiled, as casually he began to walk towards her. "Can I get you a drink?"

There was no answer, just the sound of a striking match. "Would you like one?"

"Yes," he replied.

She lit the cigarette for him, blowing a wispy piece of smoke into his face. He took it from her. A small, cherry-red lipstick mark contrasted with the white cigarette.

"I'll have a vodka and coke," she said, smiling, at him in a way that made him uneasy, as though gifted with the ability to read his mind.

At the bar the talk was easy. It always was, with hookers. It started with their name, then questions about you. It was easier to let the punter talk about themselves, let them do the work, just smile, and pretend to be interested. He'd missed lunch and the alcohol had started to rampage through his empty stomach to his brain.

"Are you hungry, Anna, shall we go for something to eat?"

"I've eaten, but I'll come with you."

They walked along the first line of the port, deftly avoiding the cars cruising the narrow road. Then stopped at Red Pepper restaurant, where Giorgio, the owner, was as usual holding court, dispensing his wisdom to all that would listen, from the table he rarely moved from.

"Have you ever seen Giorgio move from that table?" asked Jason.

She laughed. "No, if the most successful restaurant owner did the least amount of work, then Giorgio would be the king of them all."

"Hello, Jason, how are you? Table for two?"

"Good thanks, Giorgio, OK to sit here?" It was a corner table looking onto the gleaming white yachts, twenty feet away.

"Of course." He motioned to a waiter, who rushed over with a complimentary bottle of Veuve Clicquot. Jason was enjoying himself. This was the easiest task ever, he thought.

He turned and saw Anna looking at him. Her face was as beautiful as it had been a few minutes before, except that now one eyebrow was raised, as if to say, "Not Dom Perignon?"

He looked at the waiter and saw the odd way he was looking at him, a mocking sort of look. Christ, he thought, I'm becoming paranoid. Maybe I just need some food.

"The mezze, please," he said.

The food arrived, plate following plate.

"You know, this is far too much for one. Are you sure you don't want some?" he asked.

"Are you sure you want to share? Because you seem to be managing quite well on your own. When was the last time you ate?"

"Been too busy looking for the best-looking girl in the port to eat. I'm just catching up with lost time."

She smiled. "That's the worst line, I've ever heard."

He returned her smile. "It wasn't a line." He washed down the last mouthful of a fine Rioja Reserva. Harry had taught him well about wine, and Jason was certain he knew more about it than any other nineteen-year-old kid from the East End.

"Are you not having dessert?" she asked.

"Not only beautiful but funny. No, I've had enough. Let's go to the piano bar."

They walked forty yards along the marina to 'Marvellous,' the piano bar. Paul, aka the Piano Man, was halfway through a medley of Sinatra songs, and the crowd were swaying like a September cornfield.

They sat down. "I love this place."

She looked at him. "Yes, it's great." There was something in the answer, that didn't sit right with him.

Four drinks later the inevitable question came. "Do you want to come back to mine?"

"Will it cost me?"

"I feel awkward with that question, but the truth is I have to live."

"Anna, I won't pay for you, I like you a lot but if I pay it will spoil this. I think we could be more than that, I'm sorry."

She looked at him and he saw the look in her eyes, unable to work out whether it was anger or disappointment. She got up, smiled, bent down, kissed his cheek and left.

Shit, that didn't go well, he thought, I should definitely have left earlier, as Mickey said. Maybe he was right about Russians; maybe, she was Russian. He hadn't thought to ask.

Then a scarier thought struck him. There was no way he was going back to the villa to listen to Harry and Mickey telling him what a failure he was. Russian or not, this wasn't over.

He worked his way through the crowd to the exit. Rushing through the door, he ran into a girl knocking her to the ground and was horrified to realise it was Anna.

"Shit, I'm so sorry!"

She looked up at him, and her anger turned to laughter. "Are you going to help me up?"

"Yes, sorry."

He reached down and pulled her to her feet. Anna's perfume made him light-headed, or maybe it was the drink, he wasn't sure. Her white jacket was torn at the elbow and the fabric began to turn red.

Her friend looked at him and then at Anna. "Is this him?"

Anna laughed again. "Yes, Lena, this is him."

"Anna you're bleeding," said Jason.

She looked at her elbow, seeing the blood on the white fabric. It didn't seem to bother her at all. He found the lack of concern for herself both attractive and strange.

"So, were you coming to look for me, or going back to the restaurant for some more to eat?"

Lena laughed. They were both looking at him. "Anna, the least I can do is buy you a new jacket." He wondered if that was somehow breaking the no-paying rule. "Let me take you shopping tomorrow and get some lunch?"

She turned, looked at him and paused for longer than he liked. "OK, El Rancho at two."

He smiled, "Great I'll see you there. By the way, are you Russian?"

She looked at him.

"No. It's OK, don't answer that," he said.

He walked past Sinatra's bar to the taxi rank and twenty minutes later unlocked the door to Harry's villa in the hills, overlooking the port.

Forty-eight hours later, Jason Warren walked into Desvan. Its dusty floors, old wood and American Indian memorabilia appealed to him. It looked as though it had been there for years and had more character than the newer bars in the port. More than the place, he liked Magrao the manager and his wife Talita. Brazilians, party people. They had a simple attitude to life, nothing was complicated, and they always looked for the best in people, so different from his life in London.

He watched them; they hadn't seen him. Magrao was strumming his guitar, singing and looking at his wife who danced as he sang.

Everyone in the bar seemed to be having fun, except him. Anna was in his head, and she wouldn't leave it. He thought about the night he'd spent with her after the meeting at El Rancho; no payment had been required. It had been so natural, as though they'd been lovers for years. She had given herself in every way and it had been better than he had dreamed it could be, but there was something about her he couldn't put his finger on, a sadness, as though haunted by something, or someone. The only time she'd become distant and pulled away from him was when he'd kissed the arch of her back; perfect, except for the deep twelve-inch scar that ran across it.

He left the bar, where everyone's happiness was so at odds with his own, and made his way to Cubanga, hoping to find her there. He frowned at the thought about the way he'd used her, knowing she had seen through his childish game. But she had told him there was something about him that had captured a small part of her, a part she thought was dead. The task was completed, sex with a hooker without paying, but celebrating was the last thing on his mind. It was another checkpoint in his life, one reminding him he was getting a bit too full of himself. Mickey would have loved the result – free sex, mission accomplished. Harry would give him a disapproving look, not needing to say anything. Good and bad, light and dark. He shrugged, no wonder he was confused, with Mickey on one shoulder and Harry on the other.

His mood lifted when he saw her. She was talking to a man, clearly a punter, and worse still, a good-looking one who was clearly intent on adding to her bank balance. He, as handsome as she was beautiful, the sort of man that should never need to pay. He wondered if he would be given the same freebie, he had received. Reflecting on the thought, he realised he was jealous.

She had seen him enter, and momentarily glanced at him. He ordered a drink to settle the grumbling anxiety forming in the pit of his stomach. It didn't touch the sides, so he ordered another, and positioned himself strategically beside them. She scowled at him, then lowered her top another inch and moved closer to the punter.

The handsome Adonis placed his hand around her slim waist. "Would you like another drink, some Dom Perignon?"

She moved even closer to him and placed her hand on his arm. "Champagne, how nice," she said, looking at Jason.

He felt himself drowning in the Shakespearian tragedy unfolding before him. He'd seen Hamlet with Harry and was now viewing himself as the sad prince, too much thinking and not enough action. Meanwhile, to teach him a lesson, Anna was putting in an Oscar winning performance.

The punter excused himself to go to the toilet. Jason recalled another play he'd seen with Harry, *Macbeth*. The hero was the opposite to Hamlet, a man of action. It was time for the Scottish general to take control. He glanced up and saw her stunning face looking back at him, then took her arm. "Come on, let's get out of here."

"I thought you would never ask," she replied.

As they turned the corner, away from the line of bars, he stopped, held her hand and very gently kissed her lips. "I'm sorry, Anna."

She looked at him. "That's OK. You're a clown, but I like you. Shall we start again?"

"Great. Can I buy you dinner?"

She laughed. "Not that line again!"

A taxi stopped beside them, they got in and in perfect Spanish, Anna directed the driver to Raphael's, which she explained was her favourite restaurant.

The curves and potholes in the road threw their bodies together, and their hands intertwined. How could a bumpy ride in an old cab feel so good? He didn't know, but it did.

The taxi came to a dusty stop twenty feet from the few rickety old tables outside, laid in red and yellow cloth. Raphael's was a small traditional restaurant in a tiny village, off the beaten track. It looked like a place only the locals would know. Inside ancient wagon wheels covered the walls and aged Rioja bottles, obscured by years of candle wax, each with a thousand table stories to tell, lay haphazardly on the battered wooden tables.

Raphael hugged Anna as she walked through the door. "Anna, my darling, it is so nice to see you!" She drew him closer and kissed his cheeks. Jason noticed the bond the beautiful young Russian and the ancient Spaniard had between them. Raphael had the face of an old sea captain. Deep canyons traversed his face, and Jason wondered how you could ever shave such a rugged terrain.

"This is Jason." Raphael looked at him, an odd expression on his face.

"It's good to meet you, Raphael," Jason said, holding out his hand.

The expression on Raphael's face softened slightly. Still staring at him, but in a warmer way, slowly he took his hand. "You must be very special; Anna has never brought anyone here before."

The next morning Anna lay in Jason's arms, head on his shoulder, their legs intertwined. She told him her story.

"I grew up in Saint Petersburg and went to a private school," she began. "That's where I learnt English and French, and most important how to be a lady." The look on her face dared him to make the obvious comment, which he quickly thought better of. "I knew from a very young age my father's business was a dark and dangerous one. I was told never to ask questions, but as I grew older, I realised he was a gangster, or as we say in Russia, *bratva*. Many strange men would be in our houses and my father always tried to keep me away from them, but I have a great skill of always finding things I should not. On my eighteenth birthday, I saw a young man who worked for my father. His name was Gregor. I started a relationship with him, and I fell in love. I gave myself to him. We loved each other, and nothing could part us. Always he told me he loved me, but we could never be together in Russia. My father would have killed him if he'd found out about us, so we ran away. We came here, to be safe and happy, our pockets bulging with the money that would let us start our life together.

Everything was perfect for a while, but Gregor's eyes were soon too big. He slept with other girls, got drunk and used drugs. We argued and the arguments became worse and worse. Then one night he returned screaming and shouting, calling me a rich mafia whore. I had never slept with anyone but him. He hit me so hard, I was so scared, tried to get out of the door and as I reached it, I felt the pain in my back. He had slashed me with his knife. 'No one will want you now!' he screamed." Jason, pulled her closer to him.

"The next thing I remember, I was in hospital. Raphael, my neighbour, had heard the screaming, and come into the house and taken me there. Raphael was so kind, paid for my treatment and has been my dearest friend since that day. When I went back to the apartment, Gregor had gone, and I have not seen him since. I searched for some money, but all I could find was a small amount I had hidden away. I could not go home because I feared what my father would do, so I used the only thing I had left, my body. My life became empty, sad and with no hope. Until now, until you."

Jason lifted himself off the pillow and gently kissed the scar on her back. The tears rolled down her face. No words were needed; they both knew their lives had changed forever.

Chapter 2
March 1968
The Marquee Club, London

Harry bounced off the brick archway and through the black doors. A cursory wave from the doorman failed to get his attention as he sauntered into his favourite club.

Mickey Warren sat at a table, a woman on either side, both identically dressed in short metallic grey dresses. The blonde to his left slid her hand inside his trousers, and he felt himself growing hard as her delicate fingers made slow teasing movements. He enjoyed it for a moment and then pulled her hand away. Good as it felt, Mickey Warren wasn't there to listen to music or be pulled off under the table. He was here to meet Harry Fleet, and he had just watched him walk into the club.

Mickey had been thinking about the meeting all day. Word on the street was that something big was about to happen. He was sure Harry was involved, and today would find out what all the fuss was about. He knew Harry was big in the underworld, at the heart of London's drug trade, and drugs were a lucrative part of the criminal world. This was the year of the Beatles' Magical Mystery Tour, and Mickey Warren was wondering exactly what magical mystery tour Harry Fleet had in mind this time.

Harry stopped at one of the floor-to-ceiling mirrors and stared intently at his own face. Even in the half-light of the club, Mickey could not help but notice how grey Harry looked. The strobe light changed the light to a warm red, but Harry's face stubbornly refused to look anything other than a fine shade of rigor mortis grey. Mickey knew Harry sometimes tried out his latest pharmaceutical creations, but this time, it looked like he had either taken too many or they were too strong. Harry moved his head to one side, but his eyes did not seem to immediately follow. He stumbled further, and finally dropped down onto a seat at Mickey's table.

"My God, Mickey, I think those pills I made were stronger than I thought. For a minute, I thought there were two of you and four of your charming companions."

Mickey squeezed their arms a little harder than necessary, they squealed in pain. Then waved them away. "Go and powder your noses," he said.

Harry slumped backwards. "Now, Mickey, let me tell you something interesting."

Mickey sank back, matching Harry's posture. It was pointless interrupting Harry. Once he started, the only way to stop him talking was to kill him or fire a dart from an elephant tranquilizer gun.

"Do you know American companies used to give cocaine to the negroes, so they'd work harder? And they gave stuff to their soldiers that turned them into killing machines. We were no better, of course we weren't. We gave amphetamines to our fellows, to make them march faster." He paused, gathering his thoughts. "That's what we need, Mickey, men who never stop marching, men like us. That's why we are winners, it's what pays for the good life." Harry paused and took a drag from his cigarette. "Rich men want to be richer, poor men want to be rich and nobody gives a fuck. So, they work." Harry let the last words hang in the air before bursting into laughter. "So, they work. See, that's all you need to understand. Laws only exist if you're caught. If you're not, it never happened. It's not about the truth, and anyway, what is the truth."

He paused again, took another drag of the cigarette, then blew neat little circles of smoke into the air, while Mickey looked on, unblinking.

"It never has been, Mickey. It's what you gain from your perception of the truth. You see, it is, what it is, what you want it to be. That's all that matters Mickey, perception, this is what we are, and this is the way of the world, as Jules Danby, my old mate from college used to say."

"Terrific, Harry, I'm glad we got that sorted. Not that I understood a word of it." He sighed as he drained the last of his beer.

Harry took a sip of the nearest drink and more or less focused on Mickey's face. "What would you like to drink?"

"A beer."

"A beer? You really have been in England too long. Try this, I think it's sauvignon blanc, it means 'savage grape'. No offence, Mickey, but a savage for a savage." He moved his glass towards Mickey, focusing on it as it moved. "That glass has just turned into a fish. I need to adjust the formula or get those bloody monkeys in the lab to have a proper go on it, they've been slacking of late."

Mickey took a sip of the wine. "That's great, Harry." He turned to the patiently waiting waitress and winked. "I'll have a beer."

Harry looked at Mickey. "Now, where was I?"

"Drugs and soldiers."

"Exactly," Harry said, lighting his fortieth cigarette of the day. "Also, scientists in the thirties across the pond discovered speed had a positive effect on the disruptive little buggers in the classroom, kept them in line. They even started to learn, almost like the normal kids. So, they started handing them out like Smarties."

Mickey nodded, wishing he had brought a couple of pillows, and regretting sending the women away. His mind began to wander. He looked for them but could not see them. What was his life coming to? One minute, sitting with two beautiful women, the next listening to a rambling Harry Fleet. The guy had clearly gone a bit too far with one of his own experiments, Mickey concluded.

"But Mickey, that's not the end of it," Harry went on. "Hitler had daily speed injections, which goes a long way to explain the outfits. You see I reckon they made a bet when they were off their heads. 'Hey, Adolf, I bet you can't make zem march like ze geese!'" Harry shouted in a convincing German accent before bursting into laughter.

Mickey laughed too. There always came a point when Harry made him laugh.

"Worse, Mickey, and this is, the worst thing. Two years ago, bloody Parliament banned LSD, which is why we will never win the World Cup again." Harry paused and placed his hands on his heart. "You will get nowhere without a free mind. Without drugs, our boys are fucked, and I know, because I gave half of them some tabs to set them up for the last game."

Mickey massaged his temples. A sinking feeling was descending on him like a foggy January morning. "Yes of course you did. Harry, is there an end to this story?"

"Oh yes, Mickey, there's an end or should I say a beginning. I'm going to make you rich. Very rich. Now, enough chat, where are those girls?"

The sun stung Mickey's eyes as it burst through the early morning clouds. He pushed down on the coffee percolator. Twice as much coffee as normal turned the water a dark ochre. His head felt as heavy as a bowling ball, and he knew it would take more than coffee to put him straight, but it was a start. He rubbed his eyes and looked at the crack in the ceiling that had annoyed him for months, making a mental note to get the repair man in. So, what was Harry's game? He shook his head, trying to clear the haze, wading through the misty backstreets of his mind. He reached to the top of the cupboard for his emergency pack of cigarettes. Slowly his head began to clear.

Harry had spotted an old boyfriend who appealed to him more than the women, so it was left to Mickey to take them both, and that's exactly what he'd done, several times, with the help of Harry's mobile pharmacy. Now though, the cocktail of drugs was wearing off and fatigue was overcoming him. Even so, the thought of one last session with the women, before the work of the day began, appealed to him.

He walked back towards the bedroom and heard them talking. He moved his head around the door slowly so they would not see him. One was on top of the other. He watched for a few minutes. The moans turned him on as they climaxed together. As they lay back on the bed, they saw him. The brunette swung her legs on to the floor and walked towards him, "I hope you're not going to waste that, Mickey."

Maybe the coffee could wait, he thought.

Chapter 3
July 1988
Puerto Banus, Spain

The planned week in Puerto Banus had stretched to two, and the plane had left without him. He knew turning up at the airport might have helped, but London could wait. The light-headed feeling afflicting him was one he was not accustomed to. He'd decided it was love — well, lust as well, but mainly love.

He slowly dialled the number. "Harry, don't think I've gone soft, but I need to get Anna back to England with me."

"Kid, you can't bring her through customs, she's Russian, and needs a visa. It takes months and she probably wouldn't get one anyway. By the way, didn't Mickey tell you about Russians?"

"I'll ignore that, Harry, I think you've been hanging around the old man too long. Seriously, what can we do? I know borders don't exist in your mind. So, you need to work a bit of your magic."

"They are indeed inconvenient lines drawn on maps by other people. Get yourself back here, cool off for a bit, and if you still feel the same in a few days we'll see what we can do."

"No, Harry, I don't need to think about it. I want her in London."

"Stubborn as always, I wonder where you get that from. I've got a boat going to Banus in a couple of weeks. We can pick her up and get her dropped off here with the other cargo."

"Harry, she's not cargo, but thanks anyway. Sounds like a plan."

"Yes, no offence, you know what I mean."

Jason kicked a stone along the *calle* as he began to walk the short distance back to the apartment. The conversation with Harry was still fresh in his mind, and he hadn't noticed the man watching him from the table in the bar, nor the one that followed him back to the apartment.

He let himself in. Anna hugged him.

"What did Harry say, can I come to England?"

He looked across at her, and saw a small tear fall on her face. "A boat's coming to pick you up in a few weeks. It's not easy, but it will happen, he's never let me down."

"I'm so happy. We will have to make the most of the next two weeks here. Shall we go to Raphael's and celebrate the beginning of our life together?"

"I'm flying back tomorrow, Anna, I need to go. But I'll be back a few days before you leave."

"Jason, why can't you stay?"

"Everything will be fine. We will have our lives together. It's only a few weeks, and I need to go back." He reached across and wiped the tear from her face, which had been joined by two others.

"You have made me cry so much, but they are all happy tears. You make me so happy, my love."

He felt inside his pocket, his hand enclosed the small box containing the engagement ring he had bought. He thought about giving it to her but decided it would be better when she arrived in England.

Passing through the departure gate, he glanced back a final time, and saw the sad look on her face, and the tears that began to fall. For a moment he thought about turning back, as he smiled at her, and mouthed the three words he had told her every day for the last two weeks, "I love you."

As the plane became airborne, his decision to leave seemed even more irrational. He tapped an unrecognisable tune on the armrest, as the doubts began to invade his head. Why had he left? He wasn't needed, he wasn't Harry or Mickey, so why didn't he just stay? He felt reassured by the small box in the palm of his hand.

His mood lifted slightly, at the sight of Paul Eastham waiting for him in the car. Eastham was always frugal with chit-chat, and today that suited him. They passed the familiar Lucozade sign on the Great West Road. It was usually his welcome home sign, but not today. Home was where his heart was, and it wasn't in London on a grey and rainy day.

He looked back at the flashing neon sign, on the side of a nondescript building, that had become an iconic landmark, a simple neon flashing bottle of the orange liquid being poured endlessly into a glass. It had originally said "Lucozade Aids Recovery" but had been changed to "Lucozade Replaces Lost Energy," because of AIDS. It had been there before he was born and would probably be there when he died. It seemed permanent, if only life was a little more like the Lucozade bottle, he thought.

He filled the days with anything that made them pass more quickly. "Harry, time is going as slowly as watching *Lawrence of Arabia* a thousand times," he said one day.

Harry looked at him. "You're not well, kid, that's one of the greatest films ever made. I've got the cinema version with ice cream breaks. You must come round and watch it. Do you know there's not a single word in the whole film spoken by a woman?"

"Harry, you do talk some rubbish sometimes."

"Seriously, Mickey told me last week, cost me fifty quid. I thought he was just being his usual self, so I watched it again and he's right."

Two weeks later the wheels hit the tarmac, the plane taxied to a stop and the greyness of London was again replaced by the bright Spanish sunshine. Jason walked through the door and down the steps onto the tarmac of Malaga Airport. The rooftops shimmered in the stifling heat of the Spanish summer. He cleared customs, more quickly than normal, ran to the taxi queue and jumped into the first taxi, ignoring the protests of the other passengers.

Forty minutes later the taxi stopped at the fountain, a few yards from the front-line of the port. He threw some notes at the driver, bolted out of the door and ran to Anna's apartment. He pressed the buzzer, but there was no answer. He fumbled for the key she had given him and opened the door. Strange, he thought, she knows I am coming today. The notion of a return to her old

46

trade flashed into his head, he felt ashamed, at the thought and pushed it from his mind as he looked at his watch. He wasn't late. Perhaps, she had just gone out for five minutes, but his disquiet was growing.

He waited in the apartment for thirty minutes and then decided to look for her. He walked the streets searching, going to all the places they normally went together. There was no sign of her. With his head lower than when he'd arrived and the doubts pushing towards the front of his mind, he walked into Desvan. Magrao and Talita were sitting at the bar chatting. Magrao saw him and walked over to him. He wasn't smiling, which was odd, Magrao always had a smile on his face.

"Magrao, have you seen Anna?"

"Something has happened. We have not seen her for a few days, but we heard she has gone."

Jason's shoulders slumped. His bad day was becoming a lot worse.

"Gone, Magrao? Gone where?"

"I did not see this myself, but this is what I was told. She was in Pappardella restaurant, you know, the one by the big boats, eating by herself. When she left, two men approached her, on the corner by Salduba. There was no argument. She looked scared but left with them, no struggle. That's all I know; except they were Russian."

Jason slammed his fist on the table. "Gregor! Who else could it be, the bastard! I will kill him! Where can I find him, do you know?"

"I don't know, no one has seen him, not for weeks."

He searched, without sleep, a long, forty-eight-hour, depressing search, and still did not have the slightest idea what had happened. He decided to fly back to the only man that could make his nightmare go away.

Harry hugged him. "So, what happened, tell me everything?"

"I don't know, Harry, I think her ex has taken her, God knows what he's done to her. I searched everywhere, nothing. Magrao, a friend, told me, she was approached by a couple of Russians, and left with them, without a struggle. I don't get it, why would she walk away with them in broad daylight, who else can it be other than her ex?"

Harry sat there, patiently listening to the rest of the story, and waited until Jason had finished. "He sounded like bad news when you told me about him. What do you want to do?"

Jason lifted his head and looked at him, frustration etched on his face. "I don't know, what can we do?"

Harry smiled. "You've only known her a few weeks, you will find someone else?"

"It's different, Harry, different, it's never been like this, she is the one. I've made promises, I've never made before. I know you think I'm mad, but I want her back, I need to find her."

Harry laughed. "You're just like your dad was. I'll send Eastham over to find her. If anyone can find her, he will. But don't get your hopes up, Spain is a big place."

Chapter 4
1968
London

The rain was keeping Harry in his car. He tapped the dashboard, singing to Amen Corner's *Bend Me Shake Me*, and glanced across at the Blind Beggar pub. There had been a boozer on the site since 1654 and it had two claims to fame. The first, a hundred years before, when William Booth gave the sermon there that led to the creation of the Salvation Army. The second, a gangland shooting two years ago, when George Cornell, a local malefactor, was put out of his misery by a single bullet through his head whilst sitting at the bar sipping a pint of mild. The Walker Brothers song, *The Sun Ain't Gonna Shine Any More* was playing on the jukebox when it was hit by a stray bullet and the words had repeated over and over again.

Harry always put the record on, hoping the song would repeat the same way it did on the day of the shooting, but it never did. The killer had not been found, but Harry and the rest of London knew exactly who he was, Ronnie Kray, one half of the East End crime kings the Kray brothers.

Harry had been devising a plan for weeks. If it worked, it would change the lives of many people for the better, his included, and if it didn't, it wouldn't matter, as he would probably be dead. He reflected on London's criminal underworld and the changes over the last two years. London was divided between two gangs, the Krays, who controlled the East, and the Richardsons, who controlled the South. Last year the Richardsons had vacated their position at the top table thanks to a court case at the Old Bailey, in a trial tagged the 'torture gang trial'. They had thought it was OK to play dentist, removing teeth from the miscreants who had somehow annoyed them; no need for anaesthetics, just a pair of pliers, and if that was not enough, maybe a few thousand volts on the testicles would do the trick. Their departure left a partial vacuum, one, according to Harry's informer at Scotland Yard, that was about to get a lot bigger.

The rain stopped as quickly as it had begun, and Harry decided to make a dash for it before it returned. He opened the car door, stretched his arms and looked at the sky. The sun was struggling to break through the re-grouping storm clouds, and he shivered as he approached the entrance. The double wooden doors creaked as they opened. It was warmer inside, but only just.

A young couple were chatting at the bar, gazing into each other's eyes on the exact spot where George Cornell had had his brains blown out. Harry wondered if they realised their love was growing in the precise place where the gruesome gangland shooting had happened. He looked at them again and reflected, yes of course they did, they were probably cops. Assuming they were he moved to the other side of the bar, ordered drinks and waited for Mickey Warren, who strolled in two minutes later.

Mickey walked slowly to the table and the beer waiting for him. He had not yet sat down when Harry started talking.

"Come on, Mickey, drink up, I don't like the look of those two at the bar, old Bill for sure."

"Harry, I've only just got here."

"No come on, your excessive drinking can wait, this is far more important." Mickey drank the pint and they walked towards the door and headed for Harry's car.

The wheels screeched as Harry turned towards the city. "Don't ever talk business in the boozer, Mickey, I didn't like the look of those two at the bar. Old Bill, I'm telling you."

"We didn't. So come on, what's this all about?"

"I'll keep this short. I've looked at the way crime works in America, and I hate to say it, but they do it a lot better than we do. If the boss is whacked, as the Americans say, the mafia structure allows for a clear successor. True, they don't always agree on who that should be, so a few more might get whacked, but they always get to the point where the firm continues. Here, firms are not

50

structured, so once the guvnor is killed, or worse incarcerated, that means nicked to you, it's often the end. Or they're so weak they're finished anyway. Vacuums, that's what I am talking about and not Hoover juniors. In short, Mickey, the Richardsons are safely tucked up at her Majesty's and the Krays are hot on their heels. London will be there for the taking. And we, my old friend, will be there to take full advantage."

Mickey's shoulders slumped, struggling to hide his disappointment. "Not that old chestnut. I've heard the rumours about the Krays, who hasn't, but things don't stick, they never go down, no one talks. We all know about the bodies, but no one is gonna be mug enough to grass."

"Oh, they will this time. Their bookkeeper Les Paine has gone AWOL, not surprising as they tried to kill him. So, fearing for his health he's turned queens, and he's singing like a canary. And worse, there was an undercover cop on the firm, a guy named Cooper."

"How do you know that, Harry? And what's it got to do with us?"

"Don't you worry how. This is one thousand percent true, and I'm about to show you exactly what it's got to do with us."

They turned left into Mansell Street and towards the Tower of London.

"Where we off to, Harry? I could do with a bit of a kip after last night."

"As I said, there's something I want you to see. Something that will change that sad little life of yours forever."

They drove into an industrial estate and through the gated security entrance.

"Very impressive, Harry."

"Can't be too careful." They came to a halt. "I think you'll like this."

Harry opened a set of airtight doors into a room where a faint yellow mist hung in the air. Through the haze a small figure was hunched over a bathtub-sized stainless-steel vat. The figure tapped a dial, which swung wildly from side to side. A puff of bright yellow smoke erupted into the air. Mickey followed Harry. His eyes were beginning to sting, and his chest tightened. He coughed, and the white ghost-like figure turned to face them.

Harry wiped his eyes. "Mickey, this is Kaitlin."

She was covered from head to toe in a white suit and facemask. "Harry, you're early. I'm nearly done, and you shouldn't be in here, please leave. Remember the last batch you made, didn't turn out too well, did it?"

"That could have happened to anyone."

"No, Harry, not everyone, only you."

"Hurtful, Kaitlin, very hurtful." He wagged his finger at her and placed his hands on his heart. "You're giving me chest pains."

"No, that's the air in here, the pressure-reducing valve failed again. Come on, get out before you kill your friend."

He coughed. "OK, good point, we'll be in the office. Come on, Mickey, stop hanging about, it's bloody dangerous in here. Look, the canary's keeled over."

Mickey looked across to see a bright yellow bird lying on the floor of its cage. They hurried through the air-tight doors into a corridor leading to a dark mahogany door that had a brass plate with 'Harry's Bar' engraved on it.

"That brass plate's a bit of a giveaway when you get raided. And who the hell was that?"

"I'm not the sort that gets nicked, Mickey, and she is my most favourite girl in the world, an absolute angel, so you make sure you keep well away from her. Not that she would mix with the likes of you. Way too much class for an East End, street urchin."

Harry's head was spinning, struggling to remember the first time he'd met Kaitlin, one freezing night in the Argyle Arms in Soho. Snow was on the ground and as usual up his nose. He liked her from the moment they met. She was smart, beautiful and drank tequila straight from the bottle, and became his number one target. He'd tried to get her into bed and failed, that night and every night after, until finally giving up trying. She'd told him that although she did not want to sleep with him, his sense of humour and offbeat view of life, appealed to her. She explained that two

52

months earlier after landing in Southampton on a steamer from Buenos Aires, adjusting back to life in London was hard. South America had changed her; she missed the place, but most of all, the people. She went there with the idea of making a difference and changing the world, instead it changed her. The two years spent in Peru assisting Dr Stanley Ablett, had past more quickly than she imagined it would. They were the first Westerners to live and work with the Ashaninka, a tribe being decimated by Western diseases.

Three weeks after meeting her, Harry was doing something he thought impossible; having a platonic relationship with a stunning woman. They sat on high-back chairs in Harry's kitchen. "You know, Kate, I'm glad I didn't have sex with you, because I don't think our friendship would have lasted."

She laughed. "Harry, what makes you think I would have slept with you? Anyway, I thought you had a boyfriend."

"Oh, you would have, it would only have been a matter of time. Some things are certain in life."

"Well, thanks for sparing me. You know, I was about to give in the very day you stopped asking. I was a bit sad we never slept together."

"Really, Kate, you're not playing with my delicate feelings, are you? There beats a very vulnerable heart in this body of mine."

She moved across the table and kissed his cheek.

"What was that for?"

"For being you, Harry." She poured two glasses of wine.

"You know, I still can't get over the concept of everyone running around that jungle of yours totally naked. I wouldn't fancy that with all those snakes and bloody insects. They must have been on drugs to do that, must have been. You see, Kate, drugs are everywhere, even in the jungle. To walk around naked with everything hanging out, you've got to be on them."

"'They're not on drugs all the time, not everyone's like you. They've been using a drug for hundreds of years in their traditional celebrations. I tried it, and after, it made me look at things in a totally different way."

"What's it called?"

"Ayahuasca. You should try it before you die, which probably won't be long the way you're going."

"I'm confused, a drug I've never heard of? Whatever next? What's it like?"

"It gave me the most intense experience ever, life changing even."

"Did you bring some back?"

"No, Harry, it doesn't work quite like that."

"Pray tell," he replied.

Kaitlin drained her glass, then refilled both.

"Well, after a while we were looked upon as part of the tribe. Taking ayahuasca is an ancient ritual of enlightenment. I watched them take it, it was scary, but I was curious to try it myself. I took the chalice and swallowed the liquid. The tribesmen who took it before me were already puking. Not that it put me off. I began to feel sick, really sick. Thirty minutes later I began to see bright lights, swirling, changing. Strange shapes moving like a river, only up, not down. The visions were so vivid. I was sick again, deep green vomit. What had I done? My death was unfolding before me. I fell into the river and was carried upwards. My lungs filled with water; I was slowly drowning. Suddenly the river slowed and ended in a deep pool, I floated towards the edge. There was nothing below. I screamed, silent screams as the water inched me agonizingly over the edge, falling for what seemed like forever, ending with my head hitting a giant rock. Nothing was making sense." She sipped her wine.

"I looked at the Shaman, who was chanting an ancient song. The terror felt uncontrollable. Wailing souls screamed as they flashed past, all white with bright red eyes. I tried to fight the horror, but I wasn't strong enough. Begging for it to end, didn't work, fighting it was pointless, so I gave in, let it take me where it wanted to go. When I stopped fighting, things began to change. I looked at the Shaman and the others and again begged them for help. They hugged me, we were suddenly naked, intertwined as the river took us upwards. We swam, bathed in a kaleidoscope of colours. I felt such empathy and love for them. It was then I saw, I was not just an individual, but part of a world of love and caring. Later, when it was out of my system, I felt more at one with the world, my fears and worries seemed less, saw for the first time how everything in the world meshed together, in a beautiful simplicity. Like a child sees the world before the world corrupts it."

She looked at him. "Am I boring you, Harry?"

"No, Kate, I'm absolutely fascinated. I'm booking a flight, that's exactly the drug for me. My God, it might even straighten me out."

She held his head in her hands. "I doubt that, Harry, it's good, but not that good."

"Harry, you deaf bastard!" Mickey grabbed his shoulder and Harry was jolted back to the present.

"Sorry, I was miles away. I'm not sure of the exact formula of the yellow mist, but it's bloody good stuff, I wonder if I can put it in an aerosol. Mickey, you don't appear to be listening, are you OK? Your eyes aren't working together, let me help you." He took Mickey's arm and led him through the mahogany door. Harry swayed towards the wooden-topped bar, reached over and pulled out a of bottle of Glenlivet with one hand and a bag of Charlie with the other. He poured two large glasses, drank his in one gulp and laid out two lines of Peruvian flake.

"What is this place, Harry?"

Harry fell against the bar. "My eyes seem to be going dark from the outside. Everything is going dark. I'm not sure that's a good thing." He tried to focus on the two lines, which were currently a hazy four. He slowly gathered his thoughts. "This, Mickey, is the dream factory."

"What did you say, Harry? I'm feeling very odd."

"Join the club. Just watch yourself for the next few days. That was bloody dangerous stuff, but don't worry, the coke will straighten you out, I'm sure of it." Harry chuckled. "Dreams must be made, they don't just exist, they must be plucked from the morbid ether of our drab lives. Dreams, good times, happiness, uninhibited fun, laughter, life on a higher level. Mickey, we are the celestial angels, the bringers of joy, and this is the land of creation."

"So, this is where you knock up your drugs then?"

Harry looked at him. "Yes, Mickey, that's it exactly. I think I need to sit down."

Mickey clutched his chest. "My heart is beating three hundred times a minute."

"The trick is not to panic, old chum, it will wear off, it normally does."

"What do you mean, normally?" said Mickey.

"Well, you saw the canary."

Harry was pouring another drink as Kaitlin walked in. She was dressed in tight jeans and a plain white top, and her blonde hair cascaded down her back, reaching the top of her jeans. Mickey felt an awkwardness not experienced for years. His pulse quickened again, and he saw his face redden in the mirror behind the bar.

"Is it a bit hot in here, Harry?"

"No, not hot at all, Mickey, it's climate controlled, state of the art." Harry was barely concealing his pleasure at Mickey's discomfort. Then he saw the way they were looking at each other. "Oh God, not you two together! Please, that's all I need."

"Harry, how can you think such a thing? We've only just met," she replied.

"No, I can see what's going on here, and to be honest I'm a bit insulted, well more than a bit. How on earth could you ever prefer him to me?"

"Well, that's easy, Harry, he doesn't nearly kill me every day."

Harry turned towards Mickey. "Well, I won't have any disruption to my production. I have very tight schedules here, this is a very professional operation, as you've seen. And remember my words Kate, you, can do a lot better."

"Professional? Well, I hope the pills you're knocking out now are better than the one you gave to Sammy the limp."

"Below the belt, Mickey, well below the belt. I never had anything but good intentions."

"Who is Sammy the limp?" asked Kaitlin.

"Has Harry not told you?"

Chapter 5
August 1988
Puerto Banus, Spain

Eastham had checked into the Benabola Hotel an hour earlier and now sat at the bar tossing peanuts into his mouth. He studied the picture Jason had given him of Gregor, Anna's violent ex-boyfriend. He looked every inch the nasty little bastard he was, thin cruel lips, and a distinctive scar across his left eye. He stared at it, memorising the features, only needing to look at the picture once for his photographic memory to permanently store the image. What on earth had she seen in him? Perhaps she was just a kid and didn't know better.

Looking at the picture of Anna. He could see what Jason saw in her, she was stunning, but he'd only known her a few weeks. He wondered if this was worth all this effort? Still, Harry was paying the bill and was clearly convinced she was special to the boy.

He had a key and directions to her apartment and decided it would be the place to start.

Walking around the apartment, it looked as though she'd just popped out and would be back any minute. Dishes in the sink, clothes in the washing machine and an unmade bed. It didn't look good, and it was clear to Eastham, this wasn't a planned departure.

On an old teak chest was a half-finished handwritten letter; he picked it up and read it. It was a letter addressed to a woman called Lena. It offered no clues. He placed it in his pocket to read later, in the vague hope, he may have missed something.

The systematic search over the next thirty minutes yielded nothing. He frowned; his hopes of a quick answer to Anna's whereabouts were fading. The dryness in his mouth reminded him of the next place on his list. He walked along the second line of the port, where street cleaners tidied the detritus from the previous night's excesses. Dishevelled middle-aged men trudged the walk of shame after a night of half-remembered sex with hookers half their age.

He climbed the step into Desvan.

"Are you Magrao?"

"Yes, I am, who's asking?" Magrao replied, eyeing the newcomer suspiciously.

"I'm a friend of Jason's, I'm trying to find Anna. Can you tell me anything?"

Magrao looked at him. "Jason said you might be coming. I can only tell you what I told him."

Eastham sat there, drinking a beer and listening to the story he had already heard at least twice. "Thanks, Magrao, you've been very helpful. I'll see what the restaurant has to say for themselves." He saw the relief on Magrao's face as he left.

He walked three hundred yards to Pappardella. This would be the last of the places where he had a decent chance of getting a lead to the whereabouts of Anna, but wasn't surprised when the staff could not, or would not, tell him anything. It was the same as London; people were none too keen on talking to the law.

He looked across at Sinatra's bar and decided it was time for another beer. Choosing a corner table with his back against the wall was second nature, giving him optimum safety and viewpoint. He mouthed 'cerveza' to the barman, pulled the letter from his pocket, and read it again.

Dearest Lena

You many times told me, in my darkest hours that life would one day be full of light and hope again. I didn't believe you at the time, but as always you were right. I cannot wait for my new life with the man that has shown me the meaning of true love. Life will be complete if you....

The second reading confirmed there was nothing of interest in the letter, other than the affection seemed mutual between Jason and

Anna. He finished the beer and ordered another. A few hours later, the sun begun to slide slowly over the horizon.

Despite the vantage point of his carefully chosen position, he didn't see the slim figure walking towards him until she was at the table. She had the street savvy air of a hooker, but was dressed in a long, elegant dress — not typical hooker apparel.

"Excuse me."

He looked at her pretty face and guessed an age of about twenty-two. "No thanks, darling."

She laughed. "Are you Jason's friend?"

"I'm sorry, I just assumed..."

She looked at him, her smile put him at ease. "That's OK, maybe another time."

Eastham was warming to the idea but remembered this was exactly the situation that made his first wife run out of the door as fast as her legs would carry her.

She sat down. "I'm Lena, Anna's friend. Magrao told me you were here, I recognised you from his description. I was not here when Jason came back, and he'd left when I returned. I can't tell you much, but maybe what I know will help."

"Anything would help, thank you."

"Anna could not stop talking about Jason and her new life in London. It was love, never saw her so happy. Never would she leave here without him, unless it was not her choice. I think her ex-boyfriend has taken her. A nasty man, what she ever saw in him is a mystery to me. I hope it wasn't him, he will do bad things to her for being serious about another man, that's for sure."

"Do you know where he is?"

"The last I heard he had an apartment in San Pedro, selling drugs in Estepona and living with a Brazilian girl, on and off, called Andrea."

"That's just the news I needed. Would you like a drink, as a thank you?"

"I have to work, but again, maybe another time."

He took her hand. "I'm sure I can cover your costs for the evening. You have been very helpful, please, what would you like?"

The door clicked almost silently as she slipped out of his room, but Eastham was a light sleeper. He had felt her movement as she got out of the bed and pretended to be asleep. He was efficient. No need for goodbyes, and the financial side of the transaction had been dealt with hours before, dressed up as a contribution for the helpful information provided about the whereabouts of Gregor.

An hour later he pulled into the sleepy village of San Pedro, parked the car and walked the short distance to Chiringuito El Madero. An old man firing up the olive wood on the antique fishing boat filled with beach sand, looked across at him. A box of sardines coated in sea salt would soon be skewered and placed over the embers.

"*Ola, señor. Seran otros veinte minutos.*"

The sardines were a favourite of his, but today it would be something a little more filling. "*Gracias, señor, pero hoy tendre, desayuno ingles completo, por favor.*"

The freshly laid tables inside were more appealing than the ones outside, which were being toyed with by a frisky sea breeze. The table next to the bar gave him a good view of the people and the opportunity to listen to them. Out of the corner of his eye was a 'looky-looky man' walking towards him, carrying on his arms a hundred or so dresses that looked like they should collapse, and topple him to the ground. A few years earlier, Eastham had been dismissive of the hordes of looky-looky men who roamed the streets and beaches, but learnt, they led precarious lives, earning, very little from their endeavours, and sending most of the money back to their families in Africa. Before the man could speak, Eastham pulled a note from his pocket and gave it to him. "*El vestido no me vendria bien, pero toma el dinero y ten un buen dia.*"

"Thank you, you are very kind," he replied, taking the note from Eastham's outstretched hand. After placing it in his pocket, he pivoted with the grace of a ballerina and continued with the day's business. Eastham watched him approach another twenty or so people setting up their positions on the beach. Every time, waved away without another sale.

A woman playfully skipping in and out of the waves as they ebbed and flowed, for some reason reminded him of last night with Lena. Fleeting thoughts of guilt fluttered through his mind, before the more pleasant memories overtook them. Regret was a pointless emotion, he reasoned, but for the sake of his girlfriend promised himself, the event would not be repeated.

He wiped his mouth with a napkin and walked to the bar. *"La cuenta por favor."* He pulled some notes from his pocket, took out the picture of Gregor and showed it to the staff. *"Que sabes de este hombre?"* he asked.

He watched their body language; one of the most valuable lessons learned from his time in the police. Hours of interviewing cons had taught him to spot a lie from a hundred yards.

"No, señor."

"Gracias." He was convinced, they knew Gregor. They were lying, probably through fear. Silence or denial protected the innocent from a careless remark that could result in a visit from the guilty. It was a barrier, one he knew, would be difficult to overcome.

A small crowd had gathered at a tiny church in the distance, he walked towards it, mindlessly kicking stones along the way. His pace slowed, allowing the man following him, from the bar, to shorten the distance between them.

"Señor." Turning he found himself looking into the craggy face of the old man. Faded navy tattoos smudged his tanned torso. The smell of alcohol and bad breath pushed Eastham back.

"I know this man you are looking for; I will show you where he lives, but I will need money for my time, nothing is free." He started to walk; Eastham followed. They stopped outside an apartment block, no more than three hundred yards from the Chiringuito. He turned towards Eastham. "This is as far as I can go without the money, my friend."

Eastham thought it would be money well spent and anyway, it wasn't his money, and would add his standard twenty percent on top. With a bit of luck, this would be finished by the end of the day. He pulled out a small wad of notes and gave them to the man, who looked at them, put them in his pocket and stood there looking to one side. Eastham reached into his pocket again. "This is all I can give you."

"Then I suppose it will have to do."

"Great, so can we go there now?"

"This is the place, but I don't think he lives here any more." The old man pointed to the ground floor apartment, then rushed off, counting the money Eastham had given him. The apartment looked empty, no lights on, and the dusty front door had not been opened for a few weeks at least. Sea salt and dust formed crusts around the handle. He looked through the barred window in the vague hope that an answer would present itself.

He heard a man's voice. "Who are you looking for?"

Eastham had noticed the neighbour looking at him but had chosen to ignore him. He pulled the picture from his pocket; it had begun to fray at the edges. "Do you know him?"

"Yes, I know him, he left, a few months ago, thank God, and I hope the animal never comes back."

"Do you know where he is?"

"No, I don't, but I know where his girlfriend works."

"Will you tell me?" Eastham reached for his wallet and began to flick through another small wad of notes.

"Are you a friend of his?"

"No. I'm looking for someone he may have hurt."

"Then I will tell you and you can put your money away. Her name is Andrea, a lovely girl, Brazilian. I don't know what she saw in him, he was always beating her. Works in Duquesa, a marina thirty minutes away in a bar called Kinsale."

Eastham knew Duquesa well.

"Please take this," he said, as he thrust a pile of notes into the hands of his new best friend.

The drive along the picturesque coast took forty minutes. Parking was always easy in Duquesa and free, although the entry into his expenses pocketbook told a different story.

Kinsale overlooked the marina, one level up from the white boats swaying gently in the breeze. There was no mistaking her; the name badge helped. She had long black hair, tall, hourglass figure, barely a size ten. That guy must have something, thought Eastham. He certainly attracted some beautiful women.

He chose a stool by the cash register. She had noticed him walk up the stairs to the bar. A broad smile welcomed him.

"Hello, beer, please. I'm Paul, I see you are Andrea?"

Fear spread like a shadow over her face. He knew like most Brazilians working on the coast, she was probably an illegal, certainly for work purposes. The fact that the mayor might decide to do a round-up to impress his voters was a daily reality. Not that it would result in deportation, just a contribution to the mayor's latest charity, generally designed to buy him a new *finca* in the countryside.

"Don't worry, I only want to ask you about Gregor. I'm trying to find him, and I'm told you know him."

He could see the relief on her face. "Well, you're in the wrong country, he's in England, London, I hope he stays there. Why do you want him, money I guess?"

It was Eastham's turn to look surprised. "When did he go? Did he tell you exactly where in London?"

"I can't help you there, but definitely London, he called last week."

"Do you have the number?"

"No, I threw it away, why would I keep it? My life is much better without him."

"If he calls again, will you let me know? There will be five hundred pounds in it for you."

"Of course. I never thought I would say it, but I hope he calls." Just then a man waved to her from across the bar. "Excuse me," she said, and scurried over to the man, Eastham assumed was the owner. Eastham walked to the other side of the bar and gave her the number, noting that she seemed awkward in the man's company. Guessing she had been told to stop talking to the Englishman, thinking he was trouble.

Eastham left in search of a well-earned meal. He was certain she had told him the truth but decided to hang around for a few more days. Four days later it was clear; Gregor was not there, and she was telling the truth. Swaying back on his chair, balancing it precariously on two legs, he looked at the near full bottle of Rioja and decided it would be his last. He lifted the glass and took a large gulp of the wine. Yes, time to go home and tell Harry the bad news that he hadn't managed to find Anna.

The next day after returning the hire car, he boarded the plane, and relaxed into the soft leather seat. The plane taxied, then took off steeply back towards the grey skies of London.

He was puzzled, and nothing was making sense. The thought of telling Harry there was no resolution to the problem bothered him; loose ends were something he did not like.

Four hours later, Harry pressed the door entry button and Eastham walked into the office. "How did you get on, Paul, have you found her?"

"No, Harry, not her or the Russian. What I did find out, he's here in London somewhere. What are the chances of that? One good lead, an ex-girlfriend got a call from him a few weeks ago, said she would call me with his number if he calls again. Do you want me to carry on with this?"

Harry looked up and saw Eastham's eyes fixed on the top of his head. Eastham quickly looked away, but not before Harry had noticed. "Yes, Paul, keep it on the burner. I don't know what else you can do, but if you think of something, let me know."

"OK, Harry, are we done, or do you need me for anything else?"

"Yes, we're done, thanks you did a good job. Drop your sheet in and I'll get you paid. Here's a few quid to be getting on with." He pulled a thick bundle of notes from his jacket pocket and gave them to him.

As the door closed, Harry opened the drawer to his desk, pulled out a small mirror and held it above his head. He strained to see the small patch of skin that had begun to shine its way through the otherwise thick head of hair. He felt it with his fingers, then admonished himself, a frequent procedure performed several times a day. He'd begun to wonder if the constant touching was the cause of the hair loss.

He reached into the drawer again and took out a small bottle, unscrewed the cap and poured a tiny amount of the dark yellow liquid onto his hand and rubbed it into his hair. He looked at the handwritten label on the bottle, 'concentrated ostrich urine'.

"Time is a fucking bitch," he said under his breath. He was as fit as ever, still slim and quick-witted, but lately, had been struggling with the first signs of his own mortality. "Fuck, things change, friends leave, and time waits for no one," he said, looking at the bald patch again, whilst reaching across to the bowl brimming with shiny white Peruvian flake.

Chapter 6

The Tale of Sammy 'the limp' Sollis

"So, Harry, who's Sammy the Limp?" asked Kate. Harry glared at Mickey. "It's a very long story, not sure we've got time for that old yarn."

She placed an arm on Harry's and led him over to the large leather seats. "Oh, I think we've got time."

Rolling his eyes, the memories he had filed away under 'best forgotten,' flooded back. "Well, Kate, it started like this."

February 1967, CEUTA border crossing, Spain.

Something was wrong, no doubt. Harry's sixth sense was screaming at him; the only problem was making out the words. He always followed his instincts and had thought of abandoning the precious cargo hidden in the beat-up truck. It seemed the obvious choice, only now the choice had gone, it was too late.

He cast his mind back over the last few days, searching for anything that did not seem right. He'd met Mehdi, his middleman in Tetouan, as usual, and they'd driven the familiar road to Ketama. Mehdi was the same as always; he wasn't the problem; it was something else.

The Arabic name of the Riff Mountains is *bled es siba*, which translates as 'land of lawlessness', a description Harry thought perfect. He'd journeyed into the bad lands of the Riff many times. Once on the borderlands of the mountains, the roads steepen quickly and become narrow, winding and treacherous. Welcome to bandit country, and Ketama was its heartbeat, the hash capital of the Riff.

A small irritating fly appeared, one too fast to swat, with the annoying habit of refusing to leave once it had locked on to you. It flew into Harry's left ear. The instinctive slap, was immediately regretted as his ear began to throb. So where else could it have gone south? Thoughts moved to the old men drinking bitter, thick coffee in the small café on the approach to Ketama. A freshly killed sheep hung in the corner and flies buzzed around the carcass, but otherwise it seemed like all the other times; old men in Morocco sitting around tables always looked suspicious to him. Maybe it was time to lay off the pills, they were making him paranoid.

His mind hit the fast-forward button, to the exchange, the most dangerous part of any drug deal. Hassan, the normal supplier, wasn't there and a heated exchange between Mehdi and the Johnnie-Arab-Come-Lately ended without the normal handshake and kiss on each cheek. "Is there a problem, Mehdi?" Harry had asked.

"No, no problem, Harry."

The memory nagged at him, but the moment swept it to the back of his mind as he drove through customs, without a hitch. Relief, but still, doubt remained, knowing the tribal leaders and cartel bosses sometimes gave up buyers to the police to make them seem to be winning their war on drugs, but Harry always paid well to avoid that problem. Surely, they wouldn't do this to him? Apart from not wearing a turban, he was almost one of them.

Ten vehicles behind, the van that was loaded with a ton of hashish edged forward. Harry parked his car in a good vantage point on a hillside overlooking the border and customs control area and watched. Nine vehicles through, eight, seven, six, five, four, this was good, the border cops were having a lazy day. Three vehicles remained, then two. The battered, brown van was next.

The cop stepped in front of the van and put his hand in the air.

"Shit," muttered Harry.

Sammy 'the limp' Sollis stopped the van and smiled at the cop, who ignored him completely. He walked around the van and stopped at Sammy's door. He looked at Sammy for far longer than seemed necessary. The tap on the window and downward motion of his hand ordered Sammy to lower it. There was far more sweat on Sammy's face than the Spanish winter should have allowed. It was a bust, Harry was sure. The bastards were stringing it out to make it look more random than it was. He preferred the European runs; they were much safer, but this was the most profitable route, as well as the one that supplied the best product.

Sammy was five when he tried to jump on the back of a horse-drawn milk wagon, missed, and caught his leg in the spokes of the turning wheel. Three or four times his small body turned in time with the spinning wheel, but his screams went unheard by the deaf driver. It was only when a passing copper grabbed the reins of the horse that Sammy's nightmare stopped. The upside was his family never paid for milk again. The downside, Sammy would never walk again, without a limp. Worse for Sammy, as he grew older, his odd way of walking caused his spine to deform and develop a small hump.

Harry thought a cripple was less likely to arouse the suspicion of customs, so was glad to offer Sammy some well-paid work. Sammy would also put on a bad stutter when needed, to further discourage any nosy cop from being bothered with him for too long.

But today would be different. The cop looked towards the guardroom, then nodded and four more walked out of the building and dragged Sammy out of the van. He started to say something but was stopped by the hand of the largest cop, who slammed his head against the side of the van. "Shut up, we are not interested in what you have to say." Two of the officers opened the back doors of the van and disappeared inside. Harry listened to the sound of metal on metal as panels flew from the back of the van. They knew exactly where to look.

"Shit," said Harry again. "Now I need a new driver, and supplier, how bloody inconvenient." He watched as Sammy hobbled away in handcuffs and saw the blood pouring down the side of his head. Sammy was shouting at the cops. Still keeping up the stutter. Sammy, ever the professional, Harry thought.

August 1967, Modelo Prison, Spain.

Modelo prison, in the centre of Barcelona, opened in 1904. It was designed to provide a model for social rehabilitation and re-integration, rather than being a regular get-the-shit-beaten-out-of-you environment as prisons were before, but that wasn't how Sammy was seeing it.

He had a visitor, Paul Eastham, Harry's Mr Fix it. They sat at a grey battered table, which like everything else was bolted to the floor. The fluorescent light above their heads flickered annoyingly, casting an eerie light onto the face of the guard, who could barely stay awake. His three days of stubble and half-closed eyes suggested this wasn't his only job. The noise of twenty prisoners and their wives, mistresses and screaming kids completed the madness that was visiting time at Modelo.

Sammy looked a lot older than a few months before. His skin was sallow, so out of place in Spain, and was at least a stone lighter. His watery eyes and sagging jowls gave him the appearance of a bloodhound.

"Paul, I can't stand it here, they have stairs, I'm on the top floor and by the time I get to the canteen for breakfast, it's time for lunch."

Eastham laughed, ignoring the fact Sammy was being serious. He didn't care for the half-man he was having to spend a few minutes with as long as he was being paid.

"I want out. Can you sort it, Paul? I'm going crazy in here."

Eastham yawned. "Yes, look, Harry is working on it, we will get you out, keep the faith. Try to enjoy yourself. Not many people get to do what you're doing, this is a true money can't buy experience."

Although Eastham had crossed to the other side of the tracks, corrupted by easy money, he still despised villains who were too far down the food chain, and in his mind, Sammy was as low as they got. To get his respect you needed to be someone like Harry or Mickey, but respect aside, thought Harry had made a poor call.

For the reward of springing a bottom feeder like Sammy, this was risk off the scale.

"Well now, 1 — loo — look I'm not sure that's ve — very funny, and I have started stuttering for real, like I'm being punished. I tell you, when I get out of here, I'm going straight. Like it's not bad enough nearly being killed by a milk cart, I end up in here for doing a bit of driving."

Eastham shook his head, laughing. "Sammy, you were carrying a ton of hash. Anyway, I'm out of here, not my sort of place, Harry will visit in a few days, when everything is sorted. Try and cheer up a bit, get out in the yard, get some sun on that skin of yours, you look like a ghost."

A week later Harry Fleet walked through the heavy double doors into the prison visiting room and spotted Sammy straight away.

"Sammy, how are you?" As usual, it was rhetorical. "Sorry I'm a few days late. I tell you what, this city is some place. Well, you wouldn't know that, but let me tell you it is." He passed a packet of cigarettes to Sammy, who immediately took one and lit it. His eyes rolled back as the nicotine calmed his craving. "Now are you ready for the good news, and my great escape plan? I've put in a lot of effort and hard work, Sammy, because as you know, no one ever gets left behind on my team."

"What's the plan, Harry, a helicopter, tunnelling out? Sneaking me out dressed as a priest? What is it? I knew you'd never let me down."

"Don't be a clever bastard. I thought about those things, but I'd be some sort of madman to do any of that nonsense. No, I'm a professional as you know, and the man charged with the success of this escape mission. And believe me that's exactly what I will do, succeed. This place is awful, I wouldn't fancy a night in here, but what do you expect when you get caught and put me to all this trouble? Anyway, don't dwell on what you did wrong, try and enjoy your last few days, I'm sure it's not as bad as it looks." Harry stopped, exhaled, and wiped his face with his handkerchief. "What do you have to do to get a drink in here? Its

71

bloody roasting, I think you might want to write a letter to the governor."

"Welcome to my world, Harry, and it is just as bad as it looks."

Harry wasn't listening; the exertions of the night before were beginning to catch up with him. "I guess you get used to it, Sammy, better hot than cold. Some old people back home would love this heat, no more freezing winters huddled by some old gas burner. It's all about perception, you moan about the heat, the old people moan about the cold, and I have to listen to it all." Harry looked at him. "Anyway, my plan is very simple, but at the same time brilliant." He looked into the expectant eyes and held out his hand.

Sammy felt something in his palm and looked down at a small grey pill.

"Now look, Sammy, I need to go. I'll be back in two days. Got a few more things to sort, but don't worry about me. I like this town. I'd like to stay here for a few more weeks to be honest, but I guess you're in a hurry. All about you, Sammy. Two days and your nightmare will be over, what's more I've got a great boat trip planned for you, and a couple of ladies to keep you company. You will love them; I have personally tried both myself."

"Oh thanks, Harry, what ca, ca, can I s-s-say?"

Harry smiled. "Nice one, Sammy, still not lost it I see with the stuttering. Oh, and don't do anything with that pill till I get back."

Harry rushed out of the prison, reflecting on the environment Sammy had so suddenly found himself in. It was certainly a little sparse compared to his hotel suite.

Mickey and Paul Eastham were waiting in the convertible, and Harry jumped in without opening the door. Moments later, they were speeding through the streets of Barcelona.

"Only two days boys, two days," said Harry.

"Yes, I bet Sammy can't wait. How was the old fella?"

Harry looked at Mickey, his face contorted into a mask of mocking amusement. "No, Mickey, we've got two more days in Barcelona, I love this place."

Forty-eight hours later, Harry, feeling as tired as he could ever remember, walked into Modelo, went through security and into the visiting room, where Sammy sat, ashen faced.

"My God Sammy, you look rough, like you haven't slept for days. Anyway, we're all set to go. Now, you haven't sold or lost the pill, have you?"

"No, I still have it, and yu, you don't look too good yourself."

"Well as you can imagine, I haven't had a lot of sleep, what with all the bloody arrangements and things. Non-stop, that's what it's been, people don't realise how difficult it is being a leader. Always putting other people before yourself."

"You have lipstick on your shirt."

Harry followed Sammy's gaze to a bright red stain on the shoulder of his shirt. "You haven't lost more weight, have you?"

"Yes, I have. It takes me so long to walk to the fo, food that by the time I get there, it's gone."

Harry tried to rub the lipstick from his shirt, but his efforts were making it worse. "Facetiousness is not an asset, Sammy, I am trying to do a professional job here. Now I thought you would be a bit fatter, you know, with having nothing to do, lazing about all day. Anyway, might be best if you nibble a little bit off the pill and throw it away. Yes, that will be about right, what with your weight, about a hundred and forty pounds I guess?"

"Guess! Harry, shouldn't you have a pair of scales and a chart or something? What does the pill do? Does it grow me wings so I can fly out of here?"

"As I said, facetiousness is not an attractive trait. No, you swallow the pill, and it slows down your heart. Makes it look, well, like you're having problems with your ticker. You'll collapse, and I have to say, it might be a bit painful, but needs must Sammy. No half measures, no need for acting, this pill does it all."

The colour drained from Sammy's face. "That doesn't sound like much fun."

"You might want to be a bit more thankful. I lost one of my favourite dogs testing this, and I'm not sure the other one is going to pull through."

Sammy laughed nervously. "Harry, you kill me, you're a ve, very funny man."

Harry's eyes narrowed. "Funny, Sammy, funny how? Like I make you laugh, like I'm a clown?" Sammy began to tremble. "I'm kidding, great line for a film though. Right, tomorrow, you need to swallow the pill half-way through breakfast. Set off early, don't be having a lie-in and getting there late. Timing is everything in life, and the opposite of timing and life, is lateness and death."

Sammy subconsciously filtered out the word death. "So, it's gonna be, OK?"

"Sammy, please, this is me. Have I ever let you down? Anyway, I'll be getting off now, things to do, people to say goodbye to, big day tomorrow. See you at the hospital."

Sammy walked back to his cell more slowly than normal and sat on the bed. This was ridiculous. What kind of choice was this, take one of Harry's Frankenstein pills or rot in a Spanish jail for years? And what was that about the hospital? It wasn't really a choice, the legal system in Spain was stacked in favour of the law. He was bang to rights, and his lawyer had told him to expect at least five years. He thought about the irony; Harry's charity case was being given Harry's charity drug.

He lit another cigarette, his hands shaking. The same question turned over in his mind, Do I feel lucky? Harry was a great pill maker. They were the best in London and the punters loved them, always coming back for more, never a complaint and always happy. But this was different, this was to make someone ill, and that someone was him.

It was then the thought of being dragged along by the milk cart came flooding back, reminding him that luck was not his closest friend. He was grateful to Harry but had never fully trusted him. Harry was a straight shooter and as honest as anyone in his trade could be. What made him uneasy was, Harry's brain wasn't wired the same as the rest of the human race. He meant well but didn't think like other people. Harry had given him a job; his life without Harry's timely intervention would have been a continual flow of pity and poverty. For that, he was grateful. But for that, he was in jail.

He lay on the bed, as a small cockroach disturbed from its slumber scurried over his arm and ran into a crack in the concrete floor. Sammy closed his eyes and remembered the first time Harry Fleet, entered his life.

1965
The Marquee Club, London

Sammy opened his eyes, after closing them to heighten the fragrance hanging in the air. His leg was beginning to ache as he made another circuit of the club, collecting glasses and wiping tables. He liked his job, or more accurately, liked looking at the women who came in, the glamorous clothes, their beautiful bodies and the way their perfume lingered in the air.

Sammy was the guy with the limp and the hunchback, who had never read the book *Chat Up Lines and the Art of Getting Laid*. He was a virgin, and that didn't look like changing any time soon.

Again, pausing at a table, he inhaled the faint scent of the woman who had just passed him. His head raised like a meerkat, his nose quivering, as though sniffing for food. A woman tapped him on the shoulder. "Hello, handsome."

The shock of the extremely rare occasion of physical contact in his life, almost caused him to fall, as his one good leg struggled to keep him upright. Was this really happening to him? I think I'm in love, this must be what it feels like, he thought. His face reddened and his lips quivered, struggling to force the words out. "C-c-c-can I buy you a drink?"

She moved closer to him, and her breast touched his shoulder. "No, I'm good, thank you." The kiss on his cheek made his head spin. "You are a very brave man to hobble about like that." He thought she was the most caring, beautiful woman he had ever met. What he hadn't noticed were her friends, laughing at him from across the room. That should have been the end of it, but Sammy didn't get it, he never did, sure that she meant that kiss, and more would follow. Maybe, even, this would be the night of his dreams. The glasses shook in his hands on the short journey back to the bar, his head still spinning.

Harry Fleet reclined at his normal table, no more than five feet away, and had listened to the conversation. Weeks before, he had noticed Sammy working at the club and admired his spirit. Sammy, had a downtrodden air, but there was something about him that people liked. Harry's passion for opera knew no bounds, his favourite was Giuseppe Verdi's *Rigoletto*. To him, Sammy was Rigoletto, a limp, a hunch and a life, as surely cursed as Rigoletto's had been.

He watched her walk back to her friends, waited for a moment, finished his drink and walked towards them. "Very funny, girls, now get the fuck out of here and don't ever come back."

"Who are you to tell us what to do?"

"Why did you do that? It was cruel. Now like I said it's time to leave."

"It was only…"

"Is there a problem?"

They looked at the doorman. "Yes, this man is picking on us and telling us to leave."

He slowly turned towards Harry. "Is this true?"

"Yes, it is, Joe, they were very disrespectful to one of your staff, Sammy."

"Well, in that case, ladies, let me show you where the door is."

Harry returned to his table just as Sammy walked back from behind the bar, looking for the woman who kissed him. A kiss that lingered in his mind, despite not being able to see her. He sniffed again, trying to pick up the trail of her perfume.

Harry was watching him. "Sammy."

"Oh, hello, Mr Fleet."

"Sammy, the girl who kissed you has left."

"But… why?"

He saw the disappointment on Sammy's face. "My name is Harry. Call me Harry, would you?"

"Yes, sorry, where did she go?"

"Sit down, you've had a very lucky escape, believe me."

Sammy did so and was immediately distracted by the woman sitting by Harry's side. "Sammy, the woman who left has been married twice and both her husbands died. I think she may have killed them. Looking for number three, no doubt, so don't let that be you. Anyway, I hope you don't mind but I asked her to leave. Thing is, Sammy, this is my friend Mary. She has been looking at you for weeks and trying to catch your eye and would like to spend some time with you."

Sammy looked at the woman again trawling his memory, trying to recall seeing her before, let alone her looking at him. To him, she was the most beautiful woman he had ever seen, he was sure of it. How could he not have noticed her? Her hair was the colour of raven's wings, that fell in curls to her waist, perfectly framing her pale porcelain face. Dark eyebrows, arched delicately, over feline eyes, Sammy thought her body had surely been carved with the very chisels of Michelangelo himself.

She smiled and reached to touch his hand. "Could we go somewhere when you finish?"

Sammy's good leg started to tremble again, the vibrations travelling up his body like a shock wave. "Come over when you finish, we can leave together," she added. He tried to regain his composure, but now had a new problem to deal with, the bulge in his trousers. He waited a few awkward moments, trying to think of things that would make it disappear, it didn't work.

Harry smiled and passed him a white table napkin. "This might help."

He took it and placed it over the top of his trousers. "Thank you, Mr Fleet."

As Sammy disappeared through the crowd back to the bar, Harry and Mary looked at each other and burst out laughing. "I think you're going to have quite a night," Harry said, pressing a bundle of ten-pound notes into her hand.

The cigarette stub burned his fingers, returning Sammy to the present. He quickly lit another. The smoke rose, dancing, wispy curls cut through the sunlight from the barred but open window. The breeze caught it and the smoke moved in a sudden urgent migration, like wildebeest on the savannah seeking the safety of the open plains. Once outside the window, it disappeared, free, liberated.

Sammy stood, shuffled to the window, peered out, took another drag, and blew the smoke through the window. "Free," he said under his breath, "free." He stayed at the window until the light faded, then lay on his bed.

The morning sun came slowly, but still outran his effort to sleep. He looked at the little grey pill in his hand, as Harry's words rang in his ears, 'nibble some off, so it will be the right amount.' How much should be nibbled off? He wondered. Was he seriously thinking of taking a pill that would give him a heart attack? It sounded crazy. It was crazy!

A bluebottle clumsily crashed into the wall, fell to the floor and spun around frenetically attempting to prolong its life. It momentarily distracted him from the squalid cell he shared with the cockroaches. As a child, the family house in Stockwell was infested with roaches. After the first few encounters, he had grown to like them and count them as friends. A few were kept as pets in a goldfish bowl, covered to keep them in. Early experiments and dead bodies taught him the need to punch small air holes in the linen cover so they would not die. Now he welcomed them into his cell like old friends. He'd read cockroaches were once revered in English homes, centuries before, even released into new homes for good luck. How the cockroaches luck had changed — how his luck had changed. Such irony, he thought, 'Sammy the cockroach.' The simple facts of life, where clear to him; they had been made abundantly clear by a milk cart.

Decisions made today would change the course of his life, but decisions, were not his favourite thing. Going back in time, to the Marquee collecting glasses again, would make him a very happy man. Certain now, he had seen the light, crime was a thing of the past, a better future was on the horizon. But the problem remained, of securing his freedom. Could Harry really get him out of the hospital? Would the prison guards even take him there? Maybe they would throw him back into his cell to die in agony, surrounded by the applauding roaches dressed as the nobleman in Harry's twisted version of *Rigoletto*. It was Rigoletto who perished and not his beloved daughter. He had heard Harry compared him to the hunchback in the opera, but it hadn't bothered him at the time. In fact, it had made him feel special, in an odd kind of way.

Sammy tried to calm his racing mind. Harry had never let him down. The decision was made, as the pill was placed in his pocket, and he began the longest walk of his life. Slow, then quick, then slow again, a physical battle to match the mental one.

The smell of the food made him nauseous, as he picked up a plate of the pale grey sludge and sat at a table on his own. Pretty patterns formed on the plate by the involuntary movement of his spoon. He looked down and saw three numbers on the plate, all sixes. "Jesus, an omen!" he muttered. The guards and prisoners looked at him, but said nothing, thinking, here is another Englishman slowly losing his mind in their prison. The sweat and fear seeped into every bone in his body, including the broken ones. Unblinking, and the fear pushed to the back of his mind, he swallowed the tablet.

Five minutes passed, and nothing had happened. Harry has made a mistake; the pill doesn't work, and it won't give me a heart attack at all. Thank God, what was I thinking? He laughed as a wave of relief swept over him and the smoke of a newly lit, sweet tasting cigarette rescued him from the madness of what he had just done.

Suddenly the room began to spin. He rubbed his eyes and felt sweat drip into them, as a sharp pain dug into his stomach, he collapsed onto the table, coughing violently. A mixture of spit and smoke fell from his mouth. The attempt to stand failed, as his leg gave way beneath him, his body shook, and the sweat burned his eyes. His vision closed in from the edges until all that remained was a blurred light in the middle that slowly began to disappear. He dragged himself up from the table, then lost his footing, crashing onto the cold concrete floor. He rolled onto his front, now on all fours, and screamed as the pain in his chest intensified. "Jesus, Harry!"

Froth formed around his mouth. Then waves of vomit hit the floor in front of him. His head swirled, and everything faded to black.

Mickey, Harry and Eastham sat in the convertible across from the entrance to Modelo Prison. The early morning had started as it meant to go on, clear blue sky and a fast-rising temperature. Harry had forgotten his hat and was beginning to worry about the effects of the sun on his head. He yawned. "I bet that lazy Sammy's still in bed. Mickey, give me your cap, would you? You don't need it."

At that moment, an ambulance swung slowly into view and entered the prison gates.

"Well, they don't seem to be in much of a hurry, it must be for Sammy," said Mickey as he tossed Harry his cap.

Thirty minutes later the ambulance reappeared. Eastham put the car into gear and followed. They tailed the ambulance to Hospital Saint Joan and pulled discreetly into the parking area just as a motionless Sammy was taken out of the ambulance on a gurney.

"I hope you gave him the right amount, Harry," said Mickey.

"I'm a professional, how many times do I have to say it," replied Harry, but the thought had already entered his head, seeing Sammy's left arm hanging lifeless to the side of the gurney, and the lack of urgency.

"Is that our man with him?" asked Mickey.

Harry yawned. "No, that's not him. This might be a long wait Paul, I need a lie down, it's wearing me out, all this rescuing lark.

Drop us off and you wait here 'till he turns up, you know what he looks like, then come and get us. I think I might have burnt the top of my head. Things I do for other people, never a word of thanks."

"No prob, Harry, back to the hotel?"

"No, drop us at the bar on Via Augusta."

Hospital St Joan, Barcelona.

The intense pain in Sammy's chest slowly faded. Remembering nothing after collapsing, he looked up at the doctor, who was taking his blood pressure. "You are very lucky to be alive," said the doctor. "If it hadn't been for an Algerian doctor in your prison for smuggling drugs, you would be dead. Your heart stopped for a full minute. Did you take something?"

Sammy tried to look him in the eye but couldn't. Lying, was second nature to him, but he didn't like lying to a doctor who was trying to save his life. "No, I didn't take anything. Am I going to be OK?"

The doctor looked at him. "Yes, I think so, I gave you something to help with the pain." A long needle punctured Sammy's arm and the doctor faded into a misty spectre as he walked towards the door. The room began to spin, as Sammy drifted out of consciousness with the happy thought of being alive, and the plan working. "Bless you, Harry, bless you," he murmured, before he fell into a deep, peaceful sleep.

A few minutes before three p.m., officer Rodrigo Garcia arrived at the entrance to the hospital and hung around for a few minutes smoking a cigarette. He walked in circles, trying his best not to look awkward or out of place, which was clearly harder than he'd imagined it would be. He threw the cigarette packet into the bin and walked into the hospital. Eastham got out of the car, walked to the battered metal bin, threw in a cigarette packet and then, as though making a mistake, took out the other packet. Five minutes later, he pulled up outside Bar Aurelio.

Harry and Mickey were sitting outside, and Harry was lining up empty shot glasses on the table. Eastham looked at Harry, who, as expected, looked a little worse for wear. He tossed the cigarette packet to him.

"Beer, Paul?"

"No thanks, I'll have a drink when we're back in London."

Harry opened the packet and pulled out a small piece of paper. "He's in room 51, third floor, so I guess the lazy bugger will need a wheelchair. Beggars belief, lying in bed all day, then we have to wheel him about. We need to be there at seven, so time for a few more beers."

At 6.53 p.m., Harry and Mickey walked into the hospital and into the toilets, where they changed into sets of porters' clothes, stolen from central stores three days earlier. Harry glanced across at the collection of battered old wheelchairs by the reception. "Go on, Mickey, go and get a wheelchair, I'm feeling a bit pissed."

"Can you ever take anything seriously? And take that bloody cap off. There can't be a single Spanish porter who supports West Ham and wears the cap to work."

Harry's eyebrows lifted, he shook his head, "I think I've done rather well so far."

Mickey walked over to the row of wheelchairs. The first two had arms missing and the third had no seat. The next in line looked to be complete, so he took it, realising the danger of attracting unwanted attention. He pushed it towards Harry and then noticed the row of gleaming new wheelchairs to Harry's left. "Hang on, I thought you'd checked the layout of the place. There's a load of new wheelchairs over there."

Harry placed his hand on Mickey's shoulder. "Mickey, stop moaning, it's too late now. I'm pretty sure they weren't there a few days ago."

At 6.58 p.m., Rodrigo Garcia arose from his chair outside room 51 and walked along the corridor. As he passed the foul-smelling toilet, the sight of two pale-looking porters, surprised him. One looked decidedly the worse for wear and had a West Ham United cap hanging out of his pocket.

As Harry and Mickey entered the unlocked room they were surprised by the sound of Sammy's snoring. "Lazy little bastard," said Harry, poking his ribs through the single bedsheet. Mickey pushed past him and lifted Sammy's, motionless body into the wheelchair. The added weight made the wheelchair screech as Mickey pushed it down the corridor. A nurse looked at them and smiled, as the noise got louder.

Harry shook his head and wagged an unsteady finger at Mickey. "One thing, Mickey, one thing that's all I asked of you. You've put the whole mission in jeopardy. Have you not got any oil?" Sammy groaned and was regaining consciousness. "Look, you've woken up the patient," said Harry.

"Shut up, you're going to get us nicked," replied Mickey.

A small dribble of vomit rolled down Sammy's chin, he lifted his head and stared at Harry. "*Harry, el medico me ayudo cuando estaba enfermo.*"

"Jesus, Mickey, the little fucker has learnt Spanish!"

"What's he saying?"

"Probably asking for another one of those pills I gave him, greedy little bastard."

They pushed Sammy out of the hospital and into the service area, where Eastham was waiting.

"How'd it go, Harry?"

"Like clockwork. Mickey fucked up as usual, but all's well that ends well, as the bard would say."

Mickey lifted Sammy into the car. "Give it a rest, Harry."

"You need to relax a bit more, Mickey, maybe you should take one of those pills Sammy had, calm you down a bit. Come on let's go unless you want to take the wheelchair back."

Harry placed the West Ham cap back on his head as Eastham put the car into gear and slowly drove out onto the main road.

Barcelona Port

Eastham pushed his head against the headrest and slowly exhaled as the convertible came to a stop. Harry and Mickey helped Sammy out of the car. "Well done, Paul," said Harry. "You did a good job."

"Thanks. Good luck on the boat. I'll see you back in London." Eastham gently squeezed the accelerator and made his way back to the airport.

"There it is, Mickey, what do you think?" Mickey looked at the gleaming yacht. Two beautiful women, and a man he guessed was the skipper, stared back at him. Harry waved to them as though they were guests arriving at a party.

"Permission to come aboard skipper," Harry said. Not waiting for the answer, he bounced along the gangway, leaving Mickey with Sammy. "Cast off when ready skip, no time to hang about. Right, I need to get out of these ridiculous hospital clothes. Ladies, give me a hand would you." He disappeared down the stairs with the two women. Mickey turned to help Sammy aboard, but Sammy had already rushed ahead. Mickey groaned. The day was becoming ever more bizarre, he thought. One minute Sammy couldn't move, the next he was hopping along the gangway like a fucking kangaroo.

Mickey was drifting in and out of sleep; the adrenalin surge from the escapade with Harry had left him tired. The land had disappeared, and the movement of the yacht encouraged his slumber. His sleep was broken by Harry's reappearance with the women, both wearing nothing but a smile.

"Ladies, let me introduce you to my friends, this is Mickey, my assistant on this voyage, and Sammy the jailbreaker. Gentlemen, meet Christine and Mandy, the best-looking women in London, and I have to say, both bloody good in the sack."

Sammy shuffled across to Harry and grabbed both his hands. "Harry, I can't thank you enough." Tears were rolling down his cheeks.

Harry pulled his hands away from Sammy's. "Not a time for tears, Sammy, let's not hear any more of it. Anyway, we need you back, I've lined up a nice bit of work for you." Harry patted him on the back and scurried off to get another beer, grabbing Mickey's arm along the way. "That was close. Watch Sammy for a bit, the pill I gave him is a right layer cake. When it's almost worn off it makes you want to shag anything, and I'm sorry, you know I'm very accommodating, but he's just not my type. Did you see the foam coming out of his mouth?"

"My God, you've got limits, I never thought I would see the day, even if it is a rampant one-legged foaming at the mouth hunchback."

"Fuck off, Mickey, that's bloody rude. Anyway, come and meet Skip, he's an old friend of my granddad." He passed Mickey a beer.

"Harry, that would make him eighty-odd."

"That's right."

Mickey looked at the skipper, who had the body of a thirty-year-old and the darkest, fullest head of black hair he'd ever seen. "Yes, right," said Mickey, laughing.

"It's true, the old fella spent fifteen years wandering around China annoying people, sailing up and down the Yangtze. Anyway, he came across some old guy who was about five hundred years old. The skip beat him at Mah-jong or dominoes, or some other game, and couldn't pay the winnings, so the ancient Chinaman gave him the secret of his eternal youth. Wu Shou it's called, keeps him young and his hair as black as coal. It also gives him the sex drive of a rabbit. Come to think of it, you might want to get some yourself. I put it in some of the pills I make, just as a healthy little bonus. I call it customer service, the key to running a successful business." Harry stumbled forward and thought it better to take a seat. "Bloody rough sea this."

Mickey looked over the side of the yacht; the water was dead calm. "Does it really work, skip?" He regretted his words as soon as they left his mouth. The skipper took a large swig of rum and looked at the women. "Oh yes, it works, doesn't it?"

They giggled, and everyone looked at the bulge that had formed in the old man's trousers. Mickey shook his head, then went to the refrigerator and took out another beer.

They had been sailing for two hours and the moon reflected in the dead calm sea. Harry and Mickey were relaxing on the deck drinking beer. Below deck, Sammy was being entertained by the women, and on the bridge the skipper was three quarters through the bottle of dark rum, singing what were probably ancient Chinese folk songs.

"Harry, is he OK driving this boat half-pissed?"

"It's sailing, not driving. Anyway, he's better when he's pissed, it calms him down."

"Where are we going?"

"South of France, we need a break and that's the place to go. I bet Sammy can't believe how his life has turned around. One day a stinking Spanish jail, the next in bed with two of the sexiest women on the planet."

"Yes, I doubt we'll see much of him. Seems to be getting his money's worth by the sounds of things," Mickey replied.

In the master cabin

"Sammy, Harry told us you must take it easy and let us do everything.'

"Don't worry about me, I've never had so much energy." He stood, uneasily at the end of the bed holding Christine's thighs with his hands, her ankles wrapped around his ears, his withered leg supported by an old oak chest. He was close to his third climax and could hold on no longer. Mandy sat opposite him; her legs parted on Christine's face. His thrusts became faster and more erratic. Suddenly he fell forward and collapsed, knocking Mandy over. They both screamed. They'd seen many things in their time, including cabinet ministers and even the occasional Russian spy, but this was weird, even for them.

Harry heard the screams. "Jesus, Sammy must be good."

The door crashed open, and Mandy rushed out, sobbing, "Harry, it's Sammy, there's something wrong with him!"

Harry laughed. "There's been something wrong with him for years, he's making up for lost time. You'll just have to ride out the storm. It's the pill I gave him. It'll wear off soon, go on, off you go, I'm sure you've been with worse."

"No, Harry, he's not moving."

"He's probably taking a breather. I knew you two would be too much for him."

Mickey pushed past Harry, knocking his beer from his hand, as he charged down into the cabin and saw Sammy's motionless body. He turned him over and placed two fingers on his neck.

"Bloody right there's something wrong with him, he's snuffed it."

Harry stumbled down the stairs. "Damn, I've hurt my leg, Mickey, what's all the fuss about?" He looked at Sammy, who was a dark grey colour. "Jesus, Mickey, he's dead!"

Harry focused on Sammy's face. It might have been a trick of the light, but he seemed to be smiling. "Girls, what the fuck did you do to him? You weren't doing that little trick you do, were you? That would kill most men." He glanced at the skipper, whose head had appeared at the top of the stairs. "And be careful with the skipper, he's the only one who can sail this thing."

The skipper was smiling and swaying, holding a new bottle of rum in his hand. "What trick would that be, ladies?"

"Not now, Skip. Stay off those pills for a day or two, would you? I think these two have killed him. I knew I should only have brought one of them, I'm too bloody generous for my own good."

"What the fuck are we gonna do now, Harry?" said Mickey.

"All I can say is this is bloody inconvenient. After all the effort, time and money I've put in, that's without the fact, I should be at the West Ham game tomorrow." He turned towards the skipper. "Have we got a flag?"

"No flags, Harry. Well, I've got an old pirate flag, I run up the mast for a bit of a laugh sometimes, will that do?"

"Really, Skip? Good man, off you go and fetch it, I think Sammy would appreciate that. We can wrap him up in it and say a proper goodbye, give him a good send off. You'll have to bury him at sea, captains can do that can't they?"

The skipper glanced over at Mandy, as he took the flag out of the oak chest beside him. "Yes, marriages as well."

"Give it a rest, Skip, I'm not sure everyone is treating this sad moment with the gravitas it deserves. Come on, Mickey, give me a hand." They hauled Sammy on to the deck and wrapped him in the flag. "There we are, Mickey, let's put him on the back of the boat, on that wooden ledge." They placed the body on the edge of the large rail at the stern of the ship and Harry picked up an old iron winch and tied it around the body so it wouldn't float. They stood back a respectful distance and waited for the skipper to do whatever skippers did when there was an inconvenient death onboard. He took his captain's hat off, held it against his chest and began.

What delightful guests are they
Life and Love!
Lingering I turn away,
This late hour, yet glad enough
They have not withheld from me
Their high hospitality.
So, with face lit with delight
And all gratitude, I stay
Yet to press their hands and say,
Thanks. So fine a time! Goodnight.

He raised his head. "Let us remember and say goodbye to our fine shipmate Sammy."

At that moment, the body moved.

"By Christ, he's still alive," said Mickey. The body moved again as Mickey moved slowly towards it. Another more violent jerk took it in the opposite direction and just as Mickey reached for the body, it slipped over the side. A moment before the body hit the sea and sank beneath the waves, everyone heard the plaintive cry:

"Harreee!"

"Jesus, It's a miracle."

"No, Harry, it was, a bloody miracle."

"Well, jump in and get him!"

Mickey looked at him. "The only thing I'm getting is a beer."

Harry peered over the side. "Well, it could have been worse. It's a great way to meet your maker."

"Yes, Harry, except he wasn't dead."

Harry took his arm. "Yes, well, I think that's something we should keep to ourselves. Come on, let's get that beer."

Chapter 7
1968
London

Harry was on the phone discussing the merits of tomorrow's 1.30 at Kempton. He had the inside track on the long price winners that would gallop home alone, thanks to the unforeseen laziness of the favourites who, twenty minutes before, had, had the benefit of a Ketamine injection. Today though he seemed unusually distracted.

Mickey wandered unnoticed through the doors of the laboratory and looked at Kaitlin, who was checking some dials on Harry's brand-new distillation unit. She had two small flasks in her hands and was dancing and singing, not spilling a single drop from the near full flasks.

When I met you and you changed my life
All the hurt and pain, just disappeared

He walked up behind her and put his arms around her waist. She spun around and looked into his eyes.

"Were you singing that for me?"

"No, I wasn't, don't flatter yourself, Michael Warren." She kissed him on the lips.

"What are you working on, nothing dangerous, I hope? It's about time Harry paid you some danger money."

"It's one of Harry's new wonder drugs, to make his hair grow back, so not too much danger this time."

Mickey laughed. "What's his latest idea, not more sea otters I hope?"

"Sea otters? What on earth's that all about?"

Mickey laughed. "Harry read the hairiest animal in the world is the sea otter. Each one with over a billion hairs, apparently. He'd worked out, if it was good enough for the otter it was good enough for him, so, off went a fishing boat to catch a couple of them. He told the crew to bring them back alive, thinking, if they were dead, they might lose whatever it was that made them so hairy. It was a month before the lorry turned up, with two otters. All the way from Alaska, soon they were happily swimming around in the purpose-built tank Harry made for them. He galloped over to the tanks, sure this was finally it, the formula that would make his fortune, and at the same time cure his impending baldness. He peered into the tank, and one of the otters surfaced and swam up to him. Harry placed his hand on the top of his head and felt the thinning patch and sighed, "Mickey, take them back, I can't kill him, now I've seen his face." So, they went back all the way to America."

She kissed him again. "I'm not sure I believe that, anyway he's made me sign a secrecy agreement to protect his ideas. Do you think that includes you?"

"Don't answer that question, of course it includes you." Harry was grinning for the first time that day.

"Kaitlin, please promise me one thing."

"Yes, anything."

"Please don't end up as mad as Harry."

"There's no chance of that, no one's as mad as Harry." She looked across at Harry, "Are you OK? You've been stressed all day."

"Yes, I'm just a bit stressed, big day tomorrow. Come on let's get a beer."

Mickey looked at Kaitlin and then Harry. "Sorry, mate, gonna have to take a rain check, we've got other plans."

"Bloody hurtful you two. Don't forget who brought you formerly sad and lonely people together, me, in case you've forgotten, and now you can't even be there for me in my small hour of need. A drink with an old friend."

They looked at each other and knew sometimes in life giving in is easier. "OK, we're coming," said Mickey.

Kaitlin took Harry's arm as they walked to the car. "I think we may be onto something with the new hair formula, do you want to test it on the monkeys?"

"No, Kate, give it straight to me, I'm not sure testing on animals is right. I keep having nightmares about otters, and there were a couple of protesters in Hyde Park last week with pictures of dogs smoking cigarettes on their T-shirts. Progress always has its price, but not everyone sees that."

Mickey looked at her and saw the ability she had to distract Harry and cheer him up. In fact, it wasn't only Harry, everywhere, she brought light into people's lives, most of all his own.

Harry's driver was driving too slowly for his liking. "Come on, Lewis, put your foot down, there's no chance of you ever being Formula One world champion is there?" Harry's impatience was returning.

"Probably not, boss. Are you staying at the Astor, or do you want me to pick you up from somewhere else?"

"Have the night off, we'll get a cab back," Harry replied.

Inside the club, Harry walked straight to the barman. "Hello Max, three double vodkas and coke, and whatever my friends are having."

"Is he always like this when he's with you?" said Kaitlin.

"No, he's behaving, if you weren't here, he would have jumped over the bar and helped himself."

She looked at the top of Harry's head. "Hey, I think I can see some new hair coming through."

Harry felt the top of his head. "Really? I thought we were on to something. If this works it will make us a fortune, come on let's dance." He turned to Mickey. "You should watch me and pick up a few of my moves, because I've watched you, mate, and you dance like my old dad used to."

The evening of the seventh of May turned quickly into the early hours of the eighth. A few miles away were the men Harry hoped would change their lives forever. Detective Chief

Superintendent Leonard "Nipper" Read headed a squad charged with the sole job of putting the Kray brothers in prison. Little did Mickey and Harry realise that in their hands lay the power to change London's criminal set up for decades to come and give rise to something more powerful than they could ever have imagined.

The ninth of May was Kaitlin's birthday. She lowered the window and held her hand against the rushing air, as Mickey drove towards Soho and a birthday lunch. On the radio Louis Armstrong's *Wonderful World* was playing, she sang along. Mickey looked at her. "I love it when you sing, don't ever stop."

She turned and placed her hand on his shoulder. "I love you, Mickey Warren."

He was about to reply when the song was interrupted by a news flash. Mickey swung the car around, put his foot to the floor and sped through the streets. Ten minutes later they walked into Harry's office. Harry had heard the news three hours earlier and had already started his own one-man party. He sat at the bar with a half-finished bottle of Talisker.

"You heard then?" he said.

"How the fuck did you know? I can't believe they've got almost all the firm banged up."

"Yes, and they won't be coming out. Anyway, we've got a meeting with the Arikans, Adamses, Gormans, Vareys and Johnsons. Times are changing, Mickey."

"I don't think, I've ever seen you so happy."

"This is it, the big time. Now the Krays are gone, we're taking over. I've been waiting for this day, now it's here. Not bad for a couple of kids from the East End."

"We're not big enough, Harry, we can't compete with those boys. You've lost the plot. They're the five most powerful firms in London."

"Exactly, they are the most powerful, and we're not going to compete. We're going to supply the families north of the river with their pharmaceutical needs. Has the penny dropped?"

"Fuck me, Harry!" Mickey looked at his friend and realised what he had said. "Well, you know what I mean."

Chapter 8
May 20th, 1968
Kensington

Solomon Gorman had organized the meeting and security at the Belmont Hotel in Kensington, one of five the family owned in the capital. Mickey's eyes moved around the table, and the most powerful crime families in London looked back at him.

The Gorman family were the oldest, and by some margin the most powerful. Solomon gently tapped the table with his fist. "Gentlemen, the Krays are history. They will never see the sunrise again outside a prison cell. Any issues we have between us end now. This is a new beginning, there must be no bad blood. We will keep our manors as they are now, outlined on the map on the wall." He pointed to a large multicoloured map of London. "Don't get up, it's in the envelopes in front of you. The West End is open to all of us, but once a firm are in a club or business, it's out of bounds for the rest. We're not individuals any more, we're a syndicate, a commission if you will, one that works together. If we can do this, gentlemen, we will become rich beyond our dreams. Things will go wrong, of course, there will be misunderstandings, but we will sort our problems out by meeting and talking." He scanned the room and bore the expression of a man who thought things were going better than he had expected.

"Major things we will vote on, and the head of the commission will have the casting vote, if it is needed. You all know Terry Marsh, an advisor to us, so listen to him, he has a wise head. Let me tell you one more time, there is no room for petty arguments." He looked around at each of the faces at the table, looking for any dissent; there was none. "Harry and the Bishes will be on the commission, but they'll have no say in how it's run. They can run clubs, as long as they clear it with the boss whose manor it is and pay a tribute." He looked around the table again. "I will be the head of the commission, but at any time, if three out of the four of you want me to step down I will."

The meeting continued for another hour, but Harry wasn't listening. He was going over the figures in his head.

Mickey looked at Harry as they walked through the double doors. "That went well."

"Yes. It won't last, Mickey, but by the time it finishes we'll be so rich it won't matter. Someone will screw up or get too greedy." They walked to the car. "Can you hear that faint rumbling?"

Mickey stopped and listened. "No?"

"Yes, you can, if you listen hard enough. It's the sound of the gravy train departing London Paddington. In the front carriage, along with the crime machine that is the five families, are sat you and me."

Mickey laughed. "I'm not sure even Solomon can keep the other four families in order."

"He will, if he does what he said, and make them richer than they believe possible. It's a new beginning. I have no idea how the train will crash, but it surely will. There are some very dangerous locos on that loco, some who kill for fun."

"Do you expect trouble?"

"Yes, there will be trouble, but not for us. We are the suppliers, no one has the contacts me and the Bishes have. You're gonna have to step on a few people's toes, but once the word is out about the families, no one will take them on. They're too big. We have good suppliers of hash from Europe and Thailand and the coke through Africa is as regular as clockwork. I've already scaled up the orders and I've got another factory opening up in Uxbridge, making our own stuff. You, Mickey, have got to keep order, and make sure we get paid. Solomon is a clever man and we've been planning this for months. The families aren't taking over all the crime in London, that would be impossible. What they're doing is taking out the arguments that use up so much time and money. If anyone outside the commission gets out of order, the commission will sort them out. It will have its own pest control team, and you, no doubt will be part of it."

"Sounds good."

"Anyway, the drugs pipeline, as I call it, works on the simple basis that we supply the families north of the river with whatever they want, in bulk, and at a good price. They'll be happy because the price is good, and the quality is guaranteed."

"But the big money will be made in the clubs like it is now," Mickey pointed out.

"True. Solomon is old school, anti-drugs as you know, so he's given us the doors on his manor and a good share of the West End. It's not for nothing of course — there's a very good drink in it for him. You're going to have to scale up and bring in a team to handle it. Your old school mates and the West Ham boys won't be enough."

"You were reading my mind, Harry. How do we split the profits?"

"At last, the final question, straight down the middle. I wouldn't have it any other way." He held out his hand. "Deal, Mickey?"

"Deal, Harry."

Chapter 9
1968
A well-earned break

"Mickey, we need a holiday. Pack your bag, we're going to Brazil."

Mickey had laughed when Harry said those words, but now, was listening to Harry tell the driver to take the tourist route, denying Mickey's request to go straight to the hotel after the long flight. Harry, map in hand, was playing tour-guide.

"Mickey, that's the Maracana stadium, the home of Brazilian football, and there to the right is the statue of Christ Redeemer, can you see it?"

"Harry, I'm not blind. It's impossible not to see it. The statue is 120 feet tall give or take, and is on top of Corcavado mountain, which translates as hunchback."

"Very good, Mickey, although I call it Sammy. I know it's impossible not to see, but this is your chance to absorb a bit of culture for once in your life. Reading the in-flight magazine about Brazil doesn't make you an expert."

"Oh, I think we'll see what your idea of culture is while we're here Harry, and it won't have anything to do with mountains — well, maybe some white ones."

The car swung left onto Princesa Isabel and right onto Avenida Atlantico. Copacabana beach came into view, fringed by the cobalt blue Atlantic. "Señor, attende aqui," said Harry. The driver somehow understood his newly acquired Portuguese language skills, the car stopped, and they got out. They crossed the road and stopped at a small beachfront stall made of old driftwood, brightly painted in the national colours of Brazil. Harry held up two fingers and the dark leathered hands of the coconut water seller tossed a green coconut in the air, caught it and chopped off the top with a small machete, then did the same with another, and handed them to Harry and Mickey.

"Look at this, Mickey, stunning. We might have to stay a bit longer than we planned."

"It's beautiful. I wish Kaitlin was here."

"Someone had to stay. Mind you, I think she would be more fun than you, you're a miserable bugger sometimes."

"Don't start, Harry, it costs a lot of money to ship a dead body back to England."

They finished the coconut water and returned to the cab, which continued three hundred yards to the Copacabana Palace Hotel. They got out and paid the driver, while two porters took the bags from the boot. The next time they would see their clothes, they would be neatly pressed and hung in their wardrobes. "This is where all the film stars stay, and other interesting people," said Harry. "Come on, hurry up, there's someone I want you to meet."

The person standing at the bar was hard to miss. Dark ringlets framed a handsome Latino face, with delicate features contrasting with lines hewn from the granite rock that was the exploding market in cocaine. Carlos Satero was a founding member of the Barranquilla cartel, the most lethal criminal organization in South America.

"Harry, it's good to see you. Try this, it's a Caipirinha, the best cocktail in the world. Forget your James Bond martinis, this is the real thing."

"Carlos, come here you crazy Columbian." Harry kissed him on both cheeks. "Mickey, Carlos Satero, Carlos, Mickey Warren. Jesus Carlos, what is in this? I love it!"

"Enjoy it, Harry, but not too fast. It has cachaca in it, which is like your white rum in England but stronger. Come, sit on the terrace and watch the world go by."

They moved onto a roped-off area overlooking the ocean.

"Carlos, this place is fantastic."

"Yes, it is, but it is a shame that you missed carnival, the world's biggest party. You must both come for it next year. Don't let me down, it is something you must do before you die."

"Well hopefully no rush then Carlos, there's a few years left of this mortal coil, all being well. You can feel the heartbeat of this place. I think, I'll buy some bricks and mortar on the beach."

Carlos sucked the remnants of the liquid from the bottom of the glass through the straw, a waiter brought over three more; he was on a replace when empty order.

"Death lives by its own clock Harry, that is why I live for the moment. Also, my friend, this is a party place, it is not a place to buy, much better the Caribbean. I've just bought an island near Puerto Rico, a little stopover for my import business into America. There are some very good properties in Antigua, Harry, and no regulation. I will fly you there in a few days, and you'll see how beautiful and safe it is. You don't want to be mixing with the wrong type, there are some very dangerous people here."

Harry was not in the market for a Caribbean hideaway, but the thought of an adventure with Carlos was reason enough to go. His head was beginning to spin, and the fifteen hours of drinking were now sapping his energy. "Carlos, I am feeling rather pissed."

"Harry, settle into your room, meet here at nine." He finished his caipirinha and tossed Harry a package the size of an egg. "This will straighten you out, my friend." The waiter rushed over with three more caipirinhas. "Not for me, give them to my friends," said Carlos. "Harry, I need to go, I'll see you both at nine. Ciao, Mickey, good to meet you, don't let our friend get into any trouble." He pulled out a wad of notes, threw them on the table and walked out.

Three days and one long hangover later, Carlos Satero's aeroplane soared into the sky, en route to Antigua. Mickey was relieved to be in the air. He could party, but not like Harry and Carlos; no one could. He'd fallen into a long overdue sleep but was awoken by the communication system. "Gentleman, we are now in international waters." Mickey was still half asleep, but over the years had learned to detect when there was stress in a voice, and to him the pilot was showing high levels of it. Mickey looked across at Harry, who was rhythmically swaying holding on to the mane of dark hair, controlling the movement as the flight attendant moved up and down on him. He smiled at Mickey and then saw Carlos stumbling toward him. Carlos grabbed him. "Come on, there's plenty of time for that later." Carlos pulled her off him. "Harry, come on."

Harry stumbled forward, pulling his clothes back on. "Carlos, you crazy bastard what are you doing?"

"I need to show you something, this is a very good moment for me. How long do you think it takes to become a great pilot?"

"I really don't have the slightest idea, a couple of years maybe," Harry replied.

"Yes, for some people, that is probably true, but not for me. The captain here has been teaching me for two weeks."

"Carlos, my dear friend, I'm experiencing very sudden and painful chest pains, I fear it is not your infinite generosity that's causing it, so, let's leave the man with the nice hat and gold stripes to fly the plane." He looked across at Mickey, who was pretending to be asleep. "Mickey, come on, I don't want to die on my own, I know you're not asleep. Now, Carlos, are you sure that very experienced fellow lets you fly, or do you just take over?" Carlos neglected to answer as he made his way to the cockpit.

"Harry, you should see your face," said Mickey. "You're as white as a ghost. I thought you were the craziest man on earth, but after the last few days, I realise I'm wrong, it's Carlos, but you're, a very close second."

"Yes, you might be right there. This won't end well. Look at the pilot's face, he's petrified."

"Harry, if I die today, I will never forgive you, and neither will Kate."

"No one's going to die... well, I don't think so."

"Very reassuring, Harry."

Carlos strapped himself into the right-hand seat. "Right, hold on, Harry, watch this. OK, I have control."

Harry noticed the pilot close his eyes and make the sign of the cross. "Carlos, please be careful. Think of my unborn children."

"Harry, always joking, trust me, you are safe in the hands of a very skilled aviator."

Carlos made some tight turns which threw Mickey and Harry to the floor, landing them in a tangled mess of limbs. Blood poured from a deep gash in Mickey's forehead as they were thrown back by the sudden steep ascent, as Carlos pulled back on the yoke. The plane slowed as it lost the power to stay in the air. The yoke began to shake, and a loud electronic voice shouted from the control panel, "stall, stall." The pilot pushed the yoke hard forward, the front of the plane dropped sharply and picked up speed until the man with the nice hat and stripes levelled the plane and then began a gentle climb back to cruising altitude. Mickey, looked at Harry's face, which was about two inches away from his own, and was reassured to see it was a pale green colour.

Harry struggled to his feet. "Carlos, enough please, I don't think I've ever seen such a great pilot, but let's stop now, because if you don't, I'm going to throw up all over you."

Carlos was clearly pleased with himself, while everyone else was just pleased to be alive. They walked back into the cabin and Harry collapsed into the safety of his chair. The urge to empty his stomach was overwhelming, and his usually well-controlled gag reflex was being held just on the right side of projectile vomiting. The flight attendant began walking towards him, intent on finishing what she'd started.

"No, not now, please," he said, reaching for the sick bag, as the vomit gushed from his mouth. The realization, that for the first time in his life he had turned away a beautiful woman, made him eject what was left of his lunch. Mickey sat back in his chair, holding a white towel against his head.

The pain in his ears told Harry they were descending, and judging by the altitude guessed, they were about ten minutes from landing in Antigua. His heart rate soared, until he saw Carlos strapped into his seat, gently snoring.

Once safely on the ground they were picked up by a smartly dressed chauffeur, and thirty minutes later they stood outside a large, whitewashed villa on a small hillock that led down to the ocean.

"Carlos, this is great. I want it!" said Harry.

He grinned at Harry and tossed him some keys. "It's yours, a gift from me, I know you'll enjoy it."

"No, I couldn't, it's too generous. Your friendship is enough."

He placed his hand on Harry's shoulder. "Harry, don't insult me, please. One day, when you have too much money and you don't know what to do with it, I will introduce you to my friend who lives on the island. He's in America now, so you've missed him, but you will meet him. Remember, it is very easy to make money, but not so easy to keep it. Things will not always be as easy as they are today for us. Now I must go to Columbia. I hope to see you again soon. And, Mickey, it was very good to meet you, look after our friend." He moved closer to Harry and hugged him. "Harry, I forgot my manners, do you want me to fly you back to Brazil?"

Harry glanced at Mickey who was shaking his head. Three hours later, they walked up the steps of the British Airways flight from Bird International to Heathrow.

Chapter 10
1968
London

The hot Antiguan sun gave way to a dismal English mist, but it had the comfortable feeling of an old coat. Harry smiled. "You know what I'm thinking, Mickey?"

"No one knows what you're thinking, ever."

"We've done quite well for a couple of kids from the East End, and I think it's time we gave a bit back."

"Oh yes, and how shall we do that?"

"I was down the Whitechapel Road a few weeks back, there are so many old folks and young kids, sleeping rough. Not enough money to feed themselves. It's a bit of a piss-take, when we blow a couple of hundred a night and not bat an eyelid."

"Saint Harry."

"No, I'm serious. Anyway, I've bought the old warehouse in Sidney Street, not in my name of course. We're gonna convert it into a shelter, a place people can get some sleep and a meal without having to pay a penny."

"Not we, Harry, you. Charity starts at home and most of those lazy bastards don't want to work. I'll bung a few quid in, but it's not my sort of thing. Look, we made it, so others can, don't take away people's motivation, cos that's what you'll be doing. People have to stand on their own two feet."

"You're a heartless bastard sometimes, Mickey."

Mickey looked across at him and patted his arm. "No Harry, you're a soft bastard. Let's get back to more important things than your Moses and the five fishes trick. Like, who we are gonna get to do some of the doors for us. I was thinking of Jack Rich. He's a good operator, and it'll solve our problems in the West End."

"Jesus and the fish, Mickey, not Moses, and I'm not sure about Jack, can you keep him on side? He can be trouble. It's tempting, but the easiest road is not always the right one. Anyway, it's your call, when are you seeing him?"

"This evening. I'll see how the land lies."

Mickey walked up to Reva, one of the smarter of the new West End clubs. Jack Rich stood outside the club shuffling from foot to foot. Judging by the snarl on his face, something or someone had clearly upset him.

Jack Rich had done well for himself and ran fifty doormen, freelancing them, to whoever needed a doorman or a bit of muscle. His reputation for being tough and strong was legend. He could lift two men by their belts, one with each hand, into a crucifix pose. A man to have on your side, problem was, no one was ever sure whose side Jack was on.

"Hello, Mickey, what brings you down this way?"

Mickey lit a cigarette and offered one to Jack. "Like a word, Jack, might have a bit of work for you."

"What sort of work?"

"Let's have a meet tomorrow at the Seven Stars and have a proper chat, about four suit you?"

"All right, Mickey, see you there."

He watched Mickey Warren get back into his car and leave as quickly as he had arrived. Unusual to get a visit from the great Mickey Warren, that overrated no-neck cocksucker, clinging on to the coat tails of Harry Fleet and Solomon Gorman. Now he comes to me. Well, that could be a big mistake. When Jack Rich's foot is in the door, you might as well put the kettle on, because I am there to stay. The thoughts made him smile. He had never liked Mickey; they were too similar.

The Seven Stars was a favourite meeting place for people on both sides of the law. Roxy the landlady had a copy of her famous family cookbook in a glass cabinet above the bar. If it wasn't in the cookbook, it wasn't on the menu. Every meal was made from recipes going back generations to the family home in County Cork.

Roxy hugged him. "Hello, Mickey, how are you today? You're looking grand, what will you have? The stew and colcannon are grand, I'll get you some. It's the best of the menu today."

That was the way it always was; you never got to choose, that was Roxy's job. It was the most efficient kitchen in the world, and nothing was ever wasted.

Walking towards the kitchen, she saw the shadow cast by the colossal figure of Jack Rich and moved swiftly to intercept him. "Hello, Jack, how are you today, you're looking grand, what will you have? The chicken and leek pie with colcannon is grand, I'll get you some. It's the best of the menu today. Now, where will you be sitting?"

Jack grinned at Mickey. "That will be lovely, Roxy, I'll be over there with Mickey." He moved gracefully for a man of twenty stone, and as always, checked the strength of the chair before he sat on it. Two Guinness were placed on the multicoloured lino table by a barman, clearly keen to get back to the safety of the bar and away from the table, where two of London's most feared hardmen were sitting.

"So, what's this all about, Mickey? I heard you were struggling to cover some of your doors."

"You're never slow in getting to the point, Jack. That's exactly it, we need you to run some doors. You run a good outfit, and we could do with someone with your skills. You'll be our number one firm, and I know with you in charge I won't have much trouble. You'll be reporting to me of course, but I'll pretty much let you run things your way."

"Thanks, Mickey, but why would I? I'm doing very good on my own. Or are you saying I've got no choice?"

Mickey looked at him. "Calm down, Jack. What I'm saying is, we would like you to join us. If you don't want to, fine, I'll get someone else, but it's you we want. You'll get a percentage of the sales in the clubs, twice what you're making now."

"This is working out better than I thought. Now you're talking, Mickey. As long as you won't be breathing down my neck all the time, I think we can do business. How many of my boys do you want?"

"All of them, Jack. We're making some serious money, and it's something you can share in, but remember one thing, we can't have any fucking about."

Jack Rich crossed his middle and forefinger. "This is me and you Mickey."

"Well, that's good. But remember it's me on top," Mickey said, tapping Jack's middle finger and holding eye contact for longer than Jack was comfortable with. "I look forward to working with you, Jack."

"Me too, Mickey, happy days."

They finished their food and another drink quickly, neither wanting to hang around with the other longer than necessary.

He watched as Mickey walked out of the door, pleased with the deal. In seventy minutes, he'd doubled his income, and decided to have another drink and reflect on what had just happened. Someone was getting desperate, and that someone was Mickey Warren. Yes, you might be on top now, Mickey, but not forever. I'm coming for you.

Mickey walked through the doors into the Sidney Street Warehouse, or as he preferred to call it, Harry Fleet's doss house. It was 7 p.m. and the place was still full of workmen. Harry was at the back with a sledgehammer in his hands, knocking the last few bricks from what remained of a wall. A brick flew high into the air, Harry moved swiftly to one side to avoid it and caught sight of the grinning Mickey Warren.

"What do you think, Mickey?"

"I'm not sure the hat suits you."

"Health and safety."

Mickey looked at the rubble, the holes in the roof and what looked like an open sewer. "What the fuck are you thinking, Harry? I'm going to have to keep an eye on you. You're losing the plot. This place is massive, it will cost you a fortune to run. You're nuts, mate. Anyway, on a better note, Jack Rich is in." He sneezed.

"It's bloody toxic in here, I'm going. This dust is getting right up my nose."

Harry smiled. "Hold up, Mickey, I've been thinking about Jack, and I've still got a bad feeling about bringing him onboard, not sure you've done the right thing. He's doing a lot of Charlie lately and he's nuts enough when he's not on it. Anyway, what have you heard about the Ronsons?"

Mickey sneezed again. "Same as you probably, Baz Ronson in the 100 Club, waving a gun about, threatening to kill Solomon, crazy bastard. With your marching powder hanging out of his nose by all accounts, so probably down to you this one."

"Don't even be thinking that sort of thing, let alone saying it, people could get the wrong impression. Jesus, talk about Jack, you're both loose cannons. I'm surrounded by a team of lunatics and you're the one with the skipper's armband."

It was the first major challenge to the commission. The Ronsons were a large firm from the Seven Sisters area and their noses were well and truly put out of joint when they were not chosen to sit at the top table with the five families. Their business was mainly protection rackets, the odd long firm fraud, and prostitution. They had bullied and tortured their way to the top of their tree in double quick time. Solomon Gorman had carefully chosen the five families and had decided the Ronsons would not fit into the commission. They were at the top of the list of potential problems, and true to form, they were now causing trouble.

"Anyway, Mickey, Solomon wants you to drop by later. You might have some work to do, time to earn your money for once."

"Behave Harry, I thought I might be in the frame for that one."

"Be careful, they are nasty bastards, I heard they put a couple of six-inch nails through Johnny 'no toes,' knees last week."

"Didn't know you cared, Harry. To be honest, like I said, I thought Solomon would earmark me for the job, but I don't fancy it. There's a good chance I won't get away with it. It needs some serious talent. Fortunately, I've got just the people in mind. Chopping fingers off, arson and a spot of torture and gun work is where I draw the line. Taking out the top of a decent firm is for the professionals."

"Wise words for once, Mickey, wise words."

It took Mickey a few days to arrange the meeting with the people chosen to sort out the small spot of bother the commission was experiencing. The temperature hovered just above freezing and Hyde Park was less crowded than normal. Mickey was a few minutes early. There was no sign of the people he was due to meet, which was unusual as they were always punctual.

Two people walking towards him seemed vaguely familiar but didn't dwell on them as he scanned the path beyond. When they were shoulder to shoulder, he heard the familiar voice of Artie 'Muddy' Walters.

"Hello, Mickey, you looking for someone?"

Artie Walters and Raven Magdani were two of the most unlikely looking killers. Both wore shocks of blonde hair and looked more like half a rock band.

"Very good disguise, Artie, I didn't spot you."

"Well, let's hope for your sake, Mickey, we never get an envelope with your name in it."

"Yes, thanks for that. So, what have you got?"

"The Ronsons have gone to ground since their tantrum in the 100 Club, and will be difficult to take out together, but we might have a window next week. It won't be easy, and we'll have to go dark for a bit after, so the fee is double the normal, is that OK?"

Mickey looked at them. "Whatever it takes, just make sure you finish the job."

"Mickey, we always finish the job." Raven replied.

He smiled at her. It's a brave man that goes out with you, he thought. She was quite a number, beautiful in an understated way, a dangerous woman and made more lethal by the rumour she was Solomon Gorman's girlfriend.

"Right, I'll leave it in your capable hands," he said.

They disappeared into the dark of the evening.

Artie Walters and Raven Magdani were at the top of London's Murder Incorporated. Mickey, like everyone else, knew very little about them, but one thing he knew was they were single minded. Nothing usually got in the way of their objective, and if it did, it was neutralized. Their bodies were trained to the level of top-class athletes, and they lived completely under the radar. No one had an address for them, and Mickey had never been stupid enough to try and find it. He didn't enquire about the details; he would hear soon enough when news of the hit reached the streets.

A long line of poplar trees, straight and majestic, led to the Victorian house. Ionic columns, a late and bizarre addition, framed the solid oak doors to Baz Ronson's *pied-de-terre*. The wide metal gates opened, whisper quiet, as a car passed through. A police car parked opposite the entrance had excited the two guards, but they had long since lost interest in it after the call to Baz Ronson, who had laughed when they told him they were there. He was in good spirits today and looking forward to the eightieth birthday party of the family matriarch.

He turned to his younger brother in the car. "Chas, I can't wait to see gran's face when Georgie Fame sings happy birthday to her."

"Same, Baz, she's a great old girl."

As they turned the corner out of the village, the house came into view. They pulled up to the gate, and as they did, the driver of the police car got out and stood in front of them. "What the fuck, have they got nothing better to do?" said Chas.

"Don't worry about it, I'll slip the fuckers a few quid."

The other cop got out of the car carrying a thick folder of papers. She ignored the Ronsons, opened the boot and placed the folder inside. Baz motioned to the guards to stay where they were as he lowered the window. "Thanks for keeping an eye on the place, here's a drink for you." He opened his wallet and removed a small fold of notes held by a silver clip and held his hand out.

The copper ignored it and looked at Baz Ronson. "I need to look in the boot of your car."

"What! Are you having a laugh?"

"Just doing our job, sir, open the boot please."

"What exactly is supposed to be in the boot? Do you know who we are?" Baz reached into his pocket and pulled out another roll of notes. "Here, take this and fuck off."

"Open the boot, and then we can go."

Chas Ronson had the shorter fuse of the brothers and became impatient with the way the conversation was going. He got out of the car and released the boot lock, and it swung open.

"There you are, completely empty, are you happy now? Can we fuck off now, or more accurately can you, fuck off?"

"No need to take that tone, sir." The officer looked into the empty boot. "Sorry to have wasted your time."

Charles Ronson closed the boot and walked towards his brother, who was sitting in the car reading the *Racing Post*. He was suddenly distracted by the figure of Raven Magdani looking at them as she moved from the back of the police car. Her face would normally have been a pleasing experience, but Chas had no time to think pleasant thoughts after his eyes took in the AK47 in her small, delicate hands. It took Raven five seconds to kill the Ronson brothers, and another five to kill the two unarmed guards. Artie was already back in the driving seat. Raven placed the gun in the boot and thirty seconds later, they were gone.

Solomon Gorman was smoking a fat Havana cigar. The smoke drifted up and across his face like a veil. Harry wondered how Solomon could see them, let alone breathe.

Solomon moved slightly to one side to avoid the smoke and looked straight at Mickey. "Mickey, that was some job, the whole of London is talking about it. I hope it didn't spoil the old girl's birthday. Class act, very nice, I owe you one."

"All part of the service, Sol. It's the first serious bit of trouble we've had, and it will send a message to everyone else. I'm surprised we've had so few problems."

"It's easy being on a winning team. Everyone's loving it at the moment, even the cops. It's making them look good, crime is down and there are no turf wars for them to get involved in. The tension is there, buried just below the surface. Buried for the sake of profit. But nothing lasts forever." Solomon took a puff of the cigar and leaned back deep into his chair. "Remember those words, Mickey, and enjoy the good times." He turned towards Harry. "I have something for you. I've heard about your refuge in Sidney Street, and what you're doing for the homeless and poor. This is for you." He passed over a light brown bag. Harry went to open it. "Open it later, Harry, it's a small gesture from my family."

Ten minutes later as Mickey drove back towards the city, Harry opened the bag and looked inside. "There's got to be twenty grand in here. He's a very generous man, not like some I could mention."

Mickey reached into his pocket and took out a five-pound note and threw it onto Harry's lap. "There you go, Harry, don't spend it all at once."

Chapter 11
1969
London

"Harry, sit down, you're making me nervous."

"I can't, I'm scared to death! Never will I go through this again, mark my words. This is down to you, and if anything happens to that woman, I'll be making a call to Raven and Artie, and I'm not joking. I can't believe you've put her through this." Harry grabbed the nurse's arm. "How is it going, is it here yet? I can't believe it takes so long."

She looked at him, her patience finally wearing thin. "Mr Warren, it might be a good idea if you take your friend for a drink. It's going to be a few hours before the baby is born."

"Good idea, come on, Harry, you're driving everyone mad." Mickey looked at the nurse. "What time should we come back?"

She smiled. "About five hours."

Mickey grabbed Harry by his shoulders. "Come on, the drinks are on you."

"Good idea, I need to calm my nerves."

Eastham drove them to the Seven Stars, where Roxy's smile greeted them. "Now, boys, would I be right in saying the baby is near to coming? You don't have to tell me; I can see it on your faces. You're like a couple of scared little boys caught with your hands in the biscuit jar. Now I have something for you, to keep your energy up. It's the best of the menu and the drinks are on me, so they are, though not too many of course." As always, she was gone before a single word left their mouths. Five minutes later, Irish stew, Guinness and whiskey chasers were placed in front of them.

"Mickey, you need to listen, I'm getting tired of your in-one-ear-out-the-other attitude," said Harry. "I've said this to you before and I'll say it again, wedlock, Michael, holy matrimony, the joining together of two of God's own."

"Harry, she won't get married, I've told you, you know what she's like. I've asked her loads of times."

"There will be a change of mind when Harry is born."

"Harry! We couldn't do that to the kid, it's Jason, Jason Harry Warren."

He slapped Mickey's back. "OK, I'll take that, and I'll be a great godfather. The light in his life, to counteract your darkness. I'm really looking forward to this."

"Well, I'm happy to know I have brought something good into that miserable little life of yours."

Five hours later as they stumbled into the maternity ward, the nurse walked over to them.

"My God, Mickey, something's gone wrong, look at her face, or maybe it's because you're as pissed as a rat."

She turned to Mickey. "I am pleased to tell you, you have a son, who is looking forward to seeing his father."

"I told you everything would be OK."

Mickey smiled and hugged him. "Thanks, Harry, you've been a great help, couldn't have done it without you. Come on, let's go see our boy."

Chapter 12
1969
Harry's new business venture

The M4 was unusually quiet. The glow from the lights of Swindon lit up the moonless sky like a distant erupting volcano.

"Come on, Harry, what's the big mystery? Not all this way for another refuge for the great unwashed?"

"Mickey, you will be witness to another example of my genius. You will thank me for this, and as a special treat because you've not done a bad job lately, I am going to give you an experience you won't forget. Yes, you have been far too bloody good lately, and this will put all that right."

The sign indicated twelve miles to the old Roman town of Cirencester. Mickey was struggling to remember how he'd been good of late; he'd removed two of the fingers of a late payer last week and organized a spot of arson for tomorrow. "Harry, get on with it, I don't know why you've brought us all the way down here, it's full of bloody druids and old stone circles."

"Impatience, Michael, impatience. You're gonna meet my partner, Jules Danby. He was my quartermaster at Oxford. We met in the student bar, where we argued over who could drink the most, fuck knows who won. He was crazy from the first day I met him, and nothing has changed since. One of the cleverest guys on the planet."

"If he's so clever, how'd he end up in business, with you?"

"You're in business with me. But unlike you, I said he was clever, top of his class. After we got our degree in drink and drugs, he went into banking, straight onto the trading floor of a great big American bank, Standard Texan or something. Anyway, being a bit too bright for his own good, he soon worked out how to make a small fortune for himself with no risk. Every time he got a big share trade from one of his customers that would move the share price, clever bollocks would put a little trade of his own in first. Absolutely, raked it in, and in his eyes, doing nothing wrong. The bank, however, didn't agree with him. The new cars and exotic holidays brought him to the attention of their compliance department. They hauled him in and threw the book at him. However, his indignation and the threat to call *The Times* seemed to work, as did his argument they should pay him for highlighting a significant weakness in their system. They let him leave and keep the money he'd made, everything brushed under the dusty old corporate carpet. However, Jules, being Jules, took no time in spending the money and was soon forced to take his clever little mind out of retirement. Ended up doing a few long firm frauds when we ran into each other at a Lords and Ladies party. Later that night our great idea was born while we were snorting coke off the tits of a couple of hookers. What better place for the birth of an empire?"

"Harry, you're boring me now."

Harry tapped his fingers on the dashboard, imitating a drum roll. "Mickey, it's called the Retox Centre, and you can wipe that look off your face. What's it all about, you may ask yourself. Well, think about it, what's the biggest problem people have today? I can tell you, they are too bloody well behaved, and it's got to stop. Whenever people think they have been too good, or boring, or just want all the good things in one place at the same time, they can come to the Retox centre. Yes, forget detox, that's for timewasters. Retox is the word, and the best thing is they have to be bad, or they pay extra. Yes, they get fined if they are good, so it's win-win for everyone."

"I know you've always struggled with reality, but are you listening to yourself? I've heard enough. I'm going to get some shuteye."

"No time for that, Mickey, we're nearly there. Why do you question everything I do?"

"Because everything you do is questionable."

Ten minutes later they turned into Cirencester High Street and passed the medieval St John the Baptist Church, then turned left and drove through two large electric gates into the car park of Marlborough House. High Cotswold stone walls shielded the large country house from the prying eyes of unwelcome visitors. Jules Danby was waiting for them and strode out as soon as he saw Harry's red convertible.

"Jules, how's it going, have we got a winner?"

"We're fully booked for months. I never would have believed a pair of tits and a line of Charlie could prove so valuable."

"Jules, this is Mickey, can you give him the tour?"

"Of course. Harry has told me all about you, and you're going to love it here. Guests are our number one concern, well they would be, the daft buggers pay our wages. Now you notice we don't have any CCTV. This place is totally discreet, so you don't need to worry if any parts of you end up in the wrong place."

"I can't wait to see what your sick little mind has come up with this time, Harry." Harry shrugged as though he hadn't the slightest idea what was going on. What a gold mine, Mickey thought, knowing full well they were probably on two hidden cameras as they spoke. Harry was no fool; Jules probably had more incriminating film already on judges, politicians and the local royalty than they could use in a lifetime.

Harry saw Mickey looking up at the building and had worked out, he was searching for hidden cameras. "There are no cameras, Mickey, not one, so you can get that thought out of your head."

They walked into the reception area. On a table were a dozen silver bowls, the first full of the familiar white glistening Peruvian flake cocaine. Jules continued, "All guests are expected to have at least four of these or they are fined."

Mickey noticed a man dressed totally in white looking at him. His hair was the colour of snow, his eyes blood red. He gestured to Mickey, rubbing his thumb and first finger together and moving his white eyebrows up and down, encouraging Mickey to follow him. "It looks like you have a new friend," said Harry.

Mickey snarled. "If that weird fuck comes any closer, I'll knock him out. That will put some colour in his cheeks."

Jules looked at Mickey. "Mate, you can hit him, but it will cost you."

"Might be money well spent," replied Mickey, pointing to a door. "Is that a bar? I could do with a drink."

Harry smiled. "Yes, you'll like it in there, come on."

Mickey looked at the logo on the door, two champagne bottles with their contents fizzing out. "Very tacky, Harry."

"I'm beginning to wish I hadn't brought you. Visual reference points, subliminal imaging, all designed to make the customer spend more, all totally wasted on the less intellectual."

Mickey picked up what he thought was the drinks list. It was a room service menu. You could be whipped, stripped, asphyxiated, dressed up in a nappy, the list was endless; it was Harry's imagination writ large. Sex was available with women, men and those in between, one, two or three at a time. "Yes, Harry, I see what you mean, very subtle."

A Tory peer who Mickey recognised walked past the open door. Bright red finger marks circled his neck. In one hand a black bin liner rustled with his movement, in the other he held a small orange. He turned to Harry. "Hello, Harry, great place."

"Bobby, glad you're enjoying it," Harry replied.

Jules Danby put his hand on Harry's shoulder. "Mate, all the rooms are full, so I've booked you in at the Kings Head."

"Is that relief I see in your eyes, Mickey?" Harry quipped. They turned and passed another room with the familiar gold-leaf on the door, this time a golden peach. A white blur caught Mickey's eye; it was the albino again, and Bobby the Tory peer was following him into the toilets. "Bloody hell, Harry, this is a bit weird even for you."

"Jules, explain," Harry said.

"Mate, that's Herman the Albino, we imported him from Germany, he's like the drug dealer you find in pubs and clubs. Only there's no drugs, he sells vitamins and fruit, and bottles of water. If the punters are caught buying from Herman, they're arrested and taken to the detention area, then brought before the judge, who decides what punishment they receive for the naughtiness of being good."

Mickey was about to say something when the noise of a dog barking came from around the corner. "Harry, please tell me there are no animals here."

Harry shrugged and laughed as a man on all fours bounded around the corner wearing only a mask covering half his face. He was tethered to a lead, held by a slim woman dressed from head to toe in black leather. "Stay!" she barked. The human dog stopped as instructed, coming to a halt just by Harry's leg. He lifted his leg as though to urinate, but the whip that cracked down hard on his bare arse stopped him. "Bad dog!" snapped the woman, as the dogman cried in pain and another red mark joined the dozen or so already on his cheeks. "Walk on," she said with another touch of the whip.

"So, Harry, Jules, tell me how this is a legitimate business?" Mickey took one more look at the dog and his walker. "Hold on, Harry, that's my fucking dentist! I hope he washes his hands before he puts them in my mouth."

"Mickey, you need to keep that to yourself, I don't want you causing trouble for the customers. Anyway, apart from the drugs, it's all legal. Consenting adults doing things that come unnaturally."

"Come on, mate, there's a lot more to see," said Jules. They turned another corner and walked towards the sound of a trumpet and guitars.

"This is the Spanish bar, Mickey, you've got to see this."

The sound hit Mickey as they walked through the door, but it was nothing to the sight of the six-piece band wearing only their instruments and sombreros. Naked waiters and waitresses circled the room like buzzards waiting to swoop on the nearest punter who needed attention. Mickey watched unbelieving as a man dressed as a general, or maybe, he was a general, saluted a waitress walking past. This was his way of getting her attention. He handed her a small token and Mickey realised this was how

Harry circumvented the prostitution laws. She took the token and placed it in the small pouch hanging from her neck whilst at the same time taking down the general's trousers. She turned and rested her hands on the small table in front of her, put her hand behind her and guided him expertly inside her.

"Harry, for fuck's sake can we get out of here? I've had enough of this."

"Mickey, Jules has got some tokens for you, would be a shame to waste them."

"No, I'm good thanks, let's check into the hotel."

Ten minutes later, in the bar of the Kings Head, Mickey was listening to the conversation of three men in their early thirties. "I wish there was a bit more going on here, it's too quiet, let's go to Cheltenham."

Mickey shook his head. If only they knew, he thought.

"So, what do you think of the business?" Jules said.

"I think you're both as sick as each other, is what I think. Who really thought all that up?"

In perfect unison, they pointed at each other and said, "him."

Mickey watched as Harry passed Jules a small black tablet. "Here you are, Jules, try this, it's new." He took it with a swig of his beer. Mickey looked at them, thinking how great it would be to get back to his normal world of chopping people's fingers off and lighting up the night sky with a spot of arson.

Chapter 13
1969
London

Harry sunk back in his seat three rows back, trying to look inconspicuous, the paint barely dry on his hands, as the West Ham captain cut the ribbon to officially open the refuge. Very few people had the slightest idea he was the driving force behind the refuge, and that was the way he wanted it to stay. Not wanting nor needing the publicity for his good deed. His good friend at University, Uzi Malik had told him, 'Harry, it should be reward enough to do good deeds for others, without the need for others to pat you on the back. It is about the people receiving the charity not the ones giving it, and in my religion one of the groups who will be looked upon favourably come judgement day are those that are charitable but hide the fact.' Mickey sat to his left shuffling his feet, barely hiding his boredom as he covered his mouth to stifle another yawn.

"Come on, Mickey, let's go for a drink."

"Don't you want to hang about for the photos?"

Harry looked at him. "It's not a bloody wedding. Anyway, I'm back later dishing the food out."

"I think you should go on TV with this, you'd be bloody good as long as you didn't do that thing you do with your hair."

"What thing?"

"You know, where you're constantly touching the top of your head. A mate of mine had a kid who kept pulling her hair out in chunks, ended up bald as a golf ball. The kid wasn't quite right upstairs, Harry, if you know what I mean. Anyway, enough about that, don't you think you're taking this a bit too far? It's one thing building and paying for it, but to get your hands dirty as well. I just think it's a bit odd, and I'm worried about you. I never thought I would say it, but I prefer you at the Retox centre."

"How sharper than a serpent's tooth it is to have a thankless friend like you. The Retox is business, this place will change people's lives, give them a chance, some hope. What do you want to look back at when you're about to die? All the bad things you've done or the little bit of good you did, and the lives you changed for the better, not that you have of course. You're the Lord of Darkness. It's karma as well. You can't be a nasty bastard forever without life catching up with you. And I'm not going bald, by the way."

"Fuck me, that's a bit deep, you'll be building a church next. Come on, you do need a drink. That karma thing is a lot of shit, you make your own luck in this world, you know that."

They made their way to the Blind Beggar and ordered two beers. "It's not too late to be a part of the refuge, Mickey, we could do with those big shovel hands of yours."

"We spent long enough getting away from poverty. All this only reminds me of when we didn't have a lot of money. Just makes me a bit uncomfortable. And look at you, you can't wait to get back, can you? That's the truth of it. Playing God and saving all the cold and lonely little beggars. We have a business to run, Harry, which you would do well to remember."

"I can't remember the last time I was so enthusiastic about something and I'm not going to let you spoil it. I don't know what demons you have in your head today, but just lighten up a bit will you?"

"Harry, go on, off you go, I can see you're itching to get back. I'm going to have a few more."

Harry finished his beer, bade farewell and strode out of the door. Mickey, now alone, nodded to the barman to bring him another beer. His thoughts turned in on themselves, darkening his mood; wondering if he'd been too honest. He drank three different beers, but they all tasted bad, the fags made him cough, and the noise was annoying him.

An old fella knocked into him on his way to the toilet, Mickey grabbed him by the collar and pinned him against the wall. He was suddenly back at school. "Why the fuck don't you look where you're going, you dozy bastard?"

"Sorry, I'm sorry, I wasn't thinking."

He looked down at the wet patch forming in a puddle around the old man's shoes. Mickey could not believe what he was doing, after looking at the man's trembling face, one, that was at least seventy years old. Shame washed over him, the other customers were looking at him, disgusted but too scared to intervene. Mickey released him, "No, I'm sorry." Shaking his head, he decided it was time to leave. Jesus, Harry was feeding people and here I am beating up pensioners. The thought depressed him, wondering for the first time if the opportunity should have been taken to join Harry and be part of building the Refuge. Never could he remember feeling bad about dishing out a beating or intimidating people, even the old ones. It was an uncomfortable feeling.

He started the engine and instead of turning right, to go home, turned left, towards the Refuge. As he passed the Refuge, there was Harry, true to his word, passing out sandwiches and soup to a small line of people. Laughing and joking, patting them on the back and shaking hands.

Harry a man of the people, for the people, funny old world, thought Mickey, and for the first time that night, smiled.

Chapter 14
1971

Jack Rich had been on the firm for two years, a lot longer than most thought likely. He'd toed the line, but for the last few months, Mickey had begun to regret his decision to bring him into the business. The rumours about Jack badmouthing him, had reached his ears from several sources, and his coke consumption made Harry's look like an occasional hobby. He had done a good job, but now was becoming increasingly unstable, and was looking to climb the ladder. Something that could only be achieved by a confrontation with Mickey. The time for a straightener was coming, and everyone knew it.

A few nights earlier in one of the clubs, a man Mickey hadn't seen before was buying fifty-pound bottles of champagne, and the more the bottles emptied the louder he became. The three escorts sitting with him at one of the VIP tables, were slowly emptying his wallet. He snorted a line of cocaine from the table, then a second; Mickey had hoped the first was a one-off. Punters were given some leeway, especially when they were spending big, but coke at the table was a big no. Coppers on the payroll would turn a blind eye to most of the illegal practices and give him the nod if a visit was on the cards, but there were rules, and this guy was breaking them.

Mickey walked to the table. "Give the Charlie a rest or do it in the toilet like everyone else."

"Fuck off, mate, I'll do what I want, go on, off you go like a good boy, can't you see I'm busy."

Mickey picked him up by his arms, turned him around, marched him towards the door and threw him outside. He rolled over twice in the wet puddle that lay in the road.

"You bastard, I'll be back for you, you don't know who I am."

Mickey smiled. It didn't matter to him; once they were out of the club the problem was normally over.

Jack Rich was on the door, staring at Mickey. "Fuck me, Mickey, you're losing your touch mate, you're letting everyone call you a bastard these days."

"Who else is calling me a bastard, Jack? And anyway, he wasn't a problem, learn the difference. You might want to stop taking those pills and lay off the Charlie, particularly when you're working for me."

"Fuck you, Mickey, don't tell me how to do my job, if you don't like it, you can do your own fucking doors."

Mickey laughed. "Yes, Jack, fuck me. You got work to do, so do it, cos this is the last night you and your little fucking boys are on the doors." Mickey went inside, making a point of turning off the outside heater.

The next day Harry sat at his desk, tapping his foot slowly and rhythmically, chain smoking and staring at the door. It was a look Mickey had seen before. Harry wasn't happy; he hated confrontation, and a lorryload of it was about to walk through the door.

Harry's eyes drifted to the clock on the wall. "What time's he coming?"

"Four. He's gonna be full of his usual bullshit, but he's out. It will mean a sort out, but he's got it coming, I've had enough of the coked-up fuck. He punched a VIP last week at Hermes which took a lot of putting right."

"How are you gonna replace him?"

"Already spoke to Dan Harkness. He's putting his boys in tonight."

"Mickey, that's bad blood, they hate each other."

"Good, maybe the problem will sort itself out. Anyway, it's my side of the business, so let me deal with it."

"Yes, wouldn't be the worst thing, those two falling out, you're right, it's your business."

For a few moments, the room fell quiet, before the sound of footsteps broke the silence.

Jack Rich took the stairs three at a time and bounced into the open office, as high as a kite. The wooden floorboards creaked under his weight. Harry was pleased he'd arranged back-up. Eastham stood in the corner, a Beretta in his shoulder holster.

"Harry, sorry if I've been a bit out of order lately but you've had no trouble at the clubs, have you?"

Harry glared at Jack, as he walked to the drinks cabinet and poured himself a whiskey.

"Sit down, it's me you're talking to, not Harry. There's been plenty of trouble, and it's down to the way you and your boys have been throwing your weight about. Like I told you, you're out. Here's ten grand, call it severance pay. I don't want trouble, but if you bring it to my door or I hear you have been mugging me off again I will kill you. Now take your money and fuck off."

The hate burned in Jack's eyes. "Mugging you off, Mickey, you and Harry are done, a waste of time, you've gone soft. I run the clubs, I look after the people, I'm the fucking king of London." He stood and put his hands on the desk and glowered at Mickey, "I'll take your fucking money and you won't get any trouble, but let me tell you, you've got a lot of enemies out there."

"Like I said, Jack, there's the door and you have my permission to use it."

He picked up the money and walked out of the door a lot more slowly than his entrance.

"That won't be the end of that," said Eastham.

The next morning Bill Varey, the head of the Varey firm, walked through the door of Harry's office; they were expecting him.

"Billy, how are you?"

"Great, Harry. Jack Rich has been round, crying his eyes out, says you two have mugged him off good and proper."

"Bill, this has nothing to do with Harry, I dealt with it, and we can leave the commission out of this. He's just a coked-up twat who was taking the piss, he's lucky I haven't killed him. I know he's a friend of yours, but he's a liability and he's out."

"Mickey, I haven't come here for a ruck with you, I'm here to tell you I've put him to work in my manor. He's an old mate, I grew up with him. All I'm asking is, it's the end of the matter."

"Bill, he's bad news, wants to be number one, he will cause you nothing but trouble."

"Like I said, I've known him since we were kids, trust me, that's not the way it's gonna be. All I want is your assurance this is over."

Mickey moved forward and took his hand. "Bill, you have my word. I take it I will hear no more bad mouthing, because if I do, I will have to do something about it."

"Not a whisper, I guarantee it. If he does, I'll kill him myself."

Chapter 15
1973
London

Kaitlin Warren looked at her husband and wondered where the years had gone. It was the most unlikely of marriages. Everyone except Harry had said it would not get through the first year.

"Mickey, you need to sit down, I have something to tell you."

"Baby, I haven't got time, I'm late, I'll be back in a few hours, and we can get some dinner and have a chin-wag." Pulling her towards him, he kissed her and turned towards the door.

"Michael Warren, sit down, this is a bit more important than you and Harry talking about the West Ham game with Liverpool."

Mickey looked surprised, but did as she said, sitting at the table and fiddling with his watch, which seemed to have stopped.

"Yes, boss, what would you like to tell me? "

She took his hand and placed it on her flat, firm stomach. She watched the expression change as he pulled her closer and placed his ear to her stomach.

Kaitlin laughed. "It's a bit early for that. What do you think, my darling husband, are you happy?"

"How many weeks sweetheart? I dreamt last night you were pregnant."

"Twelve," she replied, as two tears fell down her cheeks.

"You know, Kate, I never thought I could ever be this happy. I thought feeling this good was for other people, you know the good guys."

"You are my good guy, Mickey, I love you so much."

He looked into her eyes and gently kissed her. "I love you, Kate. Life is perfect. Maybe I'll give up this life and go straight. We could get out of the smoke and move to the country. Come on, babe, I guess we better tell Harry, he'll be very upset if he's not the next to know."

"I thought you were busy today."

"Never too busy to tell Harry he's going to be an uncle again."

Chapter 16
1974
London

One p.m.

Jack Rich moved the coin deftly between his fingers, at the same time looking at the unshaven face of Billy Varey.

"Jack, I like the way you're running the doors and I'm going to give you a bigger cut of the profits, but Uzi Malik, and he's a very good friend of Harry's, tells me you were badmouthing Mickey Warren again. What the fuck have I told you about that?"

"Warren is getting right up my nose, Bill, the sooner that pansy's pushing up daisies the better it will be for all of us. I'd like to kill the bastard."

"I can tell by the look on your face you want me to agree with what you're saying. Let me make it clear. I don't, and I would be very careful what you're saying. Members of the commission can't be touched, and you're definitely in no position to even think about it. Let me make this crystal, if you get into a war with Mickey there is no way, I'm on your side."

"Thing is, Bill, with him out of the picture, Harry would turn to me for his muscle, one hundred percent. Warren's a pussy."

"Mickey is anything but that. Don't you realise what you're doing, if he gets to hear what you're saying, you're as good as dead, believe me."

"Bill, give me your support, there's a lot of money to be made with him out the way."

Varey glowered at Jack. "Are you deaf? Now change the subject, and while you're at it why don't you give the coke a rest."

Jack looked at him, confused. "I'm sorry, I was talking as a mate, you know, off the record. I didn't mean anything by it, you know I won't rock the boat. I appreciate what you've done for me. Anyway, I'll be going."

As the door closed, Billy Varey reflected on the conversation, not sure Jack, was being completely honest.

Three p.m.

Captain Tommy Bednar was home on leave, driving along the streets of his childhood. It was the first time in five years, that he had returned for a trip down memory lane. The next turn in the road revealed his old school. It looked smaller than he remembered. The recollections of being a little boy, persecuted every day at the hands of Mickey Warren, pushed to the front of his mind. They had never truly left, not for a single day. The missed school meals, the bruises, the nightmares, the fear on the stairs of a place that should have been safe. But worse than all the daytime horrors, was the humiliation of wetting his bed until the age of fifteen. It was written in his bones like the words in a stick of Margate rock. He wondered where the bastard was, and what the harbinger of hate was doing. No doubt still making people's lives as miserable as ever.

Five p.m.

Bernie Broadman looked at the house that was his home as a child. Trying to avoid looking at the window of the front room. The grey paint had long peeled away, the frame eaten through by mould and woodworm. His eyes were dragged towards the window of the room that had changed his life, the window to the room where his father had hung, lifeless, eyes bulging, a wet puddle of urine on the floor. Not a day passed without thinking about the moment; countless times at night woken by his own screams and the sight of his father's bloated face.

His hatred for Mickey Warren had not dimmed with the passing of time. Sometimes dreaming the same nightmare, but with Warren's face on the body. How nice that would be, the thought always turned him on. He felt the erection forming in his trousers as the chill of afternoon turned into the freezing of the evening.

A trained eye would have noticed the single set of footprints on the frost-covered road leading to the car, and away again. Under the car, mercury glistened at the bottom of a small glass tube, at the top, two wires, an inch apart, formed the connection to the electrical firing system. Packed neatly above was the small package of explosives.

A hundred yards away, the man in the dark coat sat in his car, watching. A little too close, but to miss what was about to happen was not an option. A small bird landed on the wing mirror, which flew away with the wave of a caring hand. He didn't want any innocent victims, not today. This was his day; the one imagined a thousand times. The Three Degrees' *When Will I See You Again* played on the radio, he turned up the volume and laughed. How appropriate, he thought. When would Mickey be seen again? Hopefully never. This was the day the world would be relieved of the cancer, the canker that was Mickey Warren. He had seen him yesterday from a distance, smiling and hugging his pregnant wife, looking as happy as it was possible to be.

The hoar frost made pretty patterns on the trees lining the row of neat semi-detached bay fronted 1930s houses, and the car windows were covered in a thick layer of ice. Mickey looked at his wife and her swollen stomach. "However, did I get to be so lucky to be with you?" he said.

Five-year-old Jason clung to his leg. "Are we going to see the baby today, Daddy, on that machine?"

Mickey ran his fingers through the toddler's hair. "Yes, son, she's still in mummy's tummy, but we can watch her move about, maybe she will wave to you again."

"I want her here with us, when can we bring her home?"

"Soon, son, soon." Mickey turned towards his wife. "Are you ready, love?"

Kaitlin looked at her husband. "It's me that's lucky to be with you. Other people don't see your nice side. Anyway, it's great to prove everyone wrong, still together after all these years."

"Except Harry."

"Oh yes, except Harry. I'll be a couple of minutes, just need to finish my hair."

"Your hair looks perfect. You look perfect." He moved towards her and kissed her. "I'll clear the windscreen while you finish off making yourself even more gorgeous, if that's possible." He went to the kitchen and filled a large pan with tepid water, then manoeuvred through the living room towards the front door.

"Can I come, Daddy?"

"Yes of course you can." They walked towards the car, Mickey struggling to hold both the pan and his son's hand along the icy path. He unlocked the car and turned the key in the ignition as Jason jumped excitedly into the passenger seat.

A hundred yards away the face of the dark-coated man changed, seeing Mickey Warren with his son. "You, stupid bastard," he hissed under his breath. "Get the kid out of the car!" Warren needed to die, but killing children wasn't his game. Shaking his head, he thought, even now Warren couldn't just die alone, another innocent life had to go with him. The idea of intervening, suddenly entered his head, but left just as quickly. The long, torturous years of waiting had been too long.

Mickey put the demister on and pressed the radio button, then noticed the tender look on his son's face, smiling up at him. "Don't touch anything, son." He got out of the car and threw the tepid water over the windscreen and side windows, slowly the ice began to melt. Glancing through the small, misty oval space where the ice had cleared, he saw Jason's hands on the gear stick, waggling it back and forth. The grinding gears battled against the clutch as they struggled to engage and move the car forward. Underneath, the mercury danced and reached up to the two wires. He called to him, but the sound of the radio drowned his words. He rushed to the passenger door, almost slipping over in his haste to open the door and pick up his son. "You're a bit too young to drive, sonny." They walked inside just as Kaitlin was putting her coat on.

"It's freezing out there, will you be warm enough?" The ringing of the phone interrupted them. "Leave it, babe, it can wait," he said, but Kaitlin could never leave a ringing phone.

"It's Solomon, Mickey."

This was a call Mickey would always take. "Two minutes," he whispered to Kaitlin.

"Two minutes, yes, that will be the day, I'll be in the car. Come on, Jason, let's wait for Daddy in the car."

Jason ran over and grabbed his father's leg. The relationship between Mickey and Jason always made Kaitlin feel happy inside. Never feeling more content, than when she saw them together. Soon, she thought, their family would be complete, as she instinctively felt her bump. Mickey was deep in conversation as she walked slowly along the icy path, relieved to reach the car without slipping. She opened the passenger door and sat in the warm car, waiting for them to come out. Stevie Wonder's *You Are The Sunshine Of My Life* filled the car. She sang along, in her head, she was singing to Mickey. She placed her hands on her swollen stomach again and smiled.

Five minutes later, Mickey had still not come out and the warm car was now hot. Reaching across to lower the heating, her bump pushed against the gear stick. The car fell into gear and lurched forward.

The explosion shattered the windows at the front of the house and threw Mickey and Jason to the floor. Mickey felt a sharp pain, and looked at a large shard of glass, embedded in his shoulder. His white shirt turned crimson, as he pulled the jagged shard from his flesh. Looking through the dust, he saw his son, lying motionless on the floor. He rushed over and picked him up. Jason opened his eyes. "Daddy…" Hot tears ran down Mickey's face. His first thought was that a gas explosion had caused the blast, and that Kaitlin had been outside and been spared the force of the explosion, but then he realised the blast had come from outside the house.

"Kaitlin!" he screamed, running to the gaping hole where the front door used to be. He looked at the devastation, the car, a mangled, smouldering wreck, and then, the sight of what was left of his wife and unborn child. She was unrecognisable, but he could not stop looking at her, until a small hand touched his face.

"Daddy, where is Mummy?"

The shock wave from the blast had rocked his car; the man in the dark coat liked that. Not quite the plan, but now the knowledge, that Mickey Warren would suffer for the rest of his very short life, gave him a very warm feeling. He stayed a few minutes more to watch the drama unfold before putting the car into gear and driving away, laughing, content with his morning's work. Remorse was not on the agenda. McCartney's Bond theme played on the radio. He turned the volume to full and his maniacal laugh accompanied the song.

The wailing ambulance passed him as he turned out of the street. Staying too long was a mistake and he knew it.

Mickey stood transfixed, then picked up a small piece of paper fluttering in the wind. The hospital appointment card for the ultrasound scan, charred at its edges by the blast and fire, was still warm. Looking at it, and then placing it in his pocket, it would be all that remained of the future, now stolen from him. Mickey looked at his son, still in his arms clinging to him tightly. "Where's Mummy, Daddy, where is she?" The question went unanswered.

Mickey climbed into the ambulance, not hearing the sirens until they were turned off. They pulled into the crowded emergency department drop-off.

"We need to stop the bleeding; you are losing a lot of blood."

"Check my boy first," Mickey replied. Jason sat by his dad, reluctant to move, as the doctor gently examined him.

"Your son is fine, now I need to look at your shoulder." Mickey said nothing, as the hooked needle wove in and out, bringing together the two flaps of flesh. Numb to the pain, his focus solely on the small face looking up at him, with bewildered, scared eyes.

"Let me take the boy," the nurse said.

"Leave him," Mickey snapped, then looked up, hearing the commotion outside.

"You can't go in there," the nurse said.

Harry walked through regardless. "I'm family," he said. As soon as Jason saw him, he ran to him. Harry picked him up and hugged him. "I will find out who did this, Mickey, I promise you."

Mickey did not answer. It was as though he hadn't heard him. Harry looked at him and saw a look on his face not seen before, an empty, vacant nothingness.

"You two are staying at mine," he said.

The early hours of the morning moved slowly by. "You know, Harry, the day I met her was the best day of my life, and this is the worst," said Mickey. "I have a son who won't understand where his mum has gone and has an idiot for a dad that can't explain to him what happened. I should have protected her, it should be me that's dead, not her."

Harry, for once, had no words for his friend.

In the morning, a note written for Mickey was placed on the kitchen table, as he made his way to Solomon Gorman's office.

"Harry, we will find out who did this, an attack on one of us is an attack on all of us. Thing is, Mickey has a lot of enemies. He's been a nasty little bastard over the years, it's a very long list of possibles. I'll take care of the security at the funeral because whoever did this might well come back to finish the job. What's your take on it?"

"Thanks for that, Sol, Mickey will appreciate it. Like you say, it could be anyone. Looks like a paid-for job, and I guess top of the list would be payback for one of the jobs he's done. I'd appreciate anything you can do, Sol, she was the only woman I ever loved."

"Sorry, I forgot how close you were, I won't stop, you have my word. Tell Mickey to be careful, this isn't over, it was Mickey they wanted dead, not his wife."

Harry nodded. "Yes, and his unborn child, Sol."

Unusually for him, Harry put his foot down and sped back to his friend and the young boy he viewed as his own. The struggle to deal with his own grief; never having experienced such friendship with any other woman was extreme. The sense of loss, profound, but the understanding that his pain was nothing compared to Mickey's was not lost upon him.

As he went through the door, the police were leaving. They had gained nothing from the hour with Mickey. What could they learn? That he had lots of enemies, and if he was running for an election, no one would vote for him. Everyone knew who and what Mickey Warren was.

Night came and intensified the gloom. Jason was sleeping and Mickey and Harry sat there saying nothing. They didn't need to; being there together was as good as it was going to get.

Mickey finally drifted into sleep with the help of enough sedatives in his blood to kill a rhino. Harry sat listening to the eerie silence hanging over the house, hating every minute of it.

The dark lightened and turned slowly into dawn. Another day, he thought, one to wonder exactly what sort of world it was, where women and unborn babies were killed so easily. Checking the small sleeping child, and moving towards him, he looked down at him. "I promise, I will always look after you," he murmured. "I cannot replace your mum, who was my dearest friend. But I will never leave your side." He leant over the small angelic figure wrapped warm in his blankets and gently kissed his forehead. Then closed the door softly, as the tears fell silently down his face.

Eight a.m.

The sun finally won its battle with the clouds, and the open page of yesterday's *Evening Standard* reflected the rays into Captain Tommy Bednar's eyes. Glancing towards it, and shielding his eyes from the sudden brightness, he read it again. The hustle and bustle of the café in the early morning suited him; easily fading into the crowd just as he had been taught in the Special Operations modules in Hereford. Listening to the people gossiping, normally bored him, but today all the talk was about the explosion outside

Mickey Warren's house and the death of his wife and unborn child.

He saw the waitress look at him again and knew she desired him. Studying women, as he studied everything that interested him, led him to the conclusion, they were as base and animalistic as men, when it came to their desire for sex. Being the object of their desire was nothing new in his life, but he preferred to be the one who made the moves.

She walked to his table and looked at the paper. "Terrible, that poor man, who could do such a thing? You just don't know who to trust these days."

"No, you never know who to trust, but I hear he deserved it, a nasty little bastard, a two-bob gangster."

He could see the venom in his voiced had startled her, and that now, she no longer desired the man she had wanted such a short time ago.

"I'd be careful who you say that to around here, that's Mickey Warren you're talking about, and if he heard you say that you would be a dead man."

He smiled. "Oh, I don't think it's me that needs to die, I'm sure looking for the people who killed his wife is more important." He paid his bill and left, laughing.

11.59 a.m.

"It wasn't me, Bill, honest, I hated the bastard, but a car bomb isn't my style. Where would I get a bomb from, and who would I know to do a job like that? Who would take the job from me? No, It's someone much higher up the food-chain."

Jack Rich was sweating when the temperature said he shouldn't be. Billy Varey looked at him. "Jack, you have the look of a guilty man, or more accurately a scared one. This is what you get when you open your mouth too much. You've always been the same, even at school, you just can't help yourself. If I find out you were involved, I'll kill you myself."

138

"Bill, me and Mickey had our run-ins, everyone knows that, but we were fine lately. I wouldn't know how to do a car bomb. You need to square this for me, we go back a long way."

"Now you're repeating yourself. I don't think for a minute it was you, but you don't help yourself, do you? You had a good little number with him till you mugged him off, you're your own worst enemy. I'll see what I can do. Leave town for a bit till this blows over. Or perhaps not, if you do, you'll look like you've got something to hide, so just keep your head down and lay off the Charlie. Now go on, fuck off, I don't need this shit now. And let this be a lesson, we both know it wasn't you, but your gob has put you firmly in the frame."

Jack got up and left Just as Tommy Varey walked in. "Did you hear that, Tom? What do you think?

"Bruv, there is no way in this world it was Jack, it was a professional job. Mickey Warren's days are numbered. No loss to be honest, I've never really liked the guy. Shame about his wife, but the world will be a better place when Mickey's out of it. I don't know what Harry sees in him."

Eight p.m.

Bernie Broadman was nursing his sixth beer of the evening and struggling to keep his balance on the bar stool. Three hours in the bar had elicited zero contact with another human being, other than the barman. The page in front of him had a picture of the house and the remains of the car in the murder of Mickey Warren's wife. The whole story had been read at least twenty times, and each time laughter would follow. He was a loner, damaged in his early life by the actions of Mickey Warren, never remembering enjoying life, or even the last time he'd laughed. Today was different; his jaw was aching. People were beginning to stare at him, but he didn't care. For the first time loving the attention. Even women were looking at him, for the wrong reasons, he knew, but at least they were looking. His experiences of women were few, and limited to those paid as they left, or more often, as they arrived. They thought there something very odd about him, weird even. The only thing the brasses liked, was sex was always over in less than a minute, and sometimes ejaculation occurred, before his trousers came off.

Hobbies were few; the one that consumed him and was most passionate about was his collection of dolls. They were his family. He would feed them, wash them and change the babies' nappies, chastising them if they misbehaved and punishing them when they were naughty. If they were very naughty, they would be sent to the special room, where a hangman's noose awaited them. But there would be none of that today. Tonight, a special party was planned, and they would all be dressed in their best clothes. He would take his time and dress in his favourite outfit, the one from his dead mother's wardrobe. He thought about his only friend, his childhood idol, Tommy Bednar. Tommy was his hero, they shared from childhood their hatred of Mickey Warren. Tommy would come to the party too, in fact, yes, he would be the guest of honour. He took the small doll, his favourite, from his pocket. "Come on, Tommy, we must get back to the others, it will be a very special party."

Ten p.m.

Harry sat at his desk; his eyes fixed on the front page of the *Echo*. The words stung him.

A double funeral will be held at the East London cemetery for Kaitlin Warren and her unborn baby killed by a car bomb. Kaitlin Warren died instantly when the bomb went off in a car outside the family home in Bow, East London. Her husband Michael Warren was unavailable for comment, but family have described her as 'their guiding light, a compassionate, beautiful person, and wonderful mum to son Jason, aged four.'

Close friend Dr Stanley Ablett said, 'Kaitlin worked for the Red Cross, caring for and saving the lives of others. It is a tragic day, and she will be missed so much by the people who knew her, she is irreplaceable.'

The funeral is arranged for Thursday the 28th. The family have asked it to be by invitation only. No flowers please but donations to the British Red Cross will be gratefully accepted.

This time the tears didn't come. The pain had gone too deep.

Chapter 17
1974
London

Jason was gently snoring, asleep on the sofa.

"Mickey, you need to get out of the house, you've not set a foot outside for two weeks."

"I know, I will, but Jason is my priority, each day, asking about his mum, waking every night crying by my side."

He placed his hand on Mickey's shoulder. "I know, I hear him. You're doing such a fine and difficult job, but you need to get out into the world again. Leave Jason with me for a few hours."

"I can't stop the rage building inside me."

"Mickey, you are being a great father to our little man."

"Thanks, Harry, it's just a shame it took the death of my wife to turn me into one."

"No, you've always been a good father. Don't ever believe what you just said. Stop blaming yourself, it was an accident."

"That was no accident, and I swear I will find out who it was and kill them all." His raised voice woke the small child, who was now looking at him.

"Where is Mummy, when is she coming back?" It was the question asked every day.

Mickey picked him up and held him tightly. "She is in heaven, son, but every day looks at you and kisses you when you're asleep. She strokes your hair at night and lies beside you. Mummy will always love you, always be looking out for you."

Harry could see Mickey had no intention of going anywhere. "I'm off to see Solomon," he said. Mickey nodded.

Harry shrugged as he got into his car for the short drive to Solomon Gorman's office, hoping Solomon would have some news, because Harry's own efforts to find the killer had come to nothing.

"Harry, I've got zero, whoever did this is under the radar, a pro. Jack Rich is top of everyone's list. We all know what a hot head he is, but it wasn't him. He's a solid East End boy, this is way out of his league. I checked his alibi, it's sound. What bothers me is, there are no leads, not one. It was the work of a top team, no warning. They could have killed him with a bullet, but they didn't. It's a message, a statement, maybe to us Harry, the commission. Yes, this is about us, not just Mickey. The start of a war against us. I've told the others to look at their security, and I suggest you do the same."

Harry looked at him, confused. "Sol, I don't see that if this was aimed at the commission, why Mickey? He's not front row, it would be one of the families or even myself or the Bishes. Mickey is at the bottom of the list, not the top. Also, who are we having trouble with? As far as I know, no one, unless you know different."

Solomon re-lit his Cuban cigar. "Maybe you're right, maybe I'm being paranoid, then again, maybe not. So, take my advice and look after yourself, I'll let you know if I hear anything."

Harry shuffled uneasily in his car, wary of turning the key in the ignition, and realising he was more in the dark now than when he'd walked into Solomon's office. Surely Solomon was wrong. It didn't make sense unless he knew something and was keeping it to himself.

Jack Rich was rattled, a feeling alien to him. Half of London's villains thought he had killed Mickey Warren's wife in a bungled attempt to kill the man himself. Jack's enemies were laughing at him, and his friends were telling him to leave the country. He had become a tourist attraction for people wanting to get a glimpse of him before the inevitable bullet ripped through his head.

Eastham had tailed him for the last week. He had noticed Rich become more confident as time passed since the car bomb, presuming if he was going to die, it would already have happened and it would be yesterday's news. In Eastham's experience, there was no doubt Jack Rich was not the killer, moreover, he wasn't involved at all.

Mickey's phone rang. "Yes?"

The reply was short. "Home."

Mickey drove the three miles to Jack Rich's house, parked one street away and walked fifty yards to the back garden. He crept through the unlocked gate and crossed quietly across some gravel. He looked at the flimsy door which gave way with one kick. A startled Jack Rich rushed down the stairs, intent on battering the cheeky bastard who had just kicked his door in. Then he saw who the visitor was.

"Mickey, what are you doing here?"

"Shut up, Jack." The sight of the gun in Mickey's hand, answered the question.

"Mickey, it wasn't me, I was nowhere near your place. I'm sorry about what happened, really sorry, but it wasn't me, I swear."

Mickey looked at him, "Jack, your escorts will be here in a minute. I hope you don't mind if I don't hang about."

Small beads of sweat fell into his eyes. "What escorts, Mickey?"

"The hounds of Hell," Mickey replied, raising and firing the gun. The back of Jack's head exploded. Pink brain matter dripped slowly down the wall, as the already dead body fell backwards onto the floor, it jerked again and again as Mickey fired another five bullets into him. "Goodbye, Jack," he said, quietly turning and calmly walking out.

Mickey felt better, but not as much as he had thought he would. The journey to regain control over his life had begun, and the decision to return to work the next day had been made, and God help anyone who crossed him.

Harry responded to the urgent call from Solomon, knowing what it would be about, and not looking forward to the conversation, but he would handle him, in the usual way and bring him around to his own way of thinking. He sat down. Solomon was wearing his serious face.

"Harry, help yourself to a drink." He got straight to the point. "Is Mickey becoming a problem?"

Harry looked at him. "Sol, I can see you're annoyed with Mickey's actions, and you're right to be. Killing a man in one of the families without permission is out of order, without doubt a line was stepped over. But Jack is no loss, and was a problem for all of us, Mickey's done us a favour. He's done a lot of good things, Sol. He's fine, thinks he got the man who killed his wife. We both know it wasn't Jack, but he's at peace with it now. Let me deal with him, please. I spoke with Billy Varey this morning, he said you two had a chat. If he's OK with it, then, we should be. I know Mickey acted out of turn, and he knows it, I promise you, but we need to remember what has happened and what an asset he is."

"OK, Harry, the matter is closed. What bothers me more, is we've not turned up a single thing on the bombing and neither have the cops. Whoever did this is still out there, and like I said before, I'm not sure this is just about Mickey. Killing Jack hasn't solved the problem, much as I would like it to have."

"So, what's the plan?"

"That's just it, Harry, we haven't got one."

One mile away the man in the dark coat sitting at the bar looked at the naked dancer on the pole. How well it had worked out, he thought. Mickey Warren was hurting, every single second of his miserable life. Safe for now, but a lot more pain was coming his way before the final day came. When he was happy again, maybe it would be time to kill his other child, much more fun than just putting a bullet in Mickey's head.

Thoughts played through his mind repeatedly. He tried to feel sad about Mickey's wife but couldn't. She must have been a whore to have married such a low life as Mickey Warren. As for the unborn child, it was the spawn of the devil. What would the devil-child have gone on to do itself? What evil would it have brought to the world?

He smiled and called the dancer over.

"Would you like a private dance?" she asked.

He nodded and followed her into a dingy corridor to a small cubicle and sat on a wooden bench, then pulled fifty pounds from his pocket and waved it at her. "Do you want this?"

She looked at him, not sure if he was being serious. "Sure," she replied. Looking at her, his face suddenly changed, as he placed the money on the tiny ledge in front of her. He put a finger to his lips to tell her to be quiet, then grabbed her hair and forced her head down on him. The choking sound as he pushed himself deeper into her mouth turned him on. Control was everything.

Chapter 18
1974
London

Mickey had taken Solomon's advice on moving to a more secure address and installing top-level security for good measure. A housekeeper-cum-nanny, two security guards and two drivers, were now regular fixtures. The arrangement worked well, but constantly reminded him of the day his wife was blown to bits, by the grim reaper's mistaken endeavours. A low profile had been the order of the day, knowing he was guilty of treading on a few toes when Jack Rich met his maker. There were no regrets about killing him, he knew he was not responsible for killing his wife and unborn child, but Rich was always going to die, it was only a matter of when.

His thoughts were taken away by the tugging on his shirt sleeve, and his son staring up at him. They'd grown ever closer over the last few weeks and still slept in the same room, although now Mickey had moved a small single bed into the room. Jason's life was returning to a semblance of normality, repairing itself in a way only young lives can. His father, however, would never be the same again.

He heard the postman at the door, who arrived at the same time every morning, let through the gates by the security guard. Mickey walked slowly to the door. One single handwritten envelope lay on the mat, he picked it up, walked to the kitchen, laid it on the table and finished making breakfast. He placed the plates on the table, where Jason sat waiting, knife and fork in hand, then picked up the letter and looked at the handwriting, neat but written in dark red ink. He sliced open the top of the envelope with the knife, which was still covered in butter.

A picture fell onto the table, he picked it up and turned it over. It was a picture of himself at Kaitlin's funeral. He took out the single piece of paper and began to read.

Dear Mickey

I see you are struggling since the death of your wife. Do you like the picture I took of you at the funeral? You are crying, how does it feel? I could have killed you that day, but I'm enjoying watching you suffer. I want you to suffer every day of your miserable little life. I'm watching you, Mickey, watching you, and your son. First at Harry's, and now, your new house with all its security and those two overweight thugs you have guarding you. Do you really think you're safer there? You're not. You killed Jack. What a fool you are, did you really think it was him, or were you just being your normal self, a nasty little bastard, needing to take out your anger on someone? I know what you are thinking, am I really the person who killed your woman?

I AM, I was there the day you let her die, how do you feel about that? It should have been you, yes, you, Mickey, not her.

Shall I remind you what happened? You warmed up the car, your little boy was with you. BE CAREFUL AND LOOK AFTER HIM, BECAUSE HE MAY BE NEXT. Children are very important to their fathers, are you only just realising that? You ran to the side of the car, almost slipping. Was he playing with the gear stick? You were careless, weren't you? He could have died, so you see, it's not all bad. It could have been all of you in the car. Then you went inside with a big smile on your face, she came out. You didn't look after her, you killed her. Are you proud of yourself?

Look for me, I will always be there, and when I am ready, I will kill you. I am laughing in your face.

B.B (the) King.

He placed the letter on the table. "How's your breakfast, son?"

He didn't hear the answer. Never one to be scared, but this had unnerved him. What the fuck had he done to deserve this? he wondered. Forgetting the cold-blooded killings, chopping off a football team's worth of fingers, and the countless beatings he'd dished out in the last few years.

He ran his fingers through his son's hair. "Shall we have a game of football when I get back, son?"

"Yes, Dad, can you go in goal?"

"You bet, but don't kick the ball too hard."

They finished their breakfast together. Mickey kissed him, then quietly closed the door behind him, leaving him with the nanny.

"What do you think, Harry?"

Harry put the letter on the table and picked up the picture of Mickey at the funeral.

"I think this is a whole shitload of trouble. It's you he's after, which will cheer Solomon up, no end. He still thinks this is about the commission, let's go see him. Maybe there's some tape from the funeral. Hopefully, the guy made a mistake. One thing I do know, we need to find him, and quick."

Harry felt reassured by the Mercedes' darkened windows and the fact Eastham was driving. A few minutes later, they were looking across the table at Solomon Gorman. Mickey passed the letter to the head of the five families, who read it and looked up.

"Mickey, this is about you, it's personal, it's not about the commission at all."

Harry noticed the well-disguised relief in Sol Gorman's voice. "Sol, do you think you might have picked him up on any of the tape at the funeral?"

"Good idea, Harry. Fingers crossed we'll have a picture of him and then he's as good as dead. I'm sure we can work out where the picture was taken from."

Mickey pushed his hand forward. "Sol, I owe you."

"No, you don't, Mickey, we look after each other, we are a family and that's what we do. A favour to you can be returned another time. No one is counting."

Harry smiled as he looked at Solomon. Since the Godfather film starring Marlon Brando two years before, Solomon Gorman had transformed himself into London's own version of Don Vito

Corleone. He'd slicked back his hair, grown a moustache and now smoked even bigger cigars. Life was but a stage, and Solomon's cigar smoke was filling it.

One week later to the hour, Harry, and Mickey got a call to go to Solomon's office. "Mickey, I have returned to you the favour you gave to me when you sorted the Ronson business, but we don't count these things, we are family, I have told you this." He passed a photograph across the table. "Do you know him, Mickey? This is him, standing at the place where the picture was taken."

Mickey looked at the grainy black and white photo, the face partially obscured by a cap. A camera hung around the man's neck, who was about the same age as Mickey. A flicker of recognition went through his mind, a small ember that quickly burned out. "He looks familiar. I do know him, I'm sure, but I can't place him."

"That's very disappointing. Mickey, you need to remember, search your brain, this man has one thing on his mind, you! I know you've fucked off a lot of people, haven't we all. The question is, who have you fucked so bad to do this? If he wanted you dead, you'd be dead already. He's playing with you."

Mickey smiled. "Very reassuring, Sol, thank you."

Eastham decided to take a different route back to Harry's. Mickey in the back of the car, was deep in thought. "You know, Harry, dying doesn't bother me. What does is the thought of losing the only remaining thing in the world I love. The only thing I have left, my only connection to Kaitlin. I will find this bastard and kill him. No one's ever beaten me, and I don't intend to let anyone start now."

Harry placed his hand on Mickey's shoulder. "Have you got any idea who it is?"

Mickey held the photo in his hand. "It will come to me, I'm sure. Like I said, I know him, but I'm just not seeing from where or when, let alone why the bastard wants to kill me. I will remember, Harry. When I do, liked I said, I will kill him and everyone he cares about, very slowly, and enjoy every minute of it."

Chapter 19
1974
London

The drizzle made the job a little more difficult than the man in the dark coat wanted, and the cold numbed his body. His position was exposed, and the wind blew in gusts, but the view was perfect. "When will people ever learn?" he muttered to himself. "They think they are so clever."

Mickey called in to see Harry most mornings, and his movements were becoming too predictable for his own good. Wally Fields, Mickey's day driver, got out of the car and glanced around for anything that looked out of place. It was a secure car park surrounded by high walls.

The view through the scope of the rifle showed a man bored with his job. To Wally, everything looked the same as it did every other day of the week, he did not bother to glance at the high-rise buildings around them. He was well paid for driving Mickey about and occasionally looking menacing when it was called for. Friends told him, it was a dangerous job, that an international hit man was going to kill Mickey Warren, so don't get in the way. He shivered and looked forward to returning to the warmth of the car.

Mickey opened the passenger door, got out and cupped his hands to shield the cigarette from the wind and rain as he lit it. "I'll be a few hours today, Wally, take a break, come back about twelve."

A raindrop fell from Wally's nose as the cross hairs imprinted on his face. The man in the dark coat squeezed the trigger. Wally Fields' head shot back, and a split-second later Mickey heard the shot and ran for the door. He reached the stairs at the same time as Harry's security were rushing down, having watched the scene unfold on the CCTV. Harry pressed the red button which alerted the police to a serious problem, and within minutes a police car pulled into the rear entrance, followed ten minutes later by an ambulance.

Harry and Mickey were drinking whisky.

"Fuck me, Mickey, you nearly died! You're using up your nine lives, a bit too quick for my liking."

"No, he wasn't shooting at me. People will keep dying until I find him, or he kills me when he gets bored."

"You're becoming a dangerous man to be around, my friend." Mickey laughed.

Sergeant Hone placed a hand on Harry's shoulder. He knew him well and was on the payroll. Harry passed him an open bottle of beer.

"What's the SP, Mark?"

"Professional hit, probably from the roof of the Griffin building. Two cars are there now but the shooter will be long gone. You need to sort out your security here, Harry, it's not good enough. I'll send LIA round, they're the best in the business." The cop turned to Mickey. "Do you think this is the same guy who bombed your car?"

Mickey looked at him. "Yes. Am I free to go?"

"No, sorry, we need a statement, PC Derby will take it now."

Mickey followed the PC to another office. "Stay away from Mickey for a while, Harry, if you want my advice, too many people seem to be dying around him."

Harry looked at him. "Thanks, Mark, I'll bear that in mind, and get you a copy of the CCTV. Do you need me to make a statement? "

"Yes"

Forty-eight hours later Mickey was having breakfast with his son when he heard the footsteps of the postman on the gravel. Something told him not to make the short journey to pick up the mail. He did so anyway and saw the familiar dark red ink on the letter, on the floor.

Dear Mickey

That was a good shot, wasn't it, must be getting a bit scary for you now. It's horrible not knowing what the next day will bring.

Which of your friends is going to die next? My advice, not that you probably want it, is get used to this. This is your life now, or death, depends which way you look at it.

I was thinking of shooting you. Did you feel the cross hairs on your face? I went from you to him, and back to you, I wanted to, but I couldn't, this is too much fun. How often do you think about me? I know you have a picture of me from the cameras at the funeral, but you haven't worked it out yet, have you? Otherwise, you would have been round to see me. Not that I will be where you expect, I will know you are coming, so be very careful. There is someone you trust, one of your friends. You shouldn't, he tells me everything.

I thought about you for years. Did you look at the neat bullet hole in the front of Wally Field's head and the big hole at the back? Yes, I know who he was. You probably inhaled some of his brain. Another dead body down to you, and there will be more, Mickey, lots more.

Be careful when you visit the grave of your woman, I might kill you there. If you are lucky, you could find me there, or is that unlucky? I am often there at her grave. You couldn't look after her, could you? You let her die, this is not over, and it won't be until you're dead, but that is a long way off. I'm surprised you haven't worked it out yet, maybe you need a clue. Think back, think back to the time you walked away laughing.

I forgot to mention in the last letter, you also couldn't protect your unborn child. Always protect the children, they deserve to be protected. You're better off dead, Mickey, that's the truth, leave your sick poisonous life. You could kill yourself and then the people around you will stop dying. Could you do that for them? NO, I don't think you can, but maybe you will think differently when Harry or your son are killed. Up to you, I will give you a few weeks to think about it, but remember, I will be watching! Trust no one around you.

See you soon
BB King

Mickey gave Jason his morning hug and kiss, then left to give Harry the latest news.

Harry was laying himself out two big lines of Peruvian flake. Both the length of the lines and the frequency which he took them had increased since the car bomb and untimely aeration of Wally Fields' head. Reducing his consumption was something for the future. Drugs had always been his way of coping, so why stop now.

As Mickey strolled in, Harry saw the letter in his hand and no amount of cocaine could lessen the dread he felt at that moment. His worst fears had walked in and were made even worse after reading the letter.

"Mickey, like a dog at your throat or a shark in the water sometimes life, well death in this case comes to get you. Get the kid somewhere safe until this is over, send him to my gaff in Antigua. No one else knows about it, he'll be safe there, my sister will look after him. This killer is something else, he's fucking crazy, special crazy. I spoke with Solomon who's getting very nervous."

"Good idea, Harry, let's get the boy out of here."

"What's this BB King thing? And walk away laughing? He's taunting you, but you know, I think they're real clues. Think, Mickey, the answer is in the letter."

"I have, I've thought about it a thousand times. I don't get it, do you really think it's someone from the distant past, or is it just a smoke screen, and someone more recent?"

Harry didn't answer; he just took another line. "Harry, you're doing a lot of Charlie lately, it can't be good for your health."

He lifted his head. "Yes, I am, well spotted, and you'll be getting the bloody bill for it. The only thing around here threatening my health, mate, is you." They both burst out laughing. "It's good we can laugh, Mickey, knowing there's a bullet waiting for us around the corner."

The next day they watched as the small boy at the centre of their lives boarded the non-stop flight to Antigua. On the plane with him was the ever-reliable Eastham. In the back of Mickey's mind, and those close to him was the question, would he ever see his son again?

Mickey noticed people were avoiding him. Harry looked at his friend. "It's times like this, you find out who your real friends are." He paused and inhaled the smoke from the Camel cigarette. "So that will be me and your aunt Dot, but only because she's deaf and hasn't heard you've got Carlos the Jackal stalking you."

Mickey laughed. "You sure know how to cheer me up. Fuck him, now the boy is safe I don't give a shit. I'll find the bastard and kill him. Anyway, I'm the safest man in London, the last person that's gonna die. He's having too much fun, thinking this is getting to me. It's you that needs to worry, you're right at the top of the list. Didn't you read the letter?" He grinned broadly.

"I'm serious, Harry. Listen for unusual noises as you're going to sleep. I think he might do you at your house, just to see if he can get through your security, and, my old friend, I personally wouldn't bet against it."

Harry looked at him. "Fuck off, Mickey, that's not even close to funny, you're a nasty little shit."

Mickey's words had spooked Harry, and over the next few days, varied his routine and practised some evasion techniques garnered from the latest Bond film. It was fun at first, but going around roundabouts twice, soon seemed like a lot of unnecessary effort, and taking a different route each time sounded sensible, but only resulted in getting lost. Worse, he continuously looked into the rear-view mirror muttering, "the name's Bond, James Bond." He began to question his own sanity and decided enough was enough, particularly as nothing unusual appeared to be happening.

The assassin had followed Harry for the last three days and was amused by his attempts to see if he was being followed, his various evasion techniques, and his odd habit of looking in the mirror and talking to himself. Despite not being within ten yards of Harry at any time, he liked him, and watched the way he was with people, who genuinely also seemed to like him. That was all well and good, he thought, but you are who you hang around with, so decided, Harry, would be the next to die. Mickey Warren would be very upset at losing his best friend. It was now only a question of how. It must be a spectacular death and had just the one in mind. It would be tomorrow, as long as there were no last-minute changes of plan on Harry's part.

He was at a loose end and decided to follow him again; an unnecessary risk, but he was enjoying himself, and the thought of another elimination was exciting him.

After following Harry for about an hour, he watched him stop outside a large building. The words "THE REFUGE" in bold lettering stood out in the gloom of the evening. He was intrigued. Why would Harry Fleet stop there? Even more surprising was the sight ten minutes later, when Harry came out of the building and began serving food and drink to the queue of people who had gathered outside. An hour later he followed Harry to his house before returning to his hotel room.

Sleep had been difficult. The sight of Harry serving in a soup kitchen had confused him, an unfamiliar state of mind. He decided to postpone the execution until it became clearer what Harry was up to. A visit to Companies House revealed the building in Sidney Street was owned by a Swiss company but could find no reference to who owned or ran the Refuge.

At midday, two days later a dishevelled, unsteady drunk wandered into the Blind Beggar. The tired-looking barman glared at him, his eyes stung as the odour from the dirty, torn overcoat hit him.

"Pint of mild, please."

The barman poured.

"What's that shelter in Sidney Street, can I get some food there?"

The barman rolled his eyes, not caring the drunk saw his expression. Another homeless drunk was all he needed. Ever since the refuge had opened, business in the Blind Beggar had increased; the problem was it was the down-and-outs from the shelter with a bit more money to spend on booze that frequented the place, now they didn't have to buy food. Worse, a lot of them smelled and it was beginning to get up his nose, especially this one, who smelt the worst of all.

"Yes, and you can get a few nights kip there too, and a bath." The barman wanted to move away, but the tramp had not finished.

"Does it cost anything, because I'm a bit down on my luck at the minute?"

"No, not a penny, you can pay if you can, but if you can't, it's free."

The tramp leaned closer to the barman. "Nothing's free, how can it be free, is it a charity or some church trying to convert you?"

The barman's eyes began to stream with the pungent smell of gone-off fish. "No, it's nothing like that, a guy called Harry Fleet pays for it all. Now if you don't mind finishing your pint and leaving, I would appreciate it."

After finishing his drink, the assassin glanced at the barman, and made a mental note; if he ran out of people to kill, this idiot would be added to his list.

Two days later, looking a lot cleaner and wearing a suit, he drove past the Refuge again. Harry Fleet was a lucky man; the assassin had decided as long as his good deeds at the Refuge continued, his heart would continue to beat. Harry, though not knowing, had just had his life saved by the combined hard luck stories of a thousand down-and-outs.

The killer enjoyed his benevolence; the power over life and death gave him a powerful feeling, one he loved.

Chapter 20
1974
London

Three weeks later, despite the efforts of the police and the commission, there were no new leads regarding the car explosion or the shooting of Wally Fields. Mickey's drivers were on triple time, and Harry had allocated Eastham to head Mickey's security. Eastham was enjoying the money, but had the feeling being around Mickey was like swimming with sharks, and that something was going to happen, and soon. That was where the wise money was. He had made sure his affairs and insurance policies were all in place.

"Where to, Mickey?"

"Lewisham, Paul. Henry Lightbody's place."

Eastham turned into Lewisham High Street, passing the restaurants and pubs and a small row of shops, the newsagents and Broadman's butchers. Mickey watched as a drunk thrown out of the Fleet pub, bounced along the pavement. "Ouch, that must have hurt," muttered Mickey. Then he spun his head violently backwards and felt a spasm of pain run across his back. He looked at the garish letters above Broadman Butchers shop, ASK TODAY HERE TOMORROW.

"Paul, turn around, that's him, Bernie fucking Broadman, that's him in the picture. His old man hung himself because of me. BB is Bernie Broadman. I walked away laughing when I burnt their stall to the ground. It all makes sense. It's him. Do a drive by."

Eastham turned the car around and drove slowly, but not too slowly, past the shop. He knew they shouldn't both look, but for once his discipline deserted him. There behind the counter was the man in the photograph, Bernie Broadman, serving a customer, a sullen look on his face, sloping shoulders and an awkward way of moving.

"Is it really him? Just doesn't look the type."

"Maybe that's why he's so good. I want to go in and kill the bastard right now."

"Mickey, let's do this the right way. You've got your boy to consider and remember what he said in the letter about expecting you, there's probably a shooter under the counter."

"You're right, get round to Harry's. How could I have missed it? It's so obvious."

Harry looked at the monitor and watched them run up the stairs. He pressed the button and the door swung gently open. Mickey went to the bar and got himself a drink.

"Well, someone's happy," quipped Harry.

"Got him, Harry. Found the bastard, and I'm gonna torture him until he screams for mercy."

Harry's head jerked upwards. "What, the shooter?"

"Yes, Bernie Broadman, the son of a butcher who topped himself when I leaned on him for a bit of protection. It was years ago, Jesus, when we were kids. He found his old man hanging from the ceiling. Can't blame him for getting upset I suppose."

Harry looked at Mickey. "Well, that's very magnanimous of you, Mickey. So, what's the plan? And before you go playing Superman, you might want to remember what a capable little bastard you're dealing with. Don't mess about, just kill him, nothing clever."

"I know that." Mickey turned to Eastham. "Paul, follow him, find out where he lives, then I'll take it from there, and before you say anything, Harry, that's the way it's gonna be."

Eastham looked at Harry, waiting for his approval. Harry nodded, then looked at his old friend. It was the first time in months he had seen him happy. The dark veil that hung over Mickey had lifted, but that didn't mean Harry was going to let him get his own way.

"It's all I can do to stop myself going there and killing him."

"Sounds like a good idea Mickey, a great idea. After all, I'll be there to look after your boy when Bernie boy, kills you. I'm telling you, don't fuck about, he's a professional killer and you're not in his league. Give the job to Raven and Muddy."

"Good words, Harry, well meant, I know, but I need to watch him die."

"Anger is never slated on the cold floor of revenge, Mickey, only time does that."

Eastham was careful. He had done this many times, but this was a cold-blooded killer who covered his tracks well. Only a chance drive-by had found him, and the skills shown so far would not allow him to be taken easily.

It was six-thirty p.m. Eastham parked between two Transit vans, a hundred yards from Bernie Broadman's shop. He watched him walk out of the shop and towards his car. He seemed very relaxed, either very confident or very stupid. He fumbled for his keys and dropped them. Eastham watched him move; uncoordinated, almost clumsy and not particularly fit, a roll of fat circled his trousers, evidence of having eaten too many of his own award-winning pies. It was not the profile of a cold-blooded killer.

Eastham put the doubts out of his head, reminding himself how dangerous this man was, and followed him for half a mile before pulling off the tail. Three days later in a different car, he picked up the trail and followed Bernie Broadman again. This time to Ennersdale Road, where he watched him enter his house, fumbling with his keys again. Eastham shook his head disbelievingly.

The next morning at Harry's, Eastham gave Mickey the details he'd been waiting for.

"Mickey, don't fuck about, I'm serious, no torture, no chat, just kill him, and take Paul," said Harry.

"Look, this is personal. He killed my wife and kid, and I would appreciate it if you didn't keep telling me how to do my job."

"Fair enough, don't take it the wrong way. I just don't want anything to happen to you and the boy."

"I know. Don't worry yourself, this time tomorrow we'll be celebrating the butcher joining his old dad in hell."

The day was losing the last of its light as they parked twenty yards from the drab terraced house. Fading light made the choice of the dark grey Vauxhall a good one, as it blended into the obscurity of the early evening. A light drizzle made the road quieter than normal, putting off casual walkers. Mickey turned the Beretta over in his hand; liking the feel of it. But Bernie Broadman was late, and it was making them edgy. "Never straightforward, is it. Has he rumbled us?"

"No, he's just late. Mickey, let me do this. I know what it means to you, but this job needs a clear head."

Mickey looked at him. "I have to do this. Yes, I would like to torture him for days before I kill him, but I know he's dangerous. I still have a son, and that's why I'll do it the right way. Thanks for the offer, but this one's down to me."

Before Eastham could reply, Bernie Broadman turned the corner, parked his car, got out and locked it. The bag he was carrying fell to the floor. Bending down to pick it up, he paused and looked around him, hesitating before retrieving it. Mickey wondered if his target had realised the danger that faced him. He turned and continued walking towards his house, not seeming to notice the man wearing a trench coat and hat walking towards him.

Mickey watched as Broadman raised his eyes and looked straight at him. Then noticed him slowly lift the package. Thinking for a moment Broadman had known all along they were there, he cursed at how naive he had been and waited for the bullet that would end his life. Dead before he got anywhere near the gun in his shoulder holster.

He carried on walking until the two men stood four feet from each other. Mickey knew Eastham was too far away to intervene.

"Mickey Warren!" The shock at seeing Mickey was genuine.

Mickey was confused, wondering, what would be Broadman's next move? The bag fell from his hands. Mickey pulled out the beretta and fired four bullets into the jolting torso.

Blood oozed onto the pavement, he fired a fifth shot into the head of the already dead Bernie Broadman, then kicked him, again and again.

Eastham got out of the car and ran towards Mickey. "Come on, that's enough, let's get out of here." As they turned to leave, Eastham picked up the bag Broadman had been carrying and tossed it to Mickey as they got in the car and drove away. Mickey felt the package and then opened it very slowly.

"What is it, Mickey? I thought it was a gun."

"Sausages."

Eastham dropped Mickey off and took the car to the lock up to change the number plates. He shook his head, still not quite believing what he had seen.

Chapter 21
We gotta get out of this place!

Mickey Warren placed his passport into his pocket and boarded the plane to Antigua. His spirits were high, and the thought of Bernie Broadman's blood making pretty patterns on the pavement was still fresh in his mind.

As the plane levelled out, he watched Harry simultaneously read a magazine and tilt a whole packet of nuts into his mouth, then struggle to get them down his throat without choking himself to death.

"Harry, you eat like a pig. That was a whole packet."

"Talking about nuts, Mickey, now you might live to see next week, you might want to get yourself checked for prostate and testicular cancer."

"Please stop drinking, Harry. In fact, better still, stop talking."

"No, I'm serious, it's killing a lot of men. Your prostate is normally the size of a walnut, and if it gets bigger, you've got problems, big problems. You might want to get someone to check it. It's quite simple, fun even, if it's done right, if you get my drift. Didn't you go out with a vets' nurse once? Get her to have a look."

"Harry, will you shut up? You get weirder every day. You worry me sometimes. How did we get on to talking about my prostate?

"Do you know, I can't believe you sometimes. If caring is a crime, I am guilty."

"Harry, you're guilty of many things, but worrying about my balls shouldn't be one of them."

"All I'm saying is be careful. Your testes, or balls as you call them, are easier to check than you think. You can do it yourself, what I do is look for the early warning sign, which is they get bigger. Get the vet-girl to have a look, and if she says they seem a bit bigger, get yourself down the doctor's."

Mickey looked across at the stewardess. "Could I move seats? Economy will be fine."

Mickey slept most of the way, but his dreams were constantly interrupted by visions of Harry checking his prostate. The descent, and the resulting pain in his ears, woke him as always. He looked across to see Harry's smiling face.

"Ah, Mickey, you're awake at last, thank God your snoring was louder than the engines, I'm feeling rather pleased with myself. Not only have I enlightened my old friend on the dangers of prostate cancer, but I've also managed to secure a date with that tall stewardess over there, when we get back home. Moreover, the raving lunatic Bernie Broadman is dead. And we are meeting Tobias Boswell, the man who will make us even richer. Best of all we will be seeing my sister and Jason. Yes, I think I've done rather well today."

As the plane came to a halt, a cobalt blue Bentley rolled up to it. An immaculately dressed driver got out and held up a gold-embossed placard with Harry's name on it. The doors opened and Harry and Mickey's names were called to exit the plane first. They walked out into the sweltering heat of the Antiguan day.

"It's like being royalty, Mickey, I could get used to this." Harry turned to the driver. "Don't we have to go through customs, and what about our bags?"

The driver turned to him. "No passports required. You are personal guests of Mr Tobias Boswell and our great prime minister. Mr Fleet, I will drop you off first at the offices of Mr Boswell, your luggage will follow you shortly."

Tobias Apollo Boswell sat at a huge teak desk. Looking back at Harry was a moose of a man, two hundred and sixty pounds of mainly blubber. Perched on top of his round shoulders was a bowling ball of a head, but he sprang to his feet in a manner that belied his huge bulk. "Mr Fleet, it is very good to meet you at last. Carlos Satero, our mutual friend, speaks very highly of you. He tells me you are a party animal, which is excellent. After our

165

meeting you must come to my house and I will show you how we party on this beautiful island of ours, but first to business. Please, sit down." He pressed an intercom. "Loretta, bring us some tea please." He looked up at Harry. "Now, Mr Fleet, how exactly can I be of help to you?"

"Please call me Harry. Carlos suggested I come to see you, as I have a small problem."

"What problem would that be?"

"Money, and a place to keep it."

Tobias Boswell's large hands came together, clasping each other like long-lost friends. "Ah, I see. Yes, I can help you with that problem, Harry, this is my specialty. I am an expert in this field, do you know how this service I offer works?"

Harry knew pretty well from his discussions with Carlos Satero. "Not exactly, Toby."

"Then let me tell you. I have a friend in London who owns a bank, the Bank of Credit and Commerce International, BCCI, for short. Now my good friend Mr Abedi is none too bothered if you bring in suitcases full of your hard-earned money to deposit, this is a most convenient thing for us. The account you open will be in a company name registered here; your name will not appear on the account in either London or here. That is a private matter and the documents showing you own the company will be registered with a solicitor, who, is a very good friend of mine. This too is extremely convenient, and is subject to lawyer client privilege, which means the document cannot be shown to anyone without your permission, which of course you will never give." He paused.

"So, we now have your money safely in the bank in London, but we cannot leave it there, it needs to come here. Fortunately, I have a bank here. Well, no bank as such, no building, but I have a brass plaque on the wall, which here, means it's a bank. Are you following Harry?"

"Oh yes, I'm following, Tobias."

"Then I shall continue. Mr Abedi will then transfer the money to my bank, and I, shall, with some sleight of hand, move it to a

166

bank in Chicago, then to an account in Citibank in London, to an account with your name on it."

Harry nodded. "I like the sound of that."

"There is of course a cost for all this work."

"Oh, there's always a cost," replied Harry.

Toby lifted his face, which wobbled like a jelly. "Indeed, we must all make a crust. What about your associates in London, will they be using my services? There will of course be some commission for your introduction."

Harry nodded. "I'm sure I can interest them in your services. So, let's see if I understand this. I pay money into a bank in London, it wanders around several banks around the world, a little bit is shaved off for expenses, and the rest ends up back in London whiter and cleaner than the finest driven snow."

"That is it, exactly. Now the fees, my friend, Mr Abedi will require five percent, as indeed will I. There is no room for negotiation, as these are the fees. I hope this is acceptable to you."

Harry got up and put his hand out. "Yes, it is. Now, do we have a party to go to?"

"Indeed, Harry, my parties are quite legendary in these parts."

"I've heard, Tobias."

Mickey got out of the Bentley at Harry's villa and looked at the smiling face of his son who ran into his father's open arms.

Jason's skin had turned dark brown and looked healthier and happier than the last time Mickey had seen him. The worry lines and dark circles under his son's eyes from the weeks before had gone.

A few miles away, Tobias Boswell's, other Bentley coped well with the uneven coast road that led to a pair of large golden gates, where a man in black stood bolt upright at the guardhouse. As the Bentley rolled up to the gates, the guard saluted the driver and they swung open. The car continued for three hundred yards, past rows of palms swaying in the light coastal breeze. It then swung left onto an expanse of deep gravel. Harry wiped the small beads of sweat that had formed on his forehead.

Tobias turned to the driver. "When Mr Fleet's bags arrive, take them to the south wing. Harry, a drink I think."

"Now you're talking, Tobias, this warm air has given me quite a thirst."

Tobias raised two fingers into the air, a signal for a previously invisible member of staff to appear with drinks. They walked to a terraced area which surrounded a large figure of eight pool, where the scent of bougainvillea filled the air. Harry looked towards the sea, where a large yacht and several other smaller vessels moored alongside a concrete jetty. The beaches were deserted for several hundred yards in either direction.

"Is that all yours, Tobias?

"Yes, Harry, as far as the eye can see. This country has been very good to me, in the same way that it will be good to you. Come, let us sit under the shade of the palms. Tell me all about London, I do miss the place. It's such a terrible shame I cannot return there, the authorities are being most unreasonable, for what is such a minor discretion on my part."

Mickey sat with his son, listening to everything the excited boy was telling him, feeling again the deep bond that had grown between them since the day of the explosion. Jason was a happy little boy again, and Mickey could see exactly why.

Mary was four years younger than Harry, and had the same gentleness in her actions, as her brother. He listened to the way she spoke, cared for and guided his young son. Her patience and understanding reminded him of Kaitlin, it brought a confusing lump to his throat. Throwing off his hat, he jumped into the pool, where Jason was throwing a ball into the air and catching it.

"You can swim, son?"

"Yes, Dad. Mary taught me."

Mickey looked across at her. Was there no end to her talents, he, wondered?

The breeze stiffened and the rustling palms formed an impromptu concert with the buzzing cicada and whistling tree frogs. Harry and Tobias were several Martinis into the evening when Harry's eyes were caught by movement coming from the servants' quarters. "Tobias, I think I'm hallucinating," he said.

"No, you're not Harry, the party is about to begin."

Six women walked through the open glass-panelled doors. Small thongs were all that adorned their oiled bodies. "That's quite a collection," said Harry.

"Indeed. Let me explain, the brunette is from England, the ebony beauty, from Gambia. Then my personal favourite, from China." He pointed to the next woman. "She is from Rio, and the next, from Scandinavia. My God Harry, no party is complete without a Viking. And finally, for interest, something different if it pleases you, a ladyboy from Thailand."

"Yes, a very fine selection, Tobias, truly excellent."

"Thank you, I think it's so important in life to know about three things, money wine and women."

As the last of the sun slipped under the horizon, Mickey tidied the light sheet around his son. He looked at the boy's face; the lamplight cast a warm glow on his cherubic features. Sleep had come early to him today. Mickey knew, looking down again at what remained of his family, that sleep would also come easily to himself. He leant over, kissed his forehead and whispered, "I love you, son." The threat from Bernie Broadman was gone, and seeing his son again gave him renewed hope for the future.

He walked into the kitchen, where Mary Fleet was making coffee.

"Would you like a cup, Mickey?"

He was ready for sleep, but there was something that needed to be said to the woman that had cared for his son so gently.

Tobias Boswell moved his chair slightly further away from the table and motioned to the Scandinavian to come to him. Walking slowly over, then sitting astride him, she moved her body rhythmically over his. Harry watched her massage Tobias' huge body with her breasts. He called to the rest of them to come over. "Ladies, I would like you to meet my very good friend, Harry."

Mickey and Mary sat on the terrace; the sunlight now completely gone. It was the turn of the moonlight to dance and cast delicate patterns and shapes on the waves. She smiled at him. "He is a fine boy, a real credit to you."

"I can't thank you enough, Mary, I can't believe the change in him."

"He's a child, just needing to be loved. I'm so sorry about Kaitlin, but Jason is lucky to have you. I watched you both today. You have a special bond."

Mickey felt the tears fall from his eyes. "I'm sorry, you caught me off guard."

"No, I'm sorry, I didn't mean to upset you." She moved closer and put her arms around him. He felt the tension in his body release as the tears continued to fall. Slowly his composure returned. "I don't know what just happened."

She looked into his red, glistening eyes. "I think that was long overdue. Shall we have something a bit stronger than coffee?"

As Harry rolled over, a sliver of bright sunlight stung his eyes. He turned away and buried his head in the pillow. The sheets were cold and wet, and a champagne bottle dug into his leg as he struggled to recall the previous night. His memory was refreshed as he turned to see two firm breasts with delicate brown nipples looking back at him. She'd watched him as he awoke, and now felt his desire grow as he looked at her body. She went down on him, he moaned and tugged at her now erect nipples. She moved up to him and they kissed, a passionate, hungry kiss. Harry moved his hand down her body, onto her slim waist and tight stomach, then moved further down to the softness of her inner thighs. Then further… he stopped. In his hand was a large, erect penis. The events of the night before suddenly came back to him.

Three hours later, Harry lolloped onto the terrace. Mary had been busy in the kitchen but had often stopped to watch Mickey and Jason playing in the pool. Harry had told her of Mickey's fearsome reputation, such a contrast to the gentle caring father she saw in front of her.

Mickey laughed watching Harry stagger to the table and slump into a chair. He walked over to him. "You, OK? You look half dead, and why are you walking like that?"

Harry looked at Mickey and said nothing. He tilted his head back, closed his eyes and yawned.

Harry didn't know how long he had been asleep, but looking at the angle of the sun, guessed it was an hour or so. Still feeling jaded from the night before, he rubbed his temples with small circular motions, just as Mary came onto the terrace carrying plates of food.

"Harry, you're awake at last. It's time to put something nutritious in your mouth for once."

"Awake and starving, what's for lunch? Harry replied.

Mary placed the food on the table. "This is duccana."

Mickey took a few mouthfuls. "It's delicious."

Harry gobbled the food down and was asleep before the next dish came out. "Do you think I should wake him?" said Mary.

"No, let him sleep, looks like he needs it."

Harry slept for the next few hours, occasionally calling out in his sleep. Mickey wondered what was disturbing him.

Harry knew he was dreaming, a lucid dream which at first, he did not want to end. He watched as the years rolled by and Jason grew into a young man. Harry, Mickey and the commission became rich beyond their dreams and Kaitlin, as an angel, guided them into a gentler age. Then the dream changed and turned into a nightmare. He wanted to wake up but could not. The sky suddenly darkened. A thunderous comet slammed into the ground, killing Kaitlin again, and out of the gloom, a figure dressed in black appeared and in a booming voice announced "Did you think I had gone forever? You have learned nothing. You will pay for your sins."

PART TWO

Chapter 22
1990
London

Jason let himself into the deserted office with his key, a present from Harry on his twenty-first birthday. Harry had asked him to be there at three. He snapped open a beer and sat down on the comfortable Chesterfield chair, about the only recognisable thing. The decorators had been in again. He wondered, not for the first time, why Harry hadn't moved to a bigger building in a better part of town. He'd asked him once, and Harry told him the place was home and it reminded him of 'the old days'.

Jason looked at his watch, 2.55 p.m. and took a gulp of beer, trying to remember his early childhood. He'd done this many times, but more so lately. What couldn't be accessed in his memory, the thing that bothered him most, was his mother. He remembered the bomb-blast and the hospital, but nothing of the most important woman in his life. She had faded from his mind into a dark black hole, and he felt guilty not being able to picture her. There were pictures of her, but it wasn't the same, they were two-dimensional. Real memories were three-dimensional and had sound. A dream where a small child played in the sand, and a woman was laughing, often played in his sleep. The child would turn to look at her face, but as soon as he did, she faded away.

Mickey and Harry had told him stories about her, and it was clear to him they both loved her, albeit in different ways. Those stories had left him with a different pain, that of a lost future with her, to add to the lost past. He'd asked Mickey about the day she died, but he never wanted to talk about it. A big part of his father had died that day. Mickey enjoyed the company of many women since, but never could Jason remember one hanging around for long. The big man's heart had been broken, and he wasn't about to let it happen again.

Jason's face darkened remembering the day he was told about the bomb and the man who murdered his mother. He had asked Harry several times with no response, until one night, under the influence of several drinks, Harry had told him exactly what had happened, the car, how he had nearly died playing with the gear stick, all of it, every single detail. Later when Harry was sober, Jason could see from his eyes he regretted his moment of honesty. He didn't blame him. It was the truth he had wanted, the whole truth and nothing but the truth. Harry was his rock at times when Mickey wasn't, and had finally, fully answered the question that troubled him for so long. A big hole was filled, but it brought a new guilt, the guilt of survival, blaming himself for being alive and not saving her, despite his tender years.

The grief was compounded with the thought of Anna and how she had disappeared in Spain. Why had he not stayed with her instead of returning to London? Not for the first time, coming to the conclusion, he could not keep the important women, the ones he loved, in his life. Losing Anna had put him off commitment; too scared to lose another woman and open himself to yet more heartache. Like father like son. Several attempts to convince himself he was wrong, to let those few weeks in Spain shape his life, failed, and no amount of self-delusion had worked. Like Mickey, he was no monk, but things weren't the same, Anna was still in his heart, and no one could replace her.

He noticed the price tag still attached to the Georgian bookshelf. It reminded him how much money ran through the place. Harry had moved into the straight world, in the business sense at least. With betting shops, travel agents, property, he could go completely legitimate if he wanted, but that wasn't Harry, he enjoyed the criminal environment too much. Attempts to keep his involvement in the Refuge, all five of them, on the hush, had failed, everyone knew, it was both his money and time behind it. To his credit, serving food from the kitchens was still a weekly event and he was a man Jason, was proud to know.

The noisy entrance of Harry and Mickey, jolted him, from his thoughts.

"Morning, kid," Harry shouted, making a beeline to the bar and pouring himself a gin and tonic, whilst Mickey snapped open a bottle of Heineken. They strolled over, laughing, sharing one of their private jokes. Harry was in a pinstripe suit, double breasted, with an elegant Jean Pierre pocket watch. His shoes were Italian leather, and they made a clicking sound as they hit the new wooden floor. Mickey, by contrast, wore jeans and a Boss T-shirt.

"Hi, son," said Mickey.

"So, kid, what do you think of the new place?" asked Harry.

"Great, Harry, great." He'd learnt over time to read Harry's body language, and it was clear, something was on his mind. He sat back and waited; knowing it might be a long wait.

"Did I ever tell you about my trip to Brighton with a couple of mates when I was eighteen?"

"No, Harry, I can't say you ever did. Were you ever really eighteen?"

"Umm, he's sounding a bit too much like you these days, Mickey. Anyway, we're in Brighton, the bar is packed and we're thinking we're the dog's bollocks. Three women across the bar have clearly spotted my good looks. Tight little black dresses, great bodies and tits I would have shot my grandma for a feel of at the time. Very well put together, for their age, they must have been about forty. Anyway, the boys and me are chatting and Ginger Ted decides I should go over and see how the land lies. Suits me, that way I get the first choice. I introduced myself, 'Hello, ladies!' They look at me, very odd looks on their faces."

Harry paused, sipped his drink, and smiled. "A few minutes later I can see they are interested, no doubt. I call my mates over, and very soon, my mates are laughing, the women are laughing and I'm working my arse off with all of my natural charm, which even at that young age was near perfect. About ten minutes later the women went to the toilet. So, I say, we're in here, boys." Harry paused again and lit a Cuban cigar.

"Then what, Harry?"

"My mates bottled it, scarpered. Left me all on my own. I think they thought something horrible must happen if you slept with a woman over forty."

"Then what?"

"Well, it was all a bit too exciting for me to leave, so I went back to their place. Me and three birds with a combined age of a hundred and twenty. It was a very interesting night, but not in the way I thought it would be."

Jason looked at Harry. "What do you mean?"

"Well, I haven't told anyone this story before, so you have to promise to keep this to yourself. We went to their house in the countryside. Gothic looking, bloody great turrets, like a castle. We very quickly end up in the bedroom, which had a big round bed in it, black silk sheets. There was a low stone tablet like a table about three feet wide and eight feet long. They lit candles, then took their clothes off, one by one, or more accurately, took each other's clothes off. I'd never seen such perfect bodies. Well, I thought they were perfect, but I might have been looking through young eyes. They stood there, tattoos all over their bodies, every nipple pierced. Then they began chanting, I think it was chanting, because looking back, it certainly wasn't like any song I've heard on Top of the Pops. They took my clothes off and began to kiss me, all over my body. Then got some rope and tied me to the bed. I thought I might be in some sort of danger, but to be honest, I was enjoying the whole thing a bit too much to care. I thought, if I'm going to die, what a great way to go. For hours, they teased me, never letting me finish. They were constantly doing things to each other, moaning and screaming. It went on for hours." He paused and sipped his drink.

"As the sun came up, they led me to the stone table in the middle of the room and laid me face down on it, tied my hands and feet and blindfolded me. I could have stopped them, but why would I? Then I heard a buzzing sound. I was a bit worried, but they'd given me a drink that relaxed me, took my inhibitions away, I wish I'd asked them for the recipe. I felt a sharp pain on my arse, like a needle. They were tattooing me. When they had finished, they took the blindfold off and went back to the bed and started having sex with each other again, I tell you they had some stamina. Watching them, I felt a lot happier about one day being forty, I was totally reassured about the forthcoming declining decades. Two hours later, they untied me, we had breakfast and they let me leave."

"What was the tattoo?"

Harry got up, lowered his trousers and showed them.

Jason looked at it. "Bloody hell, a pentacle."

"To be more accurate it's a pentagram," Harry corrected.

Jason looked at it again and remembered the book he had read on witchcraft. A pentagram was a five-pointed star that represented the five elements, Wind, Earth, Water, Fire and Spirit. It was one of the most powerful and ancient symbols in human history, found in most old cultures. The shape was believed to be formed by the planet Venus as it journeyed through the sky, and yes, Harry was right, a pentacle was a pentagram enclosed by a circle.

Harry continued. "They were witches, but obviously good ones, or I wouldn't be here. They had marked me, branded me. I don't regret it, and if I could have that night again, I would get the other side tattooed as well. You see for a while I thought it was the sign of the devil, as most people still do, but it isn't, I looked into it. The pentagram was the official seal of the city of Jerusalem and reputed to be a very powerful symbol against evil, shielding the wearer from disaster. Then Christianity got hold of it, like it did many ancient and pagan symbols, and turned it into a sign of evil."

"Fascinating Harry, so, there isn't a point to this story, there are five."

"Very funny, son," said Mickey. "No, the point of the story is, sometimes you have to walk alone and become a man." He looked straight at Jason. "And now it's your turn. It's time you joined the family business."

Harry listened with disquiet, not wanting him in the family business. If it had been his decision, Jason would go to university and become a doctor or a lawyer, but he was Mickey's son, and his path was set years before. Harry hoped he would not go too far down the destructive path his father had trodden, but it was a losing battle to keep the darkness from Jason's life.

Chapter 23
1990
London

Promotion had finally come Jason Warren's way, and in his mind it was overdue. He woke early the next day and looked forward to flexing his muscles officially for the first time.

He drove along the streets he knew like the back of his hand, his streets. Beside him, his childhood friend Archie Gardner, the only boy, ever brave enough to fight the son of the great Mickey Warren. The fight had ended with no clear winner, both evenly bloodied, and from that day they had been inseparable.

According to Archie, he'd a tough time growing up. His dad was a complete waste of space and hardly ever there, and when he was, it was only to beat the crap out of his mother. One day he opened the door of his car and pushed her out, breaking her arm and two ribs. When Mickey heard, he decided to make a visit. That was the last anyone saw of Archie's dad. Rumour was, Mickey had given him a bit more than a straightener. Archie knew Mickey used to give is mother a few bob to get by, whether it went further, Jason and Archie didn't like to speculate.

Berwick Road Club was a popular club, nestled amongst terraced houses in London's East End, it retained the old London feel despite all the development around the docks. They walked through the door and immediately spotted Montague Ponsford sitting in a dimly lit corner of the club. Jason had seen him a few times before, in Harry's office, and had never liked him. He saw them and got up to leave.

"Monty, where do you think you're going?" said Jason. "I need a word, your office."

"Look at his face," said Archie. "He's wearing the what a jumped-up little prick, who does he think he is talking to me like that, just because he's Mickey Warren's son."

"Yes, we might see that a lot," Jason replied. They walked through to the office. "Sit down, Monty. Have you got my money? You're late again."

"I told Harry I would have it for him next week, he was fine with that. I don't know why you're here. Business is hard enough without this, and I have a very bad heart, I can do without all this." Two small white globules had formed in the corners of his mouth.

"Monty, Harry sent me, so don't treat me like an idiot. This is my job now and you'll be dealing with me, so let's start again. Where's my money?"

"I don't know about this."

Jason moved closer to him; his breath stank. It was time to move things along and get the job finished. "OK, Monty, let me make it a bit easier for you." He grabbed his head and smashed it against the desk. "Is that any clearer? Now get the money." Blood poured from his head, as he stumbled to a cabinet and struggled to unlock it. A shaking hand wiped the blood from his head, as the keys slipped from his other hand. He picked them up and finally opened a drawer and lifted out a holdall.

Archie looked at him. "Don't get any blood on it, Monty."

He unzipped the holdall and began to take out some notes. Jason pushed him against the wall and picked up the holdall. "I'll take this. You're in credit for now. See you in a couple of weeks, and make sure you get your head looked at, that's a nasty cut you've got there."

They left the club and turned into Freemasons' Road. "Let's get a pie and mash, Arch? I think there's enough cash in here to pay for it."

"Good idea. So, what are you going to be then, the saint or sinner? One minute at the Refuge, the next rearranging Monty Ponsford's, not so good looks."

"Working at the Refuge made me look at life differently, but it's not exciting enough. Too much being good puts you off. I like this, the buzz, the power, it's where I belong."

"I see that, but what do you think your mum would have thought?" He looked at Jason. "Sorry mate, I shouldn't have said that."

"It's all right. She wouldn't have liked what we did today. In a way that's what Harry has become, a replacement mum."

"He's a diamond, you could do a lot worse than have a mum like him hanging around."

Jason laughed, lightening the moment. "I asked Harry a few years ago why he opened the Refuge. He asked me, what I thought the reason was. I figured he hated being a poor kid and was helping people that hadn't done as well as him. He laughed and said 'No, kid, that's not the reason, far too deep, it just keeps me out of trouble.' It's the only time I found out he'd lied to me."

"How do you know he lied?"

"I later heard, Harry had a troubled younger brother who left the house one day and never came back. He spent days and nights looking for him, but never saw him again. A few years later, he was told his brother had died homeless on the streets. Pneumonia, no one there to help him. Died coughing his lungs up under a railway arch. Well, I guess Harry blamed himself in some way and this was his way of turning back the clock."

Chapter 24
Autumn 1991

The phone rang unusually late, but Harry was still in his office burning the midnight oil, going over the latest figures. Business was booming and he was mulling over the purchase of an industrial unit on the outskirts of Swindon. The Jamaicans in St Paul's in Bristol had asked him to supply them with their pharmaceutical requirements. They were planning a big move on the drug distribution in the south-west. Harry liked them. They were dangerous, but they were his kind of people, and although Harry and Mickey looked a little out of place in the Black and White Cafe on the Grosvenor Road, they were always made welcome. The place would go down in history as the most raided building in the country. It was Harry's favourite place for ackee, curried goat and jerk chicken. Business could not be better. What could possibly go wrong?

He was about to find out, he picked up the phone.

"Harry, is that you? It's Tobias."

"How are you, Toby, how's Antigua?"

"Everything's good and would be even better if you came over for a visit, it's been too long. The ladies miss you. The only bad thing, my dog is sick."

"Toby, I'm sorry to hear that, will he be OK?"

"No, unfortunately he's very sick, he's going to die. I will need to get another one, you know, it's hard to live without your favourite dog."

"OK, Toby, I'll try to come over soon. Please take care, my friend."

Harry put the phone down. It was too late to do anything, and tomorrow would come soon enough. The arrangement with Tobias, the 'Laundry Man', had worked very well. Millions of pounds had been washed and returned to Harry and the rest of the commission without a single problem. Toby had taken his percentage, and Harry had received a nice little drink for the introduction of the rest of the commission, but now there was a problem; the 'sick dog' was a bank, and they had some money in it, lots of money.

Harry had heard rumours the Bank of Credit and Commerce International had run into trouble, and that trouble, was now his trouble. It was the bank used on the first leg of the laundry operation. It amazed him how you could walk into a bank with a quarter of a million of the Queen's face and no one batted an eyelid. How could it ever be anything other than hooky money, the latest proceeds from a drug deal or a bank job? If Scotland Yard had any sense, they could have got most of the faces bang to rights just by sitting outside the bank and watching who walked in.

Harry hadn't bothered with sleep. He waved to Solomon Gorman, who walked through the door of the Ritz to join him for breakfast.

"What's up, Harry?"

"I got a call from Tobias in Antigua, told me his dog was sick."

"Well, I'm sorry to hear that, I hope it gets better."

"No, Sol, the dog is the bank here in London. You need to get any money you have in it, out. Same for the others. Tobias is setting up a different bank for us. BCCI is going south."

"When?"

"I don't know, soon. The queue at the door will be very interesting."

"Why's that?"

"We'll be rubbing shoulders with the likes of Manuel Noriega, Saddam Hussein, the Medellin Cartel and I'm told even the CIA have got a few dozen accounts there."

"You serious? Why would they have accounts?"

Harry laughed. "They use the accounts for covert operations, money transfers no one needs to know about, buying weapons and supplying them to friendly countries, on the quiet."

"Really?"

"Yes. Anyway, just get your money out."

"OK, thanks. What do you think of the Eggs Benedict?"

"Very nice, Sol."

"Then that's what I shall have."

Harry thought the meeting with Solomon had gone well and was now thinking about the one scheduled with Mickey at lunchtime.

Mickey rubbed his unshaven face and looked as though sleep had not been part of the last forty-eight hours. He shovelled the food into his mouth as though it would be his last.

Harry wondered what demons were troubling his friend. "What's up, Mickey?"

"Solomon wants me to sort out a few troublemakers south of the river." He looked at Harry, but not into his eyes. "How's my son? Haven't seen him for a few days."

Harry's body stiffened. 'Troublemaker' was the word they used when it meant a kill order. "Mickey, don't break the promise you gave me twenty years ago."

"Times have changed. The kid needs to toughen up if he's ever gonna take my place."

Harry hoped this day would never come. "What do you mean, take your place? He isn't you and doesn't need to be. What are you thinking? If you make him do this, our friendship is over. He's not you. We worked all these years, so he doesn't have to be. I mean it, Mickey, this is the line in the sand."

Mickey shrugged, but Harry wasn't finished. "I suggest you think about Kate and what she would want, or have you forgotten about her?"

Mickey got up, his fists clenched, "I'm leaving, Harry. If anyone else had said that they would be dead. There are some things you don't say."

"Yes, and there are some things you don't do."

Mickey slammed the door as he left.

Jason noticed the change but had no idea what had caused the rift between them. He had not seen them together for over a week,

186

and on asking if there was a problem, no meaningful answer, from either of them was forthcoming. He would let them get through it; knowing better than to push the question too far.

Every Sunday for the last few years he went to the shooting range with Mickey, and not once had Harry joined them, it wasn't his thing. Mickey was competitive, always taking great joy in winning. Jason could not remember Mickey ever letting him win; that was Mickey. As time passed and Jason became the better marksman, he let his father win occasionally. Well, more than occasionally, about half the time, but always made it close, never letting on, leaving Mickey with his pride intact.

His time spent with Harry could not have been more different. Theatreland was Harry's playground and he had learnt to love it as much as Harry, but in a more youthful way. Harry asked his opinion of the plays they watched and encouraged his understanding of them. He smiled thinking about the times Harry never tired of giving him advice, like "Never test the water with both feet, and if you're not someone who succeeds at things first time, don't go skydiving." Funny at the time, but always a lesson hidden beneath the laughter and smiles, almost a surrogate mother.

He laughed at his fond memories of both of them and understood parents sometimes fall out. They were so different, he sometimes wondered how they had ever become such close friends, and what could have caused this problem between them.

It was an unusual summer; the first Jason could remember when the three of them hadn't spent time together. As winter arrived and the first snow lay on the ground, he strolled gingerly along the road, then paused to light a cigarette. Across the road Mickey was walking towards Harry's office, he stopped, pressed the buzzer and walked through to the enclosed courtyard.

"Did you want me for something, Harry?"

"Yes, I do, Mickey, sit down please, I want to speak with you." Mickey sat down. In times past he would have helped himself to a beer but not now, not since the day they had fallen out. "I'm sorry about what I said about Kaitlin, I didn't mean it in a bad way, I look on the kid as family."

Mickey looked at him, a new softness in his eyes. "Harry, it's me that should apologise. I don't know what I would have done without you at times, you've been a much better influence in Jason's life than me. Just promise me one thing, never stop looking out for him. I wish things had turned out different. How could I guess something I did so many years before would come back and wreck our lives? I didn't kill the butcher all those years ago, he done himself in. I only burnt down his stall, wasn't much more than a kid myself."

Harry put his hand on Mickey's shoulder. "Sometimes things like that are enough. Old sins cast long shadows. We can't turn back time, Mickey, but we can change the future."

Mickey hugged him, and they knew the words that had divided them would never be discussed again.

Christmas came, and it was like nothing had happened between them. They would never tell Jason what had caused the rift. He was just pleased it was over. In fact, to him, they seemed closer than ever.

They sat around the table, as they had for as many years as Jason could remember. Harry wore his traditional, ridiculous chef's hat as he carved the turkey. Jason looked at them. Middle age had treated them well, although Harry now let his belt out a notch or two. Harry raised his glass and the other two instinctively followed.

The sound of three Royal Brierley crystal glasses, the ones which only ever came out at Christmas, clinking together broke the silence. "To absent friends and loved ones," echoed around the room.

"Do you know why people clink their glasses?" said Harry.

Mickey looked at him. "Yes, I do, as it happens."

The furrows stayed on Harry's brow for a few seconds. "Yes, of course you do. I have a grand here says you don't, winnings to the Refuge." He looked at Jason, rubbing his hands together.

"Done, Harry. It's an act of good faith going back centuries. The thought was, when you clink cups, or glasses, that a little bit from each would spill into the other, and if there was any poison then it would affect both of you. Is that good enough for you?"

"You bastard! How did you know that?"

Mickey pointed to the *Horse and Hounds* magazine on Harry's side table. "That was the dearest magazine you ever bought."

"That's bloody cheating, Mickey."

Chapter 25
1993
London

Just as Eastham was slicing some chilled salmon to place on top of the rice he had formed into neat oblong shapes, the phone rang. The razor-sharp knife slipped and cut into his finger, turning the pink salmon bright red.

"Hello, I don't know if you remember me, my name is Andrea, from Spain, we met a few years ago. You were looking for Gregor."

"Yes, of course I do. How are you, have you heard from him?"

"I'm good, he rang me. Wanted to see me, said life was great, that he'd changed, and we should put the past behind us, meet up. I have his number, but before I give it to you, I need to be sure he won't know it came from me."

"No, of course not, you have my word and I'll send you the money I promised."

She gave him the number and details of where to send the money. The next morning, using his contacts to trace the number, the proximity of the address surprised him. It was a warehouse three miles away, but what surprised him more was the person the phone number belonged to. "Small world," he said out loud. Harry would be shocked when he heard where Gregor was.

He parked the car and bounded up the stairs, eager to see the look on Harry's face on hearing the news.

"Hello, Paul, what's on your mind?"

"Found him, Gregor, the toe-rag who kidnapped Jason's girl, and you're not gonna believe where he is and who he works for."

"Well?"

"Three miles from here, and I'm glad you're sitting down because listen to this."

"Get on with it, Paul."

"Have a guess who he works for."

"How would I know? Do I look like gypsy Rose Lee?"

"Works for you."

Harry choked on his coffee. "What!"

"It's true, working out of Dennis Whiting's crew in Canning Town. Using his own name, doing some deliveries and a bit of heavy. Hasn't changed a bit by all accounts, still a nasty bastard. Dennis didn't have an address but told me where he drinks. I've still got the picture of him, so shouldn't be too difficult to find. What do you want to do?"

"Will Dennis tip him off?"

Eastham shook his head. "No, he's not that brave. I told him; I don't want to hear the Russian has suddenly disappeared off the face of the earth."

"OK, get in touch with Mickey and fill him in. I'd better have a chat with Jason. I never thought this would come back into our lives. Should I even tell him?"

"That's your call, Harry."

"No, he needs to know, but it's a conversation that needs to be face to face." Harry picked up the phone and started to dial the number.

He watched Jason walk up the stairs and press the entry button. The door swung slowly open.

"Hi, Harry, what's up?"

"Get yourself a drink, I've got some news."

Jason poured himself a beer. "You look nervous, Harry. What's wrong?"

"We've found Gregor."

"What! that's the last thing I expected you to say. It's the news I've wanted to hear, but I've been afraid of hearing it for four years. I've never forgotten her but got resigned to never seeing her again. It scares me what he might have done to her. Where is he?"

"Mickey and Eastham are dealing with it. I know you want to, but you're not, and that's the way it is. If it comes to killing him, you can, but till then it's Mickey's job. I hope she's OK, but don't get your hopes up, four years is a long time."

"One second I'm thinking she's alive and there's a happy ending, and then I imagine her dead body lying in a ditch, battered, bruised, all alone."

"I can see that on your face. Let's play this one right, Mickey will get the answers."

"I need to talk to him. Do you know where he is?"

"Yes, come on I'll take you. Eastham is on his way over there."

They got into the car and headed towards the West End.

"Do you still think as much of her now as you did four years ago?"

"I've never stopped thinking about her. She was the one for me. No, not was, is. I still can't forgive myself for not staying in Spain with her."

"You can't blame yourself. You could never have known what was going to happen."

"Maybe. If Mickey lets me take care of this, will you promise not to try to change his mind?"

"Yes. I won't, but only because I know, he won't."

They parked outside Vadim, a new club Harry and Mickey had just opened in the West End. As they walked in, they saw Mickey drinking coffee with Eastham. He saw them and put his coffee down.

"Where's is he, Dad?"

"Forget it. If he needs killing, you can do it, till then this is my job, son, end of."

"I'm coming with you."

"No, you're not."

Harry shrugged and placed his hand on Jason's shoulder. "Come on, let's you and I sit here and have a few beers, and let them get on with it. We'll have the answers soon enough." Harry went to the bar, got out two beers and passed one to Jason.

Mickey looked at Eastham. "Come on, let's get this done."

Harry watched as Jason quickly finished his beer and get another from the bar. He looked at his watch; it was just past eleven p.m.

Mickey drove across the river to Stockwell. "I never thought we'd see this day, Paul. You've done a good job, though it might have been better never to have got the call. This won't end well, how can it?"

"You don't know that, Mickey. It's been a long time, and for all we know she might have just walked away. Who's to say she didn't want to go? There wasn't a struggle. Maybe it wasn't what Jason thought it was. He still thinks about her, doesn't he?"

"Yes, she won't be with the toerag from what you said, but if he knows where she is, I'll get it out of him. Then I'm going to kill him, the fucker's caused my family enough grief."

They walked into the club, that was a generation out of date. The walls and ceiling yellowed by the smoke of decades of cigarettes, a place the bottom-feeders dwelt, but it had its regulars and made money. If you wandered in by mistake, it was a place, you soon wandered straight back out.

As they made their way to the bar, their feet stuck to the floor. The mould from the damp caught in Mickey's throat, and old blood spots splattered the wall. "Looks like the cleaner quit and forgot to tell anyone," he said. Eastham disturbed a large silverfish which tried and failed to evade the sole of his shoe.

Mickey knew the doorman, who was expecting them, one of Jack Rich's men who had stayed on. He ordered two beers and called him over. "Is the Russian in?"

"Yes, Mickey, over there." The doorman gestured to a dimly lit corner of the bar. Eastham glanced over and saw the familiar face looking back at him. He was sitting with a woman with a barely concealed black eye.

Gregor waved his hand and slurred a sentence to the waitress, who rushed over to his table. "More drinks, and don't take too long." Mickey saw the waitress's discomfort; she was scared of him. This was the moment Mickey had waited for. He casually walked to the bar, opened the hatch and opened two more beers, drinks that would not be finished. The waitress returned; Mickey looked at the orders. "Which are the drinks for those two?" he said, indicating Gregor's table.

"These," she replied, pointing to a small scrap of paper.

Mickey poured the drinks and gave them to the waitress. He winked at Eastham and made his way back to the table with the two beers. They watched as the waitress carried the drinks to the tables.

Gregor was the last to be served. He looked at the waitress. "Take your time, why don't you! When I order drinks, you bring straight away, do you understand?"

She placed the drinks on the table without replying. He threw some coins onto her tray. "There is no tip for you, remember what I said next time."

His shouting was loud enough for Mickey to hear, he turned to Eastham. "There will not be a next time. Not only is he an ignorant bastard, he's also tight. He'll get a bit more pain for that." They watched Gregor gradually lose his ability to move and speak. "Good old Harry," Mickey said.

They walked to the table and picked Gregor up. "What's going on?" he said. His voice barely audible, the horse tranquillizer had done its job.

"You think your night is over, but the truth is it's only just beginning," Mickey whispered in his ear.

The doorman walked slowly over. "Make sure she gets home please, Tom."

"No problem, Mickey."

Eastham drove the car the short distance to the warehouse; Gregor was still drowsy and mumbling in Russian. Mickey pressed the button on the remote control and the doors opened, then silently closed behind them.

They dragged him out of the car and threw him onto the cold concrete floor. Mickey prodded him with the toe of his shoe, there was no response. "Put him in the chair, Paul." Eastham cut off Gregor's clothes and tied him to a heavy antique chair, lashed to an iron girder that reached to the ceiling. Mickey had bought the chair a few years back at auction. It was an execution chair that should have ended its time in a museum, but Mickey had other ideas for it. Leg and arm restraints and a leather tie that fastened around the neck were perfect for holding Mickey's interviewees firmly in place, while asking them a few questions. It had been the last seat of many American deviants. Mickey thought it made his infrequent question and answer sessions a little more interesting, anyone who sat in it knew straight away what it was. Sometimes it was enough for them just to sit in it, for him to get the desired answers.

"I hope he doesn't answer too quickly, I want to have some fun with this one."

He opened the small leather case beside him, took out a syringe and inserted it into a small vial of liquid. "This will wake the little fucker up." Without much care, the syringe of epinephrine emptied into Gregor's arm. Mickey walked to a slate grey cabinet. Hanging neatly inside was a pair of chef's whites, complete with a toque. He picked up the hat taking great care to place it at a slight angle on his head. He lit a cigarette, opened a beer and watched as Eastham came out of the toilet with a bucket of ice-cold water, and threw some of it over Gregor, who slowly regained consciousness. Looking up and recognising the two men who had entered the club, he tried to move his arms and legs but soon realized he was going nowhere.

"Why are you doing this? Who the fuck are you?"

"Don't you know?" said Mickey. He punched Gregor hard on his jaw, blood and a tooth spilt from his mouth. "Bit of advice. When I punch you, keep your mouth shut, that way you won't lose so many teeth."

"I work for Dennis Whiting; you don't know who you're messing with."

"Dennis works for me, so don't get your hopes up. I can't make up my mind whether to kill you now or turn this blow torch on and slowly cook you gas mark five." Mickey picked up the blowtorch and lit it.

"What do you want from me?"

"Well, you've obviously worked out you're not leaving here without some serious damage, and there will be no sudden rescue. You can scream and shout as much as you want. The building is soundproof, and no one will hear you. Do you know who I am?"

"I saw you come into the club. I don't know either of you. What I do know is you're a lunatic with a hat."

Mickey punched him again. "You know what I hate most about scum like you? Everything. You think it's OK to beat women and use a blade. Well tonight you are gonna learn what it's like to be on the other side." He turned up the blowtorch and placed a scalpel into the flame. The blade slowly turned red as he reached into the leather case and removed a small pair of pliers. He looked at Gregor. "Shall we begin?"

He spat at Mickey, who moved deftly to avoid the incoming saliva. "Levchenko sent you, I know that. Do what you want, the bastard killed my family, so finish it and fuck you."

Mickey had not expected that. He turned away to gather his thoughts, then looked across at Eastham, who shrugged, clearly none the wiser. Mickey swung around and sat on the chair facing the Russian. "Shut up, I will tell you when you can speak." He turned the flame back onto the scalpel. Then placed the blowtorch gently on the table and picked up the pliers. He placed them around the Russian's left nipple, tightened the grip and pulled the metal towards him. The flesh sizzled as the heat of the blade passed through it.

Mickey picked up a large tub of grease and began smearing it over Gregor's body. "Which part of you do you want me to cook first?"

Gregor's eyes widened. "What the fuck? You're a fucking lunatic!"

Mickey lifted his eyebrows and stared at him. "That may well be true. The grease helps the meat to cook and gives it a better flavour, which will be better for you when I cut some more off and ram it down your throat. I asked you which part you wanted cooking first, answer the fucking question." Before he could answer Mickey moved the blow torch closer to Gregor's chest and turned the newly nipple removed area into a charred smoking wasteland. Eastham winced. He had never got used to the sight of human flesh sizzling and burning, and the sweet smell similar to a pork Sunday roast. Or the desperate screams that always went with it.

It fell silent save for the whoosh of the blowtorch; Gregor had fainted. Eastham picked up the pail of freezing water and threw the rest of it over him. Gregor shuddered, raised his head and tried, unsuccessfully to keep from vomiting. Through watery eyes he looked at the crazy bastard with the chef's hat, then looked down at his smouldering flesh, the copious vomit eased the searing pain, moving him back towards the welcome world of unconsciousness.

"Now shall we stop fucking about, because it's question time?" Mickey said, lighting a cigarette with the blowtorch. "I like this, I get off on it. Don't answer too fast, hold out as long as you can, be brave, you fucking coward." Mickey stuck a finger into Gregor's smouldering chest, then took a handful of the Russian's hair and lifted his head. "Now tell me about Anna."

"Anna, what about her?" Gregor was crying, tears rolled down his face. "What has this got to do with her?"

"Tell me about you and Anna." Mickey could see Gregor could not work out what was going on.

"What are you to Anna? If Levchenko sent you, you already know the story." Mickey lifted the blowtorch towards Gregor's face, who tried to move away, but was firmly held by the leather strap. "Please, stop it, Anna was years ago." The blowtorch inched closer. "I worked for her father, a nasty bastard, Russian mafia. We fell in love, but it would not work, in Russia her father would kill me for being with her, so we went to Spain. I loved her but began to drink and take too many drugs, there were so many women, who could resist? I hit her, yes, but I was young, one day I used my knife on her. I was ashamed for what I did, so I left. She would not forgive me for that, I never saw her again."

Mickey moved forward and put the blow torch on him again. "Get on with it you miserable little bastard, I don't want your life story, where is she?"

Gregor screamed and passed out again. Eastham threw another bucket of cold water on him. Bile, sick, blood and spit ran down his smoking chest. When he awoke, he saw the hate in Mickey's eyes. "I never saw her again, never, then I heard all my family were dead, killed by her bastard father Levchenko, all of them dead including the children, dead all of them."

Mickey looked at him, contempt on his face. "Well, the good news is I don't work for him. The bad news is you're still boring the shit out of me." Mickey put the blow torch on Gregor again, this time the top of his leg. "It will be your bollocks next."

Gregor vomited again before passing out. Paul picked up the bucket again. "This is a waste of good water, Mickey." This time Gregor didn't come round. Mickey took a small bottle from his pocket, opened it and placed it under Gregor's nose. He coughed and came to.

"What did you do with her?"

His head fell to the side. "Nothing, I promise, I did not go back to see her, I was told she had gone away from the port, with Russians, it was her father's work, it couldn't be anyone else."

That made sense, and Mickey knew when people were telling the truth. "Listen you can fuck off, I'm in a good mood but remember this, I know where you are and Dennis Whiting works for me, which means so do you. You deserved what you got for cutting Anna and if I see you again or hear the woman you were with tonight has another black eye, I will finish the job." He looked at Eastham. "Get him out of here."

Mickey waited in the warehouse until Eastham returned; they drove slowly back to Harry's office. "That was disappointing, Paul. I hoped there would be some answers for Jason. I still don't understand why after so much time he still thinks about a girl he knew for two weeks. He's so wise for his age, she must have really worked a number on him. If I hadn't goaded him that night to get a brass, then this would never have happened."

They pulled into the car park and walked up the iron stairs. Harry watched them on the CCTV and pressed the entry button. They walked through and Mickey looked at the beer on the bar.

"Is that for me?" Harry nodded. Mickey looked at the expectant faces. "It wasn't him, son, it was her father who took her in Spain."

"Are you sure?"

"Positive, he wasn't lying. It's good it was her father who took her, otherwise I think she would be dead. Time to move on, there's nothing else you can do, unless you fancy nipping over to Moscow." Mickey thought of telling Jason the rest of the story, then decided against it. He figured the Russian had suffered enough for a domestic, and anyway he was Dennis Whiting's man. Why make trouble? Better to let sleeping dogs lie.

Later in the back office, Eastham was filling Harry in on the details of the night's work.

"Why didn't Mickey finish the job?" asked Harry.

Eastham shrugged. "I don't know, maybe it's because he's on Dennis's firm. If someone did that to me, I would find him and kill him. Do you want me to finish the job?"

Harry thought about it for a few seconds. "No, it's Mickey's call, just leave it."

Chapter 26
1994
London

Marshall Johnson was to all intents and purposes a successful property developer but had also been the underboss of the Johnson family. The last twenty-five years had treated him well. His hair was now greying at the sides and his body had gained a pound for each of the years, so now cut a portly figure. He had softened around the edges and his involvement in the crime business was to him a faded, distant memory. It had been an easy process to grow rich as a member of the commission's top feeders, but at the earliest opportunity had moved his money into legitimate businesses. He had just completed the purchase of a vacant building in Baker Street, and the planning permission surprisingly obtained would add one million to his bank balance. Why risk his liberty when easy money could be made in the capital's property market, with the help of a few amenable planning officers and friendly councillors? Everyone understood he was a Johnson, which opened doors for him and gave a level of respect and protection others didn't have. He might once have been the underboss of the Johnsons, but most of the commission would not recognise him if they passed him in the street. He had not been to a meeting for years, and in his mind, was completely 'legit', and mixed in a very different world from the rest of the commission.

Today he was attending a charity event at the Royal Plaza Hotel in aid of injured soldiers. He walked through the row of Corinthian columns to the richly panelled banqueting room and into the bar, which buzzed with the chatter of London's great and good.

The handsome, chiselled face of retired Major Tommy Bednar had not gone unnoticed by the women in the room. Their eyes were upon him as he moved through the crowd, glad-handing the patrons and VIPs who had come to raise money for his injured colleagues. He saw Marshall Johnson looking at him and wondered what was going through his mind. Mildly annoyed at the spectacle of ingratiating himself to all and sundry, he knew it was all part of the game, a new game, or rather the resumption of an old one. How predictable Johnson was, he thought.

Walking over to him, on the short journey, he reflected how much easier his life had become since the day, all those years ago, when the decision had been taken to take control of it. Long gone the days of being bullied in the school playground by Mickey Warren. It had shaped him, made him who he was today, and now there was nothing that could not be achieved with a little effort. The process of killing came easily, he had a natural talent for it. People were so careless, even when they knew they were vulnerable to a bullet with their name on it.

Sometimes the thought of thanking Mickey Warren, entered his head, for opening his eyes to the opportunities of making money by ridding the world of unwanted low life's. His parallel life as a contract killer had made him rich, taking a few contracts each year, sometimes more if business was good, or boredom overcame him. Being careful, and immaculate planning were central to the life of an assassin. Assets he had in abundance, which was why he had never failed, and never come close to being caught. Now here before him was one of the notorious London crime commission. It was time to revisit and disrupt Mickey Warren's little world again.

"Mr Johnson, thank you very much for the artwork you donated for the auction, it was very generous of you. I'm Tommy Bednar."

"Please call me Marshall. It was my pleasure, and if I can be of any more help, call me." He handed him a business card.

They were interrupted as the toastmaster announced dinner. Marshall made his way to his table to sit with his close friend the

Mayor of London. Sitting exactly opposite, not by chance, was Major Bednar.

Marshall Johnson turned to the mayor. "Do you know, looking around the room, I know most of the people here. What a small world it is." Tommy Bednar cringed, listening to the words. The research undertaken on every member of the commission, had taken a few months, the information on Marshall Johnson was extensive. His ego was central to his life, constantly telling anyone who listened how different he was from his brother, the head of the family crime firm. Boasting about the day the commission, learned of his departure and how they had begged him to stay, telling him he was too important to leave, and they would struggle without him. The truth was, they were pleased to see him go. There were parts of his life which they were finding increasingly embarrassing.

A smirk formed from nowhere as the plan he had for Marshall passed through his mind. It was time for some pro bono vermin control, and Marshall Johnson, was about to provide the entertainment, and be the centre of attention, his favourite pastime. Always believing he was in control, with his money and power. Money obtained by selling drugs or killing and robbing people. Not a thought for the consequences of his actions and the ruined lives he left behind.

At 1.15 a.m. Marshall Johnson left with the cocktail waitress he'd been grooming all night. She was nineteen, maybe younger, her hair tied in a bob framed an almond-shaped face with flawless tight skin, just the way he liked it. She knew about his reputation as a good payer and decided she would sleep with him. She was at college and the extra money would be useful. His face was still handsome, and his excess weight could easily be handled by being on top in the bedroom. She had just bagged Marshall Johnson, the biggest tipper in town. What she didn't know, was his obsession with young girls.

Marshall was enjoying himself. She knew her way around the bedroom, he liked women who did most of the work, and this one was doing it all. Definitely a little older than normal, but her skill in bed had pretty much made up for that. As she moved up and down on top of him, his mind wandered to the moment when the whole room had applauded him, when introduced as the man who had donated a sketch of a seventeenth-century girl on a horse that sold for sixty-two thousand pounds.

Two miles away in a bedroom bathed in pale red light, Tommy Bednar turned to the woman, led her across the room and made her kneel on the bed. He cuffed her wrists to the metal bedstead and placed a mask over her face. There were no holes for her eyes; just a small breathing hole. Her legs were tied to the end of the bed, preventing all but the slightest movement, the rope cut painfully into her ankles. He walked out of the room, there was some work that needed attending to; he would return in an hour. She would be taken, but only when he was ready.

Marshall Johnson had been at the top of his vermin control list for the last few weeks. On the negative side was his history in crime. On the positive side, he was now more or less legitimate. But his history of sleeping with under-age girls had decided his fate, and Tommy Bednar had appointed himself judge, jury and executioner.

Ten hours later he picked up the phone and dialled the number. Marshall Johnson didn't recognise the caller's number but pressed the answer key anyway.

"Hello, Marshall, it's Tommy Bednar, I hope I haven't disturbed you?"

"No problem. I didn't expect to hear from you so soon, what can I do for you, Major Bednar?"

He smiled to himself. "Well, you can start by calling me Tommy."

"Tommy, so, how can I help?"

He paused. "It is something of a very personal nature. I need help with a little problem from my past, that has suddenly reappeared. It's preyed on my mind for years. I thought it had gone away, but it's back and I'm sorry to say, worse than ever. Could we meet? But I must ask for your word you won't tell a living soul about our meeting, or what I tell you. My career would be over, and maybe even my life. If you could help me with this, I could introduce you to the young actress I left with last night. I'm sure she would like to meet you. Have you seen her on the television? She was very impressed by your generosity last night."

"Yes, I have. She's very beautiful. There is no need for that, but of course I couldn't turn her away, if you know what I mean. Now how can I help? Where shall we meet?"

He gave him the address, ended the call, sat down and poured himself a small brandy. "Let the fun begin again," he murmured, smiling. "Why have I left it so long?"

Marshall Johnson drove towards the deserted print works on the derelict industrial estate, thinking it was an odd place to meet. He'd been there two weeks before. The site was for sale, and he'd spoken with the planning department to see what could be built in place of the run-down, rat-infested buildings. The simple answer was, more or less, whatever he wanted. Brown envelopes and free holiday homes worked wonders.

Driving, he wondered what the Major's problem was. Maybe, threatened by some heavies, but he was ex-special forces, so surely it couldn't be that. If it was, it would be very easy to sort out, with just one call. No, more likely, a woman was the problem, or a secret gambling addiction, in debt with the bookies. Whatever it was, Marshall was sure the problem would be easily resolved, and then he would have the pleasure of looking forward to his reward, the young actress who had filled his thoughts, since the phone call. He would get her something to wear to make her look younger. Maybe, he would tell her to put pigtails in her hair.

He decided to stop thinking about her. He would be there in a few minutes, and a raging erection would not look good in front of his new friend.

Tommy Bednar casually dragged the emaciated body of the tramp to a less visible place. His death had come quickly, with one well aimed strike to the throat, a swift death, no blood, no mess. Innocent victims were a reality of war in Tommy Bednar's eyes, rationalising, the tramp almost certainly had a miserable life, in fact, he might even have done him a favour by dispatching him to the eternal afterlife. No longer would the old man have to worry about finding food and a warm place to stay.

He glanced at his watch. Marshall would arrive in a few minutes; on time, being late was alien to a man who liked to control every aspect of his life.

One last reconnoitre of the site, confirmed the location was a good choice. Final checks were important in his profession; you could never allow yourself to get sloppy. He stood a few yards back from the door, concealed by the semi-darkness, and peered silently through a small crack in the masonry.

Marshall's Jaguar came to a stop on the gravel. The car door opened, then shut, followed by the sound of hesitant footsteps. Tommy knew, Marshall must be questioning the wisdom of his actions. This would not feel right; instincts long dulled by time rekindling inside him. Would he have attended this sort of meeting twenty years ago? Probably not, and certainly not without a few heavies to back him up. He was sure Marshall had not brought a gun, why would he? Yet here he was on a deserted industrial estate, meeting a virtual stranger. Would he just turn around, return to his car and drive away? He would if he had any sense.

Tommy Bednar sensed the need to act. He turned the door knob.

"Major, is that you?"

Tommy Bednar's head appeared around the door, picking up on the nervousness in Marshall Johnson's voice. "Hello, Marshall, in here." The relaxed and jovial tone, put Marshall at ease. Immediately he relaxed, maybe chiding himself for feeling uneasy at meeting his new friend, probably wondering how he could have been apprehensive about meeting a fund-raising Major, ex-British Army.

"How are you, Marshall? Thanks for coming."

"This is very mysterious, Tommy, so what's the problem?"

Tommy Bednar's face became more serious. "Did you tell anyone about our meeting?"

"No, of course not."

"Then let me show you something."

They walked around the corner. Marshall followed closely behind and saw the lifeless body of the tramp as the tarpaulin was pulled from the corpse.

Marshall laughed. "So, what's the problem, some old vagrant? You want me to get rid of him? You should have said over the phone, I would have dealt with this for you. It's crazy us being here with a stiff."

Then he looked more closely at the body and realised there was something very wrong; the body looked too fresh. Now, he knew this was not as it appeared, he turned to find himself looking at the latest Special Forces issue Taser.

A cold sweat broke across his forehead. "What the fuck is this?"

"Try to control your anxiety. It must be a long time since you've been in a position like this. Does it remind you why you left your life of crime? And to answer your question, it's a Taser. If you move one inch, I will fire a few thousand volts into you. So, I suggest you don't."

"Tommy, what's this all about? What have I ever done to you?"

"What's it about? It's about being a kid, being terrorised. Wetting the bed, night after night. You've been hanging around with the wrong people. This is about Mickey Warren. Oh, and the fact, you fuck little girls."

Marshall's shoulders slumped. It suddenly all fell into place. There had been rumours that the man Mickey killed years ago had not been the killer, but time had passed, and become a very distant memory. This man was the hidden enemy, the most dangerous kind, lurking in the shadows. Well, now he was back, and it was Marshall who was going to pay the price.

"You killed Mickey's wife," said Marshall. "Look, we can sort this. Let me kill him for you."

Tommy Bednar laughed. "It's not about killing Mickey Warren; I could do that myself tomorrow. I didn't mean to kill his wife, the bomb was meant for him, but as usual someone else paid the price. I stopped, thought that was enough, but lately thought there were still some evil people who needed to die. When I researched the commission, you, seemed a good place to start."

Marshall looked into his eyes and recognised the detached look of a man psychologists would label a psychopath. "Tommy, this is not my argument. I never see Mickey, and I'm not in the crime game. You saw what I did for your charity, you're killing the wrong man. This has nothing to do with me, I don't even like Mickey Warren, never done a good thing in his whole life. Think about what you are doing."

Tommy looked at him. "You make some very good points. It's unfortunate, it's you, standing here, trembling. Of all the commission you would be near the bottom of the list, but your abuse and rape of young girls has sealed your fate. Unfortunately, for you, an enemy is an enemy. There's no difference between the most wanted and the nearly innocent. If you share the same uniform as Mickey Warren, you share the same fate. I have for the moment spared Harry Fleet because of his good work at the refuge, and I've not regretted that decision. I've watched the number of refuges grow. Harry has a genuinely good side to his character. You on the other hand are charitable for your own benefit. You bask in false charity, boasting what a kind man you are. The difference between you and Harry, is he stays out of the limelight. In another life, I could imagine being friends with him."

"Tommy, we could be friends. We have a lot in common. I can sense uncertainty in you. This is not a situation that has to end badly. Why don't..."

That was as far as the conversation went. The Taser fired, and Johnson lay on the floor convulsing, unable to control his body. Two small dart-like probes hung from his chest. The pain suddenly stopped. He looked up in despair at Tommy Bednar, who was attaching a silencer to a handgun. It wasn't the gun that convinced Marshall his life was nearly over, it was the look on the face of his killer, and the maniacal laugh, the last thing he would ever hear.

The first bullet passed through Marshall's right eye. Two more shots quickly followed, one through the heart and the other through the left eye. He bent down to admire his handiwork, then reached into his top pocket and took out two old pennies and placed them on the holes where the eyes used to be. "Another dead body down to Mickey Warren," he said to the still warm body.

He turned the corner, opened the car door, sat in the driver's seat, started the engine, turned the cassette player on and slowly drove away.

Chapter 27
Harry's office

Dennis Whiting had long since moved out of his terraced house in Canning Town, preferring the leafier lanes of Loughton. He'd worked for Harry Fleet for a decade and until recently had always welcomed a call from him, but not this time. The annoyance at the unnecessary torture of his right-hand man, Gregor, remained, not understanding the point of drugging, kidnapping, and torturing someone for a domestic. It hardly warranted a body barbecue. Gregor hadn't told him the full story, and he'd decided, not to ask Harry. Best to let it lie; rocking the boat was pointless, it was carrying too much treasure. His lifestyle was too important, and at the end of the day the Russian was expendable. Dennis had always tried to avoid Mickey Warren, believing he was a grade A psychopath.

He made his way to Harry's office more slowly than usual, unsure of what lay ahead, and reluctantly walked up the steps.

Harry and Mickey watched him on the CCTV. Harry pressed the door release.

"How are you, Dennis? Long time."

"Good, Harry, business is good."

Harry rubbed his chin, feeling the stubble, unshaven for once. "Do you still have the Russian working for you?"

"Not this again. I hoped the meeting with Mickey was the end of the matter. Yes, he's still with me. Look, I know there was some aggro, but it was a while ago. I don't want to lose him."

Harry smiled. "Only asking, there's no problem. How'd the old fella take the little straightener with Mickey?"

Dennis looked at them, clearly surprised at the question. "Well Harry, how would anyone take going to a barbecue, and finding it was them on the charcoal? I'm surprised you didn't stick a skewer up his arse and finish the job. He took it better than most, understood, shrugged his shoulders, laughed it off. 'That's the game we're in,' he said. He knows he's been a bad bastard, done some things over the years. So, in his words, it was overdue. More important, Mickey, are you sure you don't have a problem with him?"

Mickey shook his head. "No issues, Dennis."

Harry poured himself a Jack and Coke. "Drink, Dennis?"

"Beer, Harry."

"Are you sure there are no problems with the half-cooked Russian? From what Eastham said he doesn't seem the sort to roll over after the cooking lesson."

"I can only give you, my opinion. I don't think there's a problem. If anything changes, you'll be the first to know."

"Fair enough," replied Harry.

He thought back to the conversation years before with Tobias Boswell. Harry's commission for introducing the five families to Toby's money laundry was the best bit of business he had done. Almost as good, were the contacts Tobias had given him, outlets for Harry's own manufactured drugs. Russian criminals had flooded into Europe after the breakup of the Soviet Union. The FBI had warned, they now posed the greatest threat to European security, and in Harry's mind they were right, but Europe's security was not Harry's concern, there were armies for that.

Expanding into the Eastern Bloc countries was top of Harry's agenda, and the opportunity he'd been waiting for had now presented itself. This Russian outfit came highly recommended by both Tobias Boswell and Carlos Satero, and that was good enough for Harry. He looked across at Dennis Whiting, who was patiently waiting for him to get to the point of the meeting.

"Sorry, miles away," said Harry. He drained the glass and refilled it, this time straight Jack Daniels. "We have some business with a Russian firm, docked in Ramsgate. I want you to do the drop and take your boy Gregor along to have a listen. I don't want them to know we have a native speaker. I want to know exactly what they are saying."

"Nice idea, Harry. When's the drop?"

"Not decided yet, keep this week clear."

"Will do, Harry, are we done?"

"Yes, thanks for coming over." Dennis finished his beer and left.

Two days later, Dennis returned to Harry's office. "The package is ready, this is the first trade with them, so be careful. They come very highly recommended, so, there shouldn't be any trouble. Here's the address and time." He handed him a small slip of paper.

Harry never gave too much notice for a drop. Too much notice sometimes led to the person doing the exchange getting ideas of their own. Harry had known Dennis for years and was certain he would do the job without trying to rip him off, but you could never be too careful. Harry's position on the commission protected him. Stealing from him was the same as stealing from them, and that meant only one thing; retribution, probably in the form of a bullet.

Dennis and Gregor sat in the unmarked van, waiting for the minutes to tick away. Dennis, like Harry, kept the details to himself until the last possible moment.

"Five thousand pounds for me, that's a good payday," said Gregor. "And it will be good to hear my own language again. We need to be very careful with these Russians, they can be very nasty bastards."

"Well, you should know. It's the first time Harry's done business with them, so it's twice as dangerous. Everyone will be nervous, and maybe a bit trigger happy," replied Dennis.

"Yes, the Russian trigger finger is always lively. Shoot first, ask questions later. These are the worst people to do deals with. These Russian gangs are full of ex-special services, men trained to act on command, humanity, totally beaten out of them. Life is very cheap in Russia. These people will probably just put bullets in our heads."

"Very reassuring, Gregor, thank you."

"No problem."

One mile away, a large white yacht bobbed alongside those of other millionaires. Dennis Whiting had travelled down the day before on a dry run, familiarising himself with the area. He had completed many handovers and considered himself an expert, priding himself on his flawless record. Criminals that smuggled or did drug deals always tried to disassociate themselves from the event, to calm themselves. Most drug busts at airports were not actioned on information but on the unusual behaviour of the courier, who was worrying about the negative consequences of a hand on the shoulder.

A long stretch in prison or a bullet were the last things they wanted. The difference in jail time between cocaine or heroin and hash was vast. Some of the stuff Harry made wasn't even classified, so would be nothing but a slap on the wrist. The other danger was the people you were dealing with. Criminals dealing hard drugs were ten times nastier than hash dealers.

They had parked as instructed one hundred yards from the yacht. Dennis looked at his watch, eight p.m., the meeting time. He felt his pulse quicken as they walked towards the yacht. When they were five metres from it the gangway suddenly lowered and two men, each at least six foot five and two hundred pounds, walked towards them.

"This way and take your shoes off." Dennis and Gregor walked along the gangway and stepped onto a highly polished teak deck, now out of sight of any prying eyes on the quayside. "Against the wall, hands up, legs apart." They did as they were told, the search took longer than Dennis was used to. "Follow me."

They were taken to a brightly lit room inside the yacht. Behind a desk sat Arkady Litvanov. He looked at them. "Do you have the merchandise?"

"Yes, it's in the van," said Dennis.

" He pointed at Gregor. "You, go with these two." The Russians took his arms and guided him back towards the door. "I take it you are Dennis? we will wait here. Would you like a drink? Don't look so uncomfortable, this is the way we do things."

"I'm fine," Dennis replied.

"Sit, it will be a while."

The wait stretched to twenty minutes, though to Dennis it seemed longer. Arkady Litvanov had not said a word.

Thirty minutes later Gregor and the two Russians reappeared, and the taller of them nodded to his boss.

"OK, it's seems everything is in order."

"Do you have the money?" said Dennis.

Arkady Litvanov took a sip of dark coffee. "No."

The colour drained from Dennis' face. Shit, he thought, too good to be true. Thirty grand for a day's work, only problem was, there was no passing go and no collecting.

Arkady laughed looking at their faces. "Don't worry, you will have your money. It's in another place, half a mile from here. The address is on that." He pointed to a folded piece of paper on the desk, which Dennis picked up. "This is the way we do business. Now, if you don't mind, I have other things to attend to." He got up, walked through another set of doors and was gone.

Chapter 28
1994
London

Mickey had been to the gym and the two-hour midday workout had made him feel good. He moved to the kitchen, where his housekeeper had started to prepare lunch. He had missed the delivery of the morning post, which lay on the table. On top of the pile was an envelope written in red ink. Mickey's heart rate soared, then he laughed and murmured, "Sick bastard, Harry!" But then realised, Harry would never have pulled a stunt like that. Sitting down and looking at the letter, his hand began to shake as he picked it up and opened it.

Mickey

How are you? I see you're happy again and have forgotten about me. I know what you are thinking, this is a joke, played on you by one of your criminal friends, probably Harry.

Well, it isn't, you see I still hate you, and have not forgotten what you did to me. I went to Bernie Broadman's grave last week. Another innocent victim of 'Hate them all Mickey.' Wasn't it enough that you killed his father?

I saw you at your wife's grave last week; very touching. I pissed on it after you left, but I digress, back to Bernie. I told him to go to the funeral and take the picture of you. I thought you would record the funeral. You're really not as clever as you think, are you?

Well, that's about it for now, except I understand you're missing one of your friends. Just before Marshall died, and with the last few words of a condemned man, delivered with a feeble voice, told me he didn't even like you, offered to kill you for me, if I spared his miserable, perverted life. You can't trust your friends, Mickey, none of them, and it won't be me who kills you, it will be one of them. You should think of killing them first, it's your only chance, if you kill them all including your good friend Harry, I will spare you and your son.

Anyway, get yourself down to the old printworks in Rainham, that's where you'll find your friend, if the rats haven't had him by now. Keep watching.

MTB

Mickey called to the housekeeper, "Don't worry about food." Looking down he noticed his shirt moving rhythmically with the accelerated beating of his heart. He made his way to Harry's, barely glancing left or right, ignoring most of the red lights. The stairs to Harry's office reminded him of the last murder, that of Wally Fields. The entrance to the stairs had been covered with a roof after the killing, and short of a mortar attack, was safe.

He made his way into the office and slumped in the chair opposite Harry.

Harry frowned. "Mickey, you look fucked. And the look on your face is bothering me, it reminds me of a long time ago."

"That's very perceptive, and I hate to say it but you're right." Mickey took the letter out of his pocket and tossed it to Harry, who immediately saw the red ink. "Fuck me, Mickey, not this again! This was twenty years ago and now you're telling me it's back. If this is a joke, it's in very bad taste."

"It's not a joke, Harry, I wish it was." He looked across to Eastham, who was finishing a Cornish pasty. "You were right, Paul, Bernie Broadman couldn't be the killer. Looking back, he was the most unlikely, incapable assassin on the planet. We just wanted to believe it was true."

Eastham wiped the crumbs from his mouth. "Yes, it didn't add up, did it?"

As Harry read the letter, the colour drained from his face. "What do you make of this?" he asked, passing the letter to Eastham. "If Marshall Johnson is dead, there'll be hell to pay, the commission won't like this. For now, we keep this to ourselves." He glanced at Eastham, "you too, Paul."

"Of course, Harry." Eastham, read the letter again.

Harry groaned. "You were right. If we'd listened to you all those years ago, I wouldn't feel like my life could now be instantly snuffed out by the chairman of Mickey's old fan club."

"Do you want me to go to the printworks and check it out?" asked Eastham.

"Yes but take a couple of the boys with you. Ones you trust to keep this to themselves. And be careful, it might be a trap. I've got a very bad feeling about this."

Eastham moved towards the door. "You're not the only one, Harry."

Harry turned towards Mickey. "He's very clever your pen pal, divide and conquer."

"How do you fight someone you can't see? What do you think, should I do what the letter says and kill everyone, starting with you?"

Harry didn't answer, the CCTV monitors had attracted his attention. Small red lights flickered, indicating motion sensors had been activated. For a moment he thought the worst, until he saw the figure on one of the screens of Dennis Whiting carrying a Samsonite suitcase. Dennis had a broad grin on his face, at last, some good news, Harry thought.

His finger tapped the door release button. "Let's talk about this later, Mickey."

Dennis bowled through the door, too full of his successful day to notice the atmosphere in the room. He had his eye on a nice new top of the range, Range Rover, and now had the money to pay for it.

"How'd it go?" Harry asked, relieving Dennis of the suitcase.

"Sweet as a nut, Harry. Scary fuckers, but straight down the line. Good to deal with, very professional."

Harry keyed in the code only he and the Russian knew and looked down at the fifty pound and five-hundred-euro notes. The count would be made later, knowing it would all be there. He counted out Dennis' cut, placed it in a small case and gave it to him, "drink?"

"No, I'm good, got to run, cheers, Harry, there's a showroom I need to visit."

Harry was powdering his nose as Eastham walked through the door, and the look on his face confirmed his worst fears. It had been an uneasy few hours. "Jesus, don't tell me it's true?"

Eastham took a long draught of the beer he had just opened, almost emptying the bottle. "It's worse, Harry, much bloody worse, two bodies. One, a tramp, probably wrong place wrong time, and the other Marshall Johnson. No sign of a struggle, which indicates the killer knew him. Must have arranged to meet him, we're checking phone records. The killer's some operator; this was no ordinary hit, took his time. Three bullets, one in each eye, one in the heart. And that's not the end of it, two pennies were placed where Marshall's eyes used to be. A symbolic gesture, I think. He is one sick bastard, but it's a clue, I'm sure of it."

"Fuck me, why can't life be simple? I knew I should have been a doctor, wouldn't have any of this shit to deal with." He looked at Eastham, who was now on his second beer. "It's a bad day when you're worried, Paul, and I can tell you are because I've never seen you drink two beers so fast. What's the plan?"

Eastham looked at him. "The plan, Harry, would be to run and hide."

Harry's face went white. "Fuck me, don't say that."

"I mean it."

"I guess we'd better tell Mickey the news. I know I don't need to tell you again, but this is strictly between us. Mickey is a dead man if the commission find out the truth."

"I've been with you a long time; you don't need to tell me twice."

"Yes, sorry, of course I don't, but seriously, what do we do?"

"We wait for a break, Harry, a mistake. You can't kill someone if you don't know who they are. Mickey needs to think again. Trouble is, he couldn't remember years ago, so probably got no chance now. You need to watch yourself, you're his closest friend, and sure to be right at the top of the list."

Harry went even whiter. He bent down and took a line of Charlie. "Paul, life was a lot easier when Abba were number one. It was such a kind, gentle world." He opened the drawer, took out a bag and arranged the white powder into several more lines.

Chapter 29
1994
London

Dennis Whiting was studying Harry's face. "Have you lost weight? You look worried, anything wrong?"

Harry ignored the question. "We have another drop Dennis, double the amount, same place."

"Well, that's a relief. I thought it was bad news from the look on your face."

"No, no bad news here. You only have the drop this time, no money pick-up."

"Don't you trust me Harry, I would never think of doing a moonlight. Well, not unless I thought I could get away with it."

Harry laughed. He had a few things on his mind, like would the next assassin's bullet, be for him, but hadn't quite lost all his faculties. Knowing the amount of cash involved in this deal might be too tempting, the decision not to let Dennis pick it up was an easy one. He'd thought twice about letting him collect the money on the last drop. This time he'd arranged for Mickey to pick it up. Tobias Boswell had assured him the Russians were straight, and not in the business of a quick rip-off. They did deals for the long-term, and Tobias had also let slip they were as big as the commission.

"Now look, Dennis, I could give this job to quite a few people, but we go back a long way, and we've built up a lot of trust. There will be many deals with the Russians, and they'll make us a lot of money, but none of us need to get greedy. That's why you're doing the job because I know you won't." The message in Harry's words were very clear.

As Dennis walked down the stairs, Harry noticed the smile on his face, causing his doubts about him to resurface, the thought was pushed to the back of his mind; he had other things to worry about. Despite his best efforts, the premonition, the one nagging away at him since reading the letter from Mickey, of impending disaster, refused to leave his mind.

Dennis Whiting turned up the volume on the radio in the van. The sleet and rain had not dampened his enthusiasm for the task ahead. Gregor sat beside him, singing a song, he had assured Dennis was the latest music from Russia.

"Dennis, do you not like my singing? I have been told by many people all over the world that my voice is a very good voice."

"Well, I didn't know what the sound of a cat being tortured in Russia sounds like, but I think I have a very good idea now."

"Dennis, there is nothing as beautiful in this world as Russian songs, I will sing more in the days ahead, and I know, as time goes by, you will love them, as I do."

"You know, if it goes bad today, and we don't see the sunrise tomorrow, at least your singing will stop."

"You should not say that, in my country when we do these things, we do not tempt bad luck with such words. I now have a very bad feeling about this."

"You talk such rubbish, Gregor, it is so easy to make money in this country. You will be five grand richer in a few hours. Why don't you take a holiday, maybe take some singing lessons?"

"Yes, it is easy until it goes wrong."

"Why do you think they changed the location?" Dennis asked.

"They do that sort of thing all the time. It means nothing. Do not let it bother you. They play with your mind. Changes always set nerves on edge, because the mind will wonder why, which in itself can be dangerous, I have seen it. We must only think about the payday. In my country everyone plays games. Anyway, you drove down yesterday to have a look. Did you see anything that bothered you?"

"No, Gregor, everything looked fine, as far as I could tell."

"Well, there you are then. Like you say, if today is successful, and there are more drops, we will make a lot of money, and each

220

time the danger is less. But whatever happens, I've had a good life and am not afraid to die."

"I think you sometimes don't tell the truth, Gregor."

"Life is different here. You are a lot softer in this country than in mine. I don't like the thought of the process of dying, but death itself does not bother me."

"Good, thanks for that. Shall we stop talking about death now, I thought you said it was unlucky?"

"No problem. But you know the good times will end. They always do. That is the life of a criminal. A rock star life, like your favourite band, the 'Red hot chilli tomatoes,' except one day the bullet will end it all."

"Chilli peppers, anyway, give it a rest, Gregor".

"No problem."

"You did very well to let go of what Mickey Warren did to you."

"Do you really? Look, I haven't forgotten, but I saw much worse in Russia, it is nothing, the things he did. If I could get away with it, I would kill him, who wouldn't? But I'm happy here, making good money and that for now, is enough."

"Looking at your face makes me think when the time is right, you will kill him. Think of me before you do, it would cause me a shedload of problems."

"I don't see how it would cause you problems. But I will of course remember what you said. You have been good to me. This is a strange country, in my country, I would be dead. You could not do what he did to someone and leave them alive."

They were early. The meeting point, an old warehouse, stood three hundred yards from the Prospect of Whitby, a sixteenth century coaching inn, where it seemed logical to Dennis to shelter from the rain.

They walked across the flagstone floor to the pewter-topped bar. The riverside terrace was deserted, as people huddled in the bars protected from the worsening weather. The exchange was an hour away, so they sat content with the warming sensation of the double Dimple whiskies in front of them. They kept a close watch on the van parked in front of the window, as slowly the minutes ticked away.

"Time to go," said Dennis, as he drained the last of the whisky. The rain had stopped, but looming storm clouds gave an unusual darkness for the time of day. They sat in the van for a few minutes and then, just as quickly as the rain had stopped, it began to fall again, this time torrential. The windows in the van turned opaque as the moisture settled on the glass, they wiped the windows in a vain attempt to clear them. Dennis put the demister on full power, but his impatience got the better of him, driving into the road before the windows had time to clear. He immediately regretted his decision, as they struggled to cover the short distance to the warehouse.

He parked and turned the lights off, as a black Ford parked opposite the warehouse twenty yards in front of them. "Look Gregor, some of our friends are here."

Gregor glanced at the car, not believing his eyes as the passing headlights illuminated the occupants faces. He pushed his head closer to the windscreen.

Dennis looked at him. "You, OK? You look like you've seen a ghost."

Not answering he pulled his hat down covering most of his face. It was not a ghost; it was a man. Surely it wasn't possible, he thought, looking again, but the rain obscured the face he was struggling to see. Surely just a trick of the light. But then another car passed and lit up the car again. It was no trick of the light. Never had he imagined this day coming, anywhere in the world, least of all here. Was it a trap, he wondered? No, it could not be, this man would not be outside in a car, but waiting inside for him, ready to enjoy the long process of watching the unbearable pain before sanctioning his inevitable death. Gregor had made many enemies, but this man was top of the list, in a league of his own. Yes, it was him, he decided. The man was laughing and joking with the driver of the car. Gregor was sure his nemesis had no knowledge of his presence, but would soon recognise him, in the warehouse. He was trapped, and thought his only option was to kill Dennis and drive into the evening with the drugs, out of London and into a new life.

His hand reached down into the side pocket of the door, where he kept a large wrench.

"Looks like they're not staying for the main event," said Dennis.

Gregor looked up to see the Ford drive off, with its full complement of occupants inside. Dennis put the car into gear, as Gregor released his grip on the wrench. As they pulled up outside the warehouse, two doors slid apart, and they drove in.

Arkady Litvanov, greeted them. "Dennis, how are you? It's good to see you again, do you have the goods?"

Dennis nodded towards the back of the van. The boxes were removed, and a small bespectacled man, with a long ginger beard opened one of the boxes, and tore open a plastic bag, full of bright purple, oval tablets. He broke one in half, placed it in his mouth and crushed it with his teeth. His tongue moved it around his mouth. He closed his eyes and reached for the glass of water by his side, taking a full mouthful and then spitting it out, before nodding to Arkady. The layer of perspiration that had formed on Dennis' brow slowly lost itself in the cold air.

"Thank you, Dennis, our business is done."

They drove out of the double doors, which slowly closed behind them. The black Ford had returned and was parked in the same place as before. Gregor lowered his hat further and his hand covered what remained of his face. Between his fingers he could see the eyes of the man he hated most on earth looking at them.

The struggle to fall asleep that night, was lost. It was not the thought of the money earned. It was the question of what would follow having seen the man he would do anything to see begging at his feet for mercy.

Mickey got out of the car and pushed open the front door of the pawn shop. The old man's wrinkled fingers lifted up the tortoiseshell spectacles that sat crookedly on his nose. Looking up at his visitor a gentle wave motioned for Mickey to go through a partially open door. Mickey wondered how the man knew it was he who should go through the creaky old door, then saw a picture of his own face, on the timeworn counter. Slowly his eyes accustomed to the dimness of the musty, damp space that opened before him.

"Mr Warren, turn around please, I need to see you are here in good faith."

Mickey turned and instinctively placed his hands on the wall. He felt himself being efficiently frisked, military style. The owner of the hands quickly came to the conclusion their visitor was not carrying a weapon.

"Turn around."

Mickey's now dark-adapted eyes looked into the face of the man. A suitcase lay by his feet. "This, I believe, is for you. A word of advice. It has come to our attention that you, Mr Fleet and the commission have some difficulties you cannot control. We will have a lot of business to do together. If you need our help, speak with the man outside, who will arrange a meeting. This business is very important to us." He passed Mickey the case.

"Thanks. I'll pass on your words to Harry."

Mickey left the shop and strode back to his car, unlocked it, and placed the suitcase of money, from the drug deal on the passenger seat. He hesitated closing the door, thoughts racing through his mind. How did the Russian know of the troubles the commission were having? Maybe they were the trouble... but no, they couldn't be. The problem had started years before their arrival on the scene. He decided to keep the conversation to himself.

The commission sat around a large, round, oak table, the mood sombre. Solomon Gorman tapped his glass with the bulky gold ring on his index finger. "Gentleman, this is a grave time for us. Our commiserations to you, Charley. Your brother was a brother to all of us, although we have not seen much of him in recent years. We will do all we can, to find the people responsible for this and kill them."

Charley Johnson nodded but didn't reply.

"What do we have?" Solomon looked around the room, "because I have nothing, and cannot think who would kill Marshall. With respect to the rest of us, he was a straight guy." He looked at Charley Johnson, "Charley, who would have done this to your brother?"

He shook his head, raised it and slowly looked at every face around the table. "I don't know."

Every other mouth stayed silent. Harry looked at Mickey. So far, their secret was safe, they would have to hope, it stayed that way.

Three miles away Gregor sat at his usual spot in his local, steadily getting drunk. Over and over in his mind, replaying the moment, seeing the man he was desperate to kill. Two drinks later, a smile lit up his face and he began mumbling to himself in Russian. He had a plan.

Chapter 30
March 1994
London

Tommy Bednar was enjoying himself; it reminded him of his time in active service. This was his speciality, covert surveillance, weakness analysis of targets and establishing their routines. The two potential targets had decent security systems at their homes, but there would be no trouble disabling them, should he choose. However, it would be too simple to kill them in their homes. No, something special was planned. He was shocked to see how careless they were, not taking the threat to their lives seriously. He laughed; gangsters were so full of themselves; thinking they were so clever, invincible even. Well, the next execution would change that. Only one challenge remained, that of making the death as creative as possible. That was how he measured himself, not on the death, which was inevitable, but on how good was the performance.

"The end-game is coming, Mickey Warren," he muttered. "Time for you to pay the price for your evil life. The wounds you inflicted on me will finally heal, but first, some more vermin control." The chosen participants were Samuel Gorman, underboss of the Gorman family, or Tommy Varey, the Varey underboss. It made no difference to him. He would make it easy — heads Gorman, tails Varey.

He glanced across at the waitress, who was staring at him. She had been looking at him since the first step through the door. He motioned for her to come to the table. She rushed over, trying not to look too keen, and brushed against him as she wiped the table, a table that didn't need wiping. He looked at her slightly blushing face, and saw the wedding ring on her finger, but knew, that would be no defence against him if he wanted her.

"Another coffee, please."

"Would you like anything else?"

He smiled. "Yes, toss this coin for me, would you? I can't make up my mind about something."

It was the last thing she had expected but took the coin from his hand and tossed it into the air. It made a soft whooshing sound as it spun. She glanced at him. He saw the shame on her face as the thought went through her head that the toss was to decide whether he would sleep with her or not. The coin fell towards her hand, but she closed it a little too slowly, the coin bounced off her fingers, hit the table and tumbled to the ground. She bent over to pick it up.

"Don't touch it, let it stop!" he snapped, looking down to see the result. It rolled towards his foot, and stopped, the Queen's face stared back at him.

Samuel Gorman's house was a short distance from Denham aerodrome, which was convenient, as flying was his passion. Tommy Bednar was pleased when the coin had landed with the smiling face of the monarch staring back at him. A spectacular death was planned for Gorman, one that would make the TV and radio news channels.

He turned off the car ignition and tapped his fingers to the music with one hand, whilst adjusting the heating with the other. The car was hidden off road in Nightingale Wood, less than a mile from the runway, a good vantage point to see Samuel Gorman's Piper Cherokee clearly through the binoculars. Every Sunday Gorman flew his plane, and always at the same time. Usually, taking a passenger with him. Tommy Bednar hoped today would be different, not caring for any collateral damage.

The notes on Samuel Gorman documented his inflated view of himself, believing he was popular, entertaining and intelligent. Others suggested he was only half the man his brother was, basking in his reflected glory. The other commission members had little time for him, having developed a dislike for his unnecessary beatings, stripping and humiliation of his victims before they got what he thought they deserved.

Tommy Bednar wondered who if anyone would be Gorman's unlucky guest. He'd decided to abort the kill if the passenger was a child. Anyone else would share the same fate as Gorman.

Looking through his binoculars and right on cue, Samuel Gorman walked on to the tarmac. With him was a man Tommy Bednar had become very familiar with. He looked again and smiled, not believing his luck. The face of Tommy Varey looked back at him through the binoculars. He watched as they walked around the plane doing pre-flight checks.

Samuel Gorman finished as always, by checking the fuel level in the right wing. "All aboard, Tommy, you'll get the bug after today. When we're in the air, you can take the controls. It's a great sensation, the noise of the engine and wind. No one can touch you up there." His enthusiasm was infectious.

"I've been dying to have a go, Sam, been looking forward to this for weeks. Maybe I'll buy one. A plane could be very handy in our business."

They strapped themselves into the tight cockpit of the Cherokee. "These pre-take-off checks are bloody important, Tom, some people skip them. Don't ever do that, they can save your life." Gorman went through the checklist, explaining every single item to his passenger. He finished by turning the strobes and lights on. "That's it, Tom, time to get airborne. Denham tower, this is golf lima foxtrot tango, ready at runway 23, request take-off."

"Golf lima foxtrot tango clear for take-off, have a good day, Sam," replied air traffic control.

Solomon grinned. "You ready, Tom?"

Tommy Varey put his thumbs up and the plane accelerated down the runway, then powered into the air. He levelled the plane at five thousand feet and headed north, away from the restricted airspace of RAF Northolt and the Heathrow air corridor, then turned left towards the spires of Oxford. "Oxford looks beautiful from the air," he told his passenger. Turning towards a small bank of cloud and skirting around the edge of it, they felt the temperature change as they dipped in and out of the water droplets. They flew for an hour, and as Milton Keynes disappeared behind them, they headed back towards Denham Airfield. Tommy Varey was now flying the plane and enjoying the feeling it gave him.

"Tommy, that's Aylesbury and Stoke Mandeville to the left, and there's the hospital."

"I like this, Sam. It's exhilarating, but peaceful at the same time. Short of hitting another plane or a flock of birds, it's safer than driving. No phones ringing or people bothering you."

"Not that safe, you still have to take-off and land, but as long as you complete them in equal numbers the day ends well."

"Well, I'll leave that to you. What do you think is the story with Marshall Johnson? I think it was the underage girls. I heard he'd slept with the thirteen-year-old daughter of a member of parliament. I reckon he was done by the secret service. Talking of Stoke Mandeville and kiddie fiddlers, have you heard about that creepy bastard Jimmy Savile? I heard he's been abusing the patients there. I'm thinking of doing him."

Samuel Gorman glanced across at Tommy, then checked the horizon for other air traffic. "Yes, I heard that. We all have, but it's not the subject I wanted to bring up at the sit down with the other boys. As for Savile, yes, it's an open secret at the BBC. I'm thinking of not paying my TV licence. Good idea doing him in, he'd be no loss. Can't believe he was knighted. If we know about it, the Queen and the secret service do."

"Doubt the Queen knows, Sam, but you can be sure plenty others do. Yes, I'm gonna arrange it this week, that should make the ten o'clock news."

"There's the runway, Tom. I'd better take over unless you fancy having a go at landing?"

"All yours, Sam."

Tommy Bednar watched as the plane came into view. He picked up the Stinger surface-to-air missile, mounted it on his shoulder and looked through the viewfinder. He liked the feeling of the metal on his shoulder and smiled as the missile whistled through the air at 600 metres per second. They never saw it coming, as the Cherokee exploded in a ball of flames. Smiling again, he packed away the launcher.

An hour later, laughing, he listened to the news on the radio.

"News is coming in of a mid-air explosion above Denham airfield in Buckinghamshire. There are reports a private plane was struck by a missile. Early reports suggest there are two casualties."

He turned the radio off, then pressed the play button on the cassette player and listened as the song began. He had been saving this song for just such an occasion. Since a child, he had been able to recite the words of the 1927 poem *Desiderata*, translated as 'things that are desired.' He had desired many things as a child, but when hearing the words put to music by Les Crane, it had changed his life. It had reached only number seven in the music charts - a travesty, he thought, the ordinary public knew nothing about music. A tear formed in the corner of his eye.

Go placidly amid the noise and the haste and remember what peace there may be found in silence. As far as possible, without surrender, be on good terms with all persons.

Speak your truth quietly and clearly; and listen to others, even to the dull and the ignorant; they too have their story.

Avoid loud and aggressive persons; they are vexatious to the spirit. If you compare yourself with others, you may become vain or bitter, for always, there will be greater and lesser persons than yourself.

Enjoy your achievements as well as your plans. Keep interested in your own career, however humble; it is a real possession in the changing fortunes of time.

Exercise caution in your business affairs, for the world is full of trickery. But let this not blind you to what virtue there is; many persons strive for high ideals, and everywhere life is full of heroism.

Be yourself. Especially, do not feign affection. Neither be cynical about love; for in the face of all aridity and disenchantment, it is as perennial as the grass.

Take kindly the counsel of the years, gracefully surrendering the things of youth.

Nurture strength of spirit to shield you in sudden misfortune. But do not distress yourself with dark imagining's. Many fears are born of fatigue and loneliness.

Beyond a wholesome discipline, be gentle with yourself. You are a child of the universe no less than the trees and the stars; you have a right to be here.

And whether or not it is clear to you, no doubt the universe is unfolding as it should. Therefore, be at peace with God, whatever you conceive Him to be.

And whatever your labours and aspirations, in the noisy confusion of life, keep peace in your soul. With all its sham, drudgery and broken dreams, it is still a beautiful world. Be cheerful. Strive to be happy.

"If the vermin had lived by those words, as I do, they would be alive today," he thought.

Less than two hours later Tommy Bednar had changed the number plates on the Range Rover and returned the missile launcher to his weapons store. He was now watching the early evening news in a West End bar.

Harry, Mickey and Jason had finished their second round of golf and were sitting in the bar waiting for Paul Eastham to take them home. He was unusually late. They moved to the bar and ordered another drink just as he walked through the doors.

"Good God, Harry, look at Eastham's face."

Harry looked and realised something was very wrong.

Eastham turned the car radio on, and they listened to the story on the news. Eastham supplied the missing details — the names of the victims.

Chapter 31
1994
London

The remaining members of the fast-diminishing commission had not been seen in public for two days. The police had worked tirelessly to find the killer, and the two hundred-thousand-pound reward put up by the commission for information leading to the arrest, or better still the death, of the killer, had not brought a single credible lead. Solomon figured someone knew who the killer was, and it would not take long for greed to do the work the police could not. He preferred the scenario of the criminal underworld flushing the assassin out and bringing him, to him, then personally taking it upon himself to exact the slowest revenge for the death of his brother. The conclusion this was a take-over attempt and wouldn't end until they were all dead or the assassin had bled out, was fast becoming the accepted point of view. The problem was identifying the people behind it. There were no obvious candidates. No one big enough to take over London, it didn't make sense. A calm head was needed; they would find the killer or killers and things would soon be back to normal. At least, that is what he hoped.

Mickey woke up on the morning of the third day since the missile had hit the plane. Each day waiting for the post to arrive, waiting to see the familiar letter written in red. He walked to the breakfast table, and there it lay, in front of him.

Dear Mickey
Well, what did you think of that? You made the national news. Yes,
I say you because that's two more bodies down to you.

Did you not work out the clue I left you last time, the two pennies on the eyes? It wasn't to pay the ferryman to the next world, it's far simpler than that.

So, who next? What about Solomon? As you know by now, I recorded my last piece of work and sent it to the TV stations. What do you think of it? They looked so happy as they got into the plane, did you see their faces?

Mickey glanced at the TV, and there it was again, the video of the plane being hit by the missile. It was looping endlessly on the TV news channels and had been shown all around the world. He listened. "Stunning new footage shows the mid-air explosion of the piper Cherokee, killing Thomas Varey and Samuel Gorman. It is thought to be gang related. This footage is believed to have been taken by the assassin." The TV footage ended with a macabre laugh, the laugh of the assassin. A very distinctive laugh, probably a false one, Mickey thought; another red herring.

He returned to the letter.

I gave you the chance to kill all the commission and save your own life, but you didn't. Well now, it's too late and I don't think you will like what I have planned for you next. Take the easy way out, kill yourself and save your friends. Time is ticking.

See you soon.

MTB

When Mickey let himself into Harry's office, he was surprised to find its occupant snoozing.

"Wake up, you lazy bastard."

Harry grunted, "Get me a whisky, Mickey, I can't be bothered to get up. This thin stream of fear in my life has turned into a raging torrent, which is engulfing my every thought, my every laboured movement."

Mickey went to the bar and poured two large whiskies, took the letter out of his pocket, folded it into the shape of an airplane and launched it at Harry. It landed gently in his lap.

Harry looked at it. "That's rather bad taste, I'm not sure Solomon would appreciate the joke." He unfolded it and began reading. "Well, I'm glad to see the option for you to kill everyone is off the table. There's not been one solid lead, even with a reward on the table. We're all fucked. I can honestly say, I think you will be the death of me."

"What has Solomon said?"

"Not a lot. Thinks the money will flush out the grim reaper. Now he's worried, certain it's related to the commission, a takeover attempt. I'm surprised he's so sure, because there's no one I know in a position to do that."

"Maybe I should tell him," said Mickey.

Harry choked on his whisky. "You won't be doing that, you'll be signing your own death warrant and probably mine as well, there's got to be a better way. You could always kill yourself. You know, think about others for a change."

"Yes, I was thinking about that."

"Progress at last, all is not lost. Though death be poor, it ends a mortal woe. Is Jason safe?"

"Yes, he's at one of the safe houses. Do you know people are betting again, on who's going to be next, Harry?" Joint favourites, you and Solomon.

"Really? Well let's not tell Solomon that either. It'll send him over the edge if he thinks he's next. I'm sure I'm not at the top, where am I really on the list?"

"Nowhere, but then no one knows the whole truth, do they? Well, apart from us, and the killer. Truth be known, you should be right near the top. Might be worth a bob or two, might as well try to make a bit of money while we still can."

"You're a sick bastard, Mickey, no wonder you've got no friends."

"I've got you, Harry."

"You need more than just me."

"Yes, I think you're right. And I think I might just have the answer."

"Yes, course you do."

"See you later, I've got someone I need to talk to." Mickey walked out, quietly closing the door behind him.

He wandered into the pawnbrokers, trying to look more comfortable than he felt.

"Mr Warren, how can I help?"

Mickey smiled. "You've got a good memory."

"That's my job. How can I help you?"

"I need to talk to your boss."

The old man picked up the phone and his fingers tapped out a number dialled many times before.

Solomon Gorman's office

"Sit down, Harry. Did you know about this?" Solomon Gorman could barely conceal the anger in his voice as he passed him the letter. Harry looked at the familiar red ink and noticed the pile of similar letters on the desk.

Solomon

He hasn't told you, has he. Read the copies of the letters, I sent to him. He doesn't respect you. Letting you all die one by one, and Mickey Warren will soon be the death of you.

You are next. You've had a good life, so get your affairs in order, say goodbye to the people you love. Your death will be like that of a king, even more spectacular than that of your unpleasant brother. Yes, you will be on the news just like your brother and Varey. I have planned a great exit for you. Shall I tell you about it? No, let's just enjoy it as it happens.

Your death will be special, a death which befits the leader. Alternatively, we can do this another way. I'm a fair man, and like to give people a chance, unlike Mickey Warren. I expect you feel very betrayed by him. It was kind of you to offer a reward for information about me. Unfortunately for you, no one will be collecting. You should give me a bit of credit. Two hundred thousand has a nice ring to it, but five million sounds much better.

So, this is what you're going to do if you want to stay alive. You will kill Mickey Warren and donate two and a half million to the NSPCC, and the same to Barnardo's. You have one month. If not, say goodbye to your children.

The clock is ticking.

MTB

Harry placed the letter on the table. "Sol, Mickey is my friend, but nothing comes before what we have. I thought this was all over when the butcher was killed. I can assure you I knew nothing about this."

Harry thought throwing in a curve ball might help. It wasn't only Mickey's life on the line, it was his as well. If Solomon thought Harry knew, he was as good as dead.

"Sol, how do you know this is a letter from the killer and not some crank?" Harry was clutching at straws and knew it.

Solomon shook his head and tossed him four photos. "Don't insult my intelligence."

The first picture was what was left of Mickey's car on the road, and a distraught Mickey on the pavement. The second, the body of Marshall Johnson, with pennies resting where his eyes used to be, and the gun that killed him placed on his neck. The third, a picture of Solomon's brother and Tommy Varey getting into the plane. The fourth was of Sol and his family, taken last week, in what he thought was a secure location.

Harry looked at the letter and pictures that amounted to Mickey Warren's death warrant. "Sol, I didn't know. You must believe me. Shall I chip in a few quid towards the five mil?"

"Great idea Harry, great idea, five million should do it, and you need to retire. You have three months to shut down. You're off the commission."

Harry looked at him. Solomon knew almost everything; the man was no fool.

"Harry, we go back a long way. If it was anyone other than you, they would be dead already."

Harry knew better than to argue the point.

"I need to ask you one thing. The kid, is he OK?"

"Harry, both you and the kid are fine. So long as you don't discuss this with anyone including Mickey. Jason, will think it's the killer who killed Mickey, so keep it that way. What we've said today stays between us. Now, Harry, if you don't mind, leave."

Harry walked out of Solomon's office, his world changed completely, wondering how those carefree days at Oxford University had come to this. He would be losing his best friend, his place on the most powerful criminal organization in the country, and his business. The only thing that reassured him was the fact, Solomon Gorman was a man of his word.

Chapter 33
1994
London

The wind howled and violent gusts rocked the van. Rain falling by the bucketload hit the roof and windows, but Raven Magdani's view of Mickey Warren's house was clear enough.

She enjoyed her work and the pay that went with it, but for once, had mixed feelings. She had worked with Mickey and liked him. However, business was business, so he would be leaving the world of the living today, just as all her other targets had in the past. The noise of the rain would drown out any small noise from inside the custom-built Luton van — not, that there would be any. The modified van had a raised stage which lifted her above the passing cars, giving her an unobstructed view. The Blaser 93 tactical sniper rifle with custom-made silencer would reduce the discharge noise to a dull thud.

She had waited for two hours without moving from the spot, and a nagging ache had spread from her shoulders and down her back. Small price to pay; this was a big payday, she thought. How much longer until you put your head out of the door, Mickey? she wondered, visualizing the moment. It was windy and raining, but that would not affect the high-velocity bullet at this range.

She heard the wailing of an ambulance and felt the van rock as it sped by at high speed. It slowed, then came to a halt outside Mickey Warren's gates. The gates swung open, and the paramedics were met by a hysterical housekeeper. Raven watched through her riflescope as a police car pulled alongside the ambulance. She switched to her binoculars. It seemed Mickey Warren's death would have to wait.

Twenty minutes later a gurney appeared from the house and bumped along the driveway. Somebody had already died today. The body was covered by a white sheet, and a crimson stain at head level was spreading and turning lighter as the rain soaked through the material. An arm fell to the side, and she saw Mickey Warren's distinctive tattoo and gold Rolex.

The day had just got better, a hundred big ones and not a shot fired. She packed away the rifle, moved to the driver's seat and headed for Solomon Gorman's office.

"Raven, what are you doing here?"

"He killed himself before I could get a shot off. I take it this doesn't affect our agreement?"

"No, of course it doesn't. How do you know it was him, did you see the body?"

"I saw the tattoo on his arm, it was him."

"Well in that case get yourself ready, we have a dinner date."

Chapter 34
1994
London

Tommy Bednar placed the first mouthful of the Eggs Benedict into his mouth and looked at the paper. The front page was shared between two stories.

'Local businessman Mickey Warren was found dead today in his home, killed by a single gunshot wound to the head. No one is being sought in connection with the death.' The face of Mickey Warren stared out of the paper.

His eyes moved to the other story. 'Two local charities today received an anonymous donation of two and a half million pounds. Both Barnardo's and the NSPCC welcomed the donations. Richard Goodman, the local director of Barnardo's, said, "We are delighted. This shows there are some very good, kind and generous people out there who care about the lives of others."'

Tommy smiled and looked at the waitress hovering over his table. "Maybe crime does pay. Another coffee please."

He turned towards the window and looked onto the street, and at that moment saw the last two people on earth he expected to see, Jason Warren and Harry Fleet, deep in conversation. The pain on the face of Mickey's son was there for everyone to see. He threw five pounds onto the table, pushed the chair back and left the café to follow them. He was within ten feet, way too close, but they didn't know him, and he wanted to hear what they were saying.

"Things will work out, kid," Harry said.

"Life will never be the same, Harry. How did it ever get to this? Can't believe he killed himself, it wasn't in him. Someone else did it."

He saw Harry's body stiffen, had he become aware of his presence behind them? Don't turn around, Harry, he thought, because if you do, I will have to kill you. He chided himself for getting so close, slowed his pace, dropped back and turned left into a side street, wondering what else they were saying, it intrigued him. Certainly, the grief was genuine, and with more analysis he was convinced, Harry, knew it was him following them. The pleasure, he hadn't turned around was real. There had been enough killing for now.

They continued the short walk to Solomon Gorman's office. Harry had been told Solomon's attitude towards him had softened, reasoning it wasn't Harry's fault and he was just being a good friend to Mickey. More important, were the words, apparently from Solomon's own mouth, that he would have done exactly what Harry had done in his position. But his decision about Harry's future, was to stand, off the commission and out of business. It wasn't Solomon's way to change his mind. His priority, now the danger of death had faded, was to restructure the commission, and restore the status quo.

Harry had also heard Solomon was tiring of the strain of being London's crime king and was looking at an exit strategy.

"Jason, I'm so sorry about Mickey," said Solomon. "If there's anything you need, just ask."

"Thanks, Sol. I'm going to the funeral home, to say my final goodbye. You're welcome to come; I know you were close."

Solomon Gorman thought about it for a moment. "No, son, I'll pay my respects at the funeral." He had received a report of the injuries; most of Mickey's face was missing. He didn't envy the boy. Grief was etched into the young man's face; both parents, and unborn sister, lost to a silent, hidden assassin.

Solomon Gorman drew Jason to him and hugged him. "Remember, Jason, anything. Just ask."

Chapter 35
Temple Church, London

Looking up at Temple Church on any other day would have been a far more pleasant experience for Jason Warren, but not today, not on the day of his father's funeral. He placed his hand on Harry's shoulder. "You OK, Harry?"

"Yes, just getting a bit tired of going to so many funerals. I think I'll be buried at sea like Sammy 'the limp' was, when I get the knock on the door."

"Yes, not a bad shout. Hopefully though, you'll actually be dead at the time."

"That was unfortunate. Decent fellow, old Sammy. How unlucky can one man be? Everyone seems to have heard the story. So, I guess he ended up a celebrity. All he ever wanted was to be liked. Just a shame he never hung around long enough to see it."

"Come on, Harry, let's get this over with." They walked into the church.

The Reverend Canon Gareth Grierson paused and looked at the congregation from the pulpit, waiting for their full attention. "I am the way, the truth and the life," he pronounced. "No one comes to the Father, except through me."

Harry smiled and reflected how Mickey would have loved that, a heavenly protection racket, a bouncer on the door to Heaven.

"Go forth upon thy journey from this world, beloved soul, in the name of God the Father who created thee; in the name of Jesus Christ his only Son who hath redeemed thee; in the name of the Holy Spirit who gave thee life and giveth thee life still. Accompanied by angels and archangels and by all the company of heaven, may thy portion this day be in peace, and thy dwelling place the heavenly Jerusalem."

Jason looked up at the elegant curves of the church roof. Harry had taken him on a tour of the more majestic London churches when he was a child, and as always, had made the subject interesting. He admired the architecture and history; but disliked the existence of religion itself, and all it represented. Endless wars, persecution of perceived enemies, centuries of death. The hypocrisy of the words made him angry, he couldn't wait for the service to end.

They left the church, and the cortege of cars made its way to the East London Crematorium. The sun managed to poke its head out of the clouds, bringing a welcome warmth to the chill of the day. The crematorium was limited to fifty or sixty close friends. Solomon Gorman sat behind Harry and Jason, who felt his eyes boring into them. Solomon, like almost everyone, found it hard to believe Mickey had killed himself, but had reasoned not even Mickey and Harry could have staged such a show.

For Jason, the short crematorium service was not short enough. The day was more difficult than he had imagined. Mickey was not the most popular man, and the murdered members of the five families had cast a long shadow over the day. Solomon had insisted all the commission show Mickey respect by turning out, but there would be no celebration into the night, there, the line had been drawn. Jason saw through the words of kindness that the remaining syndicate members gave him. Fair enough, under the circumstances, he could see their point of view.

A few spots of rain fell on them as they walked with Eastham to the car. The three of them drove to the Mayflower Inn, one of Mickey's favourite pubs. It stood on the embankment of the Thames and was the original mooring of the Pilgrim Fathers' ship. It felt appropriate; a new beginning.

Jason watched Harry at the bar chatting to the barmaid, ordering drinks. He had lost his father, but as life, or death, would have it, still had another one, in Harry. Guilt, dwelt in his mind, when asking himself who he would choose, Harry or Mickey, to live or die, if it were down to him. The thought made him shudder, realising it would be an impossible decision to make.

Harry returned to the table and pushed the drinks over to them. They had all noticed the two men who had followed them in.

"Today was terrible, got to be a better way than that. The guys hated him, didn't they?" Jason said.

"They didn't hate him, kid, they just didn't thank him for bringing them so close to their own deaths. Mickey will have the last laugh. He left me with very specific instructions about his ashes."

"Really?"

"Yes, we were in the lab one day I was processing the Chinese herb, you know the one the old skipper used, to stay young. Thing is, it's dark brown so I have to bleach it. Mickey was watching and started laughing. I asked him what was so funny. He said if the mad bastard that's been killing everyone killed him, his ashes should be whitened and mixed in with some Charlie and given to Solomon and the other boys. Mickey liked the thought of getting up everyone's noses. In life, and in death."

"I like that idea, Harry, I like it a lot."

"Yes, I thought you would."

Chapter 36
Harry's office
A few days later

"How are you, Harry?"

"OK, what about you?"

"So, so. Things aren't the same without the old man. He filled such a huge space, everywhere I go reminds me of him."

Harry shrugged. "I keep expecting him to walk in and annoy me, like he did, every other day of his life."

"What are you going to do? Have you decided?"

"I'm in no rush, maybe just retire. The Russians want to meet, I'd like you to come. They want to chat about something that might be of benefit to both of us."

"What's that?"

"Well, for a start they want whatever we can give them before we shut down. I get the impression they could shift whatever we can make, but there must be more to it than that, let's play it by ear. It's the only piece of good news, now we're unemployed."

"Where's the meeting?"

"On the yacht, it's sailing to France."

"Not my idea of fun."

"No, nor mine. East-West detente, I think it's called. Or as Bennie Peapell used to say. 'You can't choose your friends when you haven't got any.'"

"Bennie Peapell. Whatever happened to him?"

"After he turned Queens and ratted on all his mates, he went slowly mad with the clap and withered away in the nut house."

"Kind of puts things in perspective," replied Jason.

Twenty-four hours later Eastham pulled up in front of the mooring, a happy man again. He thought it was a shame about Mickey, but that was the life he had lived. Wherever Mickey went, chaos followed. He would miss him, but life was a whole lot quieter.

The sleek lines of the yacht stood testament to the powerhouse the Russian mafia had become in European crime. When the Berlin Wall came down, they came marching through to every corner of Europe.

The gangway silently lowered, and they were invited aboard. Arkady stood looking at them. "Harry, please follow me." They handed over their luggage and went through a doorway that doubled as a scanner. There were no flashing lights, so Harry assumed they had passed the test.

Arkady motioned to a crew member. "Show our guests to their cabins." They followed him for a short tour around the yacht and then down into a wide corridor and into their cabins.

Harry looked out at the swirling mist of the English Channel and then opened the wardrobe, noting his clothes were already neatly hung. He wondered how they had managed it so quickly.

The phone rang, Harry picked it up. "Dinner will be served in thirty minutes, Mr Fleet," said a voice in perfect English.

Harry had just finished deciding which tie to wear, when a knock on the cabin door reminded him, the thirty minutes had passed. He saw Jason in the corridor, and they followed the steward to the dining room. Harry thought the Regency dining table at odds with the modern lines of the yacht, both elegant but in very different ways.

Harry had not met Sergei before, but it was obvious who he was. His stature and personality dominated the room. Handsome, with dark wavy hair that swung across his pale face as he moved. His eyes appeared first blue, then green, changing with the light. His jawline, high and firm, a nose, noble but slightly crooked, broken but not fixed years before. A curious angle to his lips, gave the impression, he was enjoying his own private joke.

"Harry, it is very good to meet you at last," said Sergei. He made an elegant quarter turn towards Jason. "I am very sorry to hear of the loss of your father."

"Thank you, have we met before? There is something familiar about you, I'm sure we've met."

"I don't think so, young man. But now we have, and I hope we will meet many times in the future, take a seat. How is Tobias, Harry? He's larger than life in every way, I think!"

"Great memories, but he makes me feel tired sometimes, there's no one like Tobias." Harry had tried to obtain information about Sergei but had drawn a blank. Even Tobias had refused to answer questions about him. He was completely off the radar. Harry, knew absolutely nothing about the man that could hold the key to his future.

"He's told me of your visits to Antigua, over the years, and how well you act in times of crisis. I should tell you; we have been following you both for the last few weeks to see if there was perhaps a threat to your lives."

"That's a relief, Sergei. I thought we were being followed, particularly on the day of Mickey's funeral."

"Yes, that was my men. They thought you noticed them. I shall tell them to be more careful next time."

"And was there a threat, do you think?" replied Harry.

"No, we could see no threat. I was concerned that someone would decide you both share Mickey's fate."

The waiter brought over a bottle of Remy Martin Black Pearl Louis XIII and poured it into three glasses. Harry swirled the deep, amber-coloured liquid in the crystal goblet, raised it and then inhaled its bouquet before taking the first sip. The flavour of ginger, cinnamon and Cuban cigars flooded his mouth. "Superb taste, Sergei," he said.

Another waiter delivered a silver platter of smoked salmon with a smattering of Beluga caviar. The message was clear; Sergei served nothing but the best. Harry wondered, was this for show, or just a normal part of his life, as he picked up one of the small hors d'oeuvres and looked at the caviar. It was very light grey, the colour of the best available.

"My God, this is delicious; I could get used to this."

"I very much hope you do, Harry."

Harry looked across at Jason, who was smiling at him, as he shovelled another hors d'oeuvres into his still half-full mouth, and then realised why he was smiling. Sergei was also looking at Harry, sharing the same joke.

"I'm sorry, Sergei, I can't resist them."

"It's good to see a man enjoying his food, have another brandy with me."

"I will, thank you."

"Harry, Solomon Gorman has replaced you on the commission, a mistake by him, I believe. Your loyalty to your friends is admirable. You supply some unique products, and your talent is undoubted. I'd like to take all the product you have left, and any more you can make for me. Then I want you to come to Russia and start producing for me. With my contacts and your skills, we can distribute product around the world."

Harry was not expecting the subject to be raised so soon. "I am honoured, Sergei. Thank you for your words. What would the deal be?"

Sergei held the brandy in his mouth, inhaling the vapour. "You can have a share of profits or be paid a fixed amount each year. What shall we say, five million pounds? The choice is completely yours. You'll stay with me for at least four years and teach my people everything you know. When the four years are over, you can leave if you wish, with a ten-million-pound goodbye. If we occasionally need your expertise after, I hope we can count on you to help us. Think about it, take your time."

Harry picked up the brandy glass and took a sip of the amber fluid. "I have thought about it Sergei, I'm in."

Sergei slapped the table. "Harry, everything I heard about you is true. We have a deal." He looked across at Jason, who had been watching the interaction of the two men. "What do you think of Harry coming to Russia, Jason?"

"It's a great idea. Congratulations, Harry. It will be a big adventure. I just hope Russia is ready for you."

Sergei moved his chair back and walked towards Jason, then placed his hands on his shoulders. "You, are very welcome to join us. It is a different country. Not what you are used to, but you will like it, I'm sure. You too will be very well paid. There is a place for you, think about joining us."

A few seconds passed; the answer not coming as quickly as the one from Harry, who was looking at him, hoping for a positive answer.

"It's a very attractive offer, and Harry would be there, but I've decided it's time to make my own way in life," replied Jason. I'm going to Antigua to see Harry's sister. She and Mickey were very close."

"Well, maybe you will change your mind when you know us a little better. I will leave the offer open. Now we have an agreement, and the business has concluded, I would like you to meet my family."

"It would be an honour," replied Harry.

Ten minutes drifted by. The door opened and two women walked through who Harry assumed were Sergei's wife and daughter, both strikingly beautiful. Harry's eye was caught by Jason rocking backwards and almost falling. Sergei had noticed it also. He looked at him. "You OK, Jason? best to stay off the brandy, I think."

But it wasn't the brandy that had made Jason stumble; it was the face staring back at him, Anna. She had aged, but in a good way. Transforming from a stunning girl into a beautiful woman. He had seen the same momentary shock in her face when she saw him, but wisely decided this was not the time for a reunion.

"Harry, Jason, I'd like you to meet my wife Valentina and daughter Anastasia."

His hand trembled slightly as Jason shook hands with Anna. He recalled the times he believed, Gregor had taken her, and the nights lying awake thinking of the bad times she might be going through. He had felt better when Mickey told him it was probably exactly as Gregor had said, that it was her father who had taken her; an act of love to protect his daughter, doing what any good father would have done.

"Anastasia, please show Jason around the boat," her mother said.

"Of course, mother." She kissed her father on the cheek. "Please, follow me, Jason."

Chapter 37
London
1994

Harry saw a look on Dennis Whiting's face he hadn't seen before, supremacy. Everyone including, Dennis, had heard Harry was being decommissioned and his star was waning. What no one else knew, other than Jason and a few Russian mafia, was that Harry was emigrating on a golden ticket to Russia.

"We have some more business with the Russians. Again, only a drop, I will collect the money." Harry was aware of his vulnerability with the protection of the commission gone. The last thing he needed was to lose a six-figure sum, or worse, join Mickey in gangster heaven. He could have dropped the drugs off to Sergei himself, but decided, fate was something not to be tempted. "You'll get paid when I get the money." He looked at Dennis and saw the disappointment in his eyes. "The boss will be there, so make sure there are no problems. Be respectful."

Dennis drove to his office, where Gregor sat smoking a cigar. "I could get used to these," he said. "They are from Cuba. Rolled on the thigh of a virgin, this is true, the man in the shop told me."

"Yes, of course they are. Did you book that holiday you were talking about?"

"Not yet, I'm still looking where to go. Why?"

"Hold on for another week. Harry's given us another job, probably the last."

"It has been a very good time. The crazy Mickey bastard is dead, and we will have some more money," Gregor replied.

"I'm not sorry to see the back of Warren, but I'll miss Harry. He's a good man and pays well."

"Is it the same Russians as last time?"

"Yes, except the boss will be there. Harry told me we have to behave. I don't see why he cares, it's the last drop."

Gregor smiled, excited not by the thought of money, but the fact, the boss would be there. The thought of killing Sergei Levchenko, who had murdered his family in cold blood, made his heart race.

"You OK, Gregor? Your heart is thumping, I can see it through your shirt. Are you listening? You look miles away."

Gregor hadn't heard a word Dennis had said. His mind was elsewhere. Thinking about his dead family and how he could kill the man who murdered them. His mind played out different scenarios, all which ended with the object of his hatred in a pool of blood. His own death would not matter. This would be his one chance for revenge.

Chapter 38
1994
London

Eastham looked at Jason. They were both thinking Harry was abnormally quiet.

"What's up, Harry?"

"Nothing, kid, just thinking about the old days, you know, the three musketeers, the Marquee, Kate, Tobias Boswell, Sammy the Limp. You know, the old days."

"That's not the first time you've mentioned my mother in the last few days. Do you really still miss her so much after all this time?"

"I do, she was so special. I'm getting very tired of life. Everything changing so quickly. I hope the move to Russia's the right one, the problem is you won't be there. Reconsider and come with me?"

Jason smiled. "Harry, I know you want me to come, and I've thought about it. The last thing I wanted was to be separated from you. You mean so much to me. But I wanted to go my own way..."

"Wanted?" Harry interrupted.

"Yes, wanted, but life's become more complicated. I might well be coming with you."

"What's made you change your mind?"

"She was on the boat."

"Who was?"

"Anna. Sergei Levchenko is her father. Anna from Spain."

Harry sat bolt upright. "What! We need to go. Now!"

"Why?"

"There's something I need to tell you." Jason saw the look between Harry and Eastham. Harry slid open the panel to a small hidden compartment, took out three handguns and tossed one to each of them. "Just when I thought things couldn't get any worse."

"What do you mean? Why am I getting the feeling everyone knows what's going on except me?"

Harry rubbed his eyes. "I'll tell you on the way."

Eastham fired up the six cylinders of the Lexus GS330. "Where to, Harry?"

"The Russians' warehouse, and put your foot down, the meeting's in ten minutes. Jason, there's something you don't know, something your dad and I didn't tell you. Mickey thought Gregor got what he deserved. He would normally have finished him, but Gregor works for Dennis Whiting, so let him live. He's his right-hand man and will be at the handover. I told Dennis that Sergei would be there. If Gregor sees him, he'll try to kill him for what he did to his family."

"Which was?"

"Sergei killed every single member of his family, revenge for the way he treated his daughter in Spain. Gregor won't care if he dies in the process. We need to get there. If something happens, it will be down to us, and we will all be dead. Can we get there in time, Paul?"

"I don't know."

"Harry, can't you call him?" asked Jason.

"No, kid, we never use phones, you know the score. I only wish it was that simple."

"Why wasn't I told? If there's one person who should have been, it's me. I don't understand why Mickey didn't kill him. What was he thinking?"

"I said at the time I thought it was a mistake, but it was Mickey's call. Now we might all pay the price for that decision."

"Jesus, Harry, just when I find her again and life is looking good, I find out we could all be dead within the hour.'

Harry laughed nervously. "At least we'll all die together."

Chapter 39
1994
London

A few short miles away, the day Gregor had waited for had arrived, and he was determined it would be the day Sergei Levchenko died. It had been a sleepless night, as scenarios looped continually through his mind. Not once had his eyes closed to sleep. He had decided his own death was probably inevitable, a price worth paying. Security would be very high, and they would all have guns. He had to gamble they would not find the gun hidden in the van. It was in a place they had not looked before. His head was shaved and had several days growth on his chin. Heavy horn-rimmed spectacles completed his change of appearance.

As the van came to a stop inside the warehouse, the steel shutters slammed shut behind them. Gregor looked around the large open space, there was no sign of Sergei Levchenko.

Arkady nodded, and two of his men searched them. He looked at Dennis's companion, the man who never spoke. "You look very different today. Where are you from? I'm sure I know you."

Gregor had rehearsed this question many times. "I am from a town in east Poland, Białystok."

"He's married to my cousin," Dennis said.

"Does she like your new haircut?" Arkady asked in Russian.

"Da."

"Very clever, Dennis, a Russian speaker to listen to us, I'm impressed. Was this your idea or Harry's?"

"Harry's of course, but does it matter? This is the last time we'll meet. Your delivery's in the van, let's get on with it?"

"Why don't we. Let's hope there are no more surprises."

A light in the office above them flickered into life. Sergei Levchenko peered through the dusty window.

Harry looked at his wristwatch as they approached the Prospect of Whitby. It was five past seven, they were five minutes late.

"Well, I can't hear any gunshots, that's a good sign, Harry."

"Very funny, Paul, very funny." A lorry reversed out of a side street and blocked their progress. Eastham blasted the horn, the driver acknowledged his mistake, but struggled to manoeuvre out of their way.

"Jesus, this is all we need," said Harry.

"Harry, this is not your problem, stay in the car, when we get there," said Jason.

Harry looked at him. "Did I never read *The Three Musketeers* to you? I'm not leaving you now. I promised Mickey I would always look after you."

"I can't remember a time when you let me down. Well other than now when we're all about to die in a hail of bullets. It's more like *Butch Cassidy and the Sundance Kid* than *The Three Musketeers*."

Chapter 40
1994
London

Olav Rebrov looked at his boss of the last twenty years. "Sergei, why do you insist on coming here."

Sergei Levchenko smiled at his consigliere. "I miss the old days, my friend. This makes me feel alive, this world of ours is too sanitized. Sometimes it is good to go back."

Olav shook his head, a gesture not missed by his boss.

"Come, Olav, let's see what's happening."

The door creaked open and a rhythmic tapping on the iron stairs announced their arrival. Arkady's face darkened. He signalled to four of his men. "Search them again." Seconds later Dennis and Gregor were against the wall.

"What the fuck do you think you're doing?" Dennis shouted.

"They know," said Gregor.

Dennis Whiting looked at him. "Know what? What are you talking about?"

"Arkady, this is no way to treat our guests, let them go." Arkady let his men finish the search. They found nothing and released them.

Sergei Levchenko stood, hands across his chest, smiling. "Olav, this is just like the old days, don't you think?" He watched as the boxes were unloaded and checked. "You know, I think my presence here is unsettling everyone. The atmosphere is very tense, look at Arkady, he wants this to be over, thinks my being here is unnecessary and dangerous, just as you do."

When the last of the boxes had been checked, Arkady looked at Dennis. "You can go," he said.

Dennis and Gregor turned, walked towards the van and opened the doors. Gregor reached for the gun hidden beneath the seat but was stopped in his tracks by rapping on the steel shutters. Arkady looked at the bank of CCTV monitors. All were clear except the one covering the entrance.

He looked at Sergei. "Three men, not police."

Sergei walked the few yards to the monitors and smiled. "It's OK, it's Harry, let them in." The doors slid open, and Harry, Jason and Eastham rushed in.

"Harry, what are you doing here?"

"I need to speak to you, Sergei."

Eastham was looking at Gregor, as was one of Sergei's men, not distracted by Harry's arrival. Gregor could not reach for the gun as it would now be too obvious; he would never get a shot fired. He whispered, "Dennis, that is the man who killed my family."

"What are you talking about, what is wrong with you?"

Gregor had an empty look in his eyes. "He must die."

"Don't you do a thing, you crazy Russian bastard. You'll get us both killed."

Jason's eyes settled on the man who had put a twelve-inch scar down the back of the woman he loved, the thought of emptying his gun into him played through his mind.

Arkady's eyes were drawn to the slight bulge in Eastham's jacket. He looked at Harry and Jason and realised they were all carrying guns. He took his gun from his shoulder holster and shouted in Russian to his men. Harry, Jason and Eastham were pinned against the wall.

"Arkady, what are you doing?" The anger in Sergei's voice was genuine.

Arkady spun Eastham round and pushed his head into the wall and pulled the handgun from Eastham's holster. "They are here to kill you, Sergei."

"Why, Harry?" Sergei asked.

Everyone's attention had turned towards Harry, Jason and Eastham. Moving slowly, Gregor reached inside the car and picked up the gun. Then raised it and aimed at Sergei Levchenko.

Jason's eyes had returned to the man he wanted to kill. "Gun!" he shouted. But it was too late. He could only look on as the bullet hit its target and Sergei fell to the floor.

Arkady emptied both his and Eastham's gun into Gregor and Dennis, then went to the two motionless bodies, replaced the clip in his gun and shot them both again.

Oleg was leaning over Sergei, a hand on the wound. "Get off, Oleg," said Sergei. Blood was seeping from the wound, as he got up. "Come on, let's get out of here, and bring those three."

The blood and brains were washed off the van and Harry, Jason and Eastham were thrown into the back, hands tied and duct tape over their mouths. Arkady hit Eastham with the butt of his newly acquired AK47. They left the warehouse, and as they passed the Prospect of Whitby, they heard the sound of police sirens.

Valentina looked at her daughter. "Anna, what has happened? You seem happier than I have seen you in a long time."

"Mother, the man on the boat the other day that you met."

She interrupted her daughter. "I thought you liked him, but your father would never approve of him, you know that don't you?"

"He is the man I fell in love with, in Spain. I still love him. I have never stopped loving him."

"You are full of surprises and have a stubbornness like your father. I have always admired it, but at times it gets you into trouble. My darling, what am I to do with you?" She hugged her daughter. "I'll talk to your father, we'll sort this out, I promise you."

Chapter 41
1994
London

They stopped and listened to the swishing sound of large gates opening and then closing, coming to a gentle halt about thirty seconds later. Harry, Jason and Eastham were dragged out of the van and thrown onto the floor of a large barn. Sergei, Oleg and Arkady walked in. Sergei had a bandage on his arm, but blood had seeped through, etching a bright red pattern which resembled the sickle on the Russian flag.

"Harry, I am very disappointed," he said. "I was fair with you and invited you to meet my family. I will kill all of you myself, but first I want to hear you beg for your life. Arkady, remove the duct tape."

"Sergei, wait, the man you killed was Russian. Someone you know, Gregor, the man who put a scar down your daughter's back. He was there to kill you because you killed his family. We only found out today, and were coming to warn you, why do you think Jason shouted when he saw the gun?"

"I thought I recognised him. But how did you know it was him?" Sergei replied.

"Mr Levchenko, please don't kill Harry, he's a kind man, a great man," said Jason. "And what he's saying is true. I met Anna in Spain and we fell in love, I was going to bring her to England, but she was gone when I returned, as you know. We tried to find her. My father found Gregor and got the truth from him, that it was you who had taken her and not him."

"He worked for one of our associates," said Harry. "Mickey tortured him and decided he'd been punished enough, so decided to let him live. We didn't tell Jason he worked for Dennis, the other body on the floor tonight. It was only an hour ago that Jason told me he'd met your daughter on the boat. I realised the danger to you, as you had offed his family, and well, that would upset most people, wouldn't it. We came as soon as we could to warn you."

Sergei looked at Jason. "You have a lot of explaining to do."

Arkady checked the mechanism of his gun. The clicking sound, like a pin dropping in a silent room, got everyone's attention.

"There has been enough killing for one day, Arkady, take them to their homes." He turned towards Harry. "Both of you come to the boat tomorrow at two, we will discuss this then. I personally have had enough excitement for one day." He left with a driver and made his way back to the yacht.

Sergei got out of the car and walked slowly towards the yacht. He saw his daughter silhouetted in the moonlight but pretended not to have noticed her. "What hidden depths you hold, my daughter," he half-whispered to himself.

She watched him board the yacht, noticing the tenseness in his walk. In the light, she saw the glistening red patch that had worked its way through his shirt. She called her mother, who was nearby, reading a book, "Mother, father is hurt!"

They rushed to meet him. "Valentina, it is nothing, please do not fuss. I will get Anthony to get his needle and thread. I hope he's not lost his skills after all this time."

The doctor began stitching the ragged piece of flesh on Sergei's shoulder. "You are very lucky this man could not shoot, Sergei, one inch to the right and I would be looking for pieces of bone. Three inches, and I would be putting you in a box."

"It is not time for me to die yet, old man. You have become my closest friend after all these years together, but would it be possible on this occasion, that you just do your job?"

Dr Anthony Barinov continued the delicate stitching. "I'm serious, Sergei, you're getting too old for these things, why were you even there? I think you sometimes yearn for the old days. They were good days, I remember them, but a man must age well, like a good wine. We must remember the important things, like our families and their happiness."

Valentina looked at the doctor, glad of the conversation she'd had with him, less than forty minutes ago.

"Please, old man, finish your stitching, you are talking like an old woman." Sergei looked at his wife. "Why do I get the impression you two have had one of your chats?"

Anna moved towards her father and held his face in her hands. "Father, are you OK? Tears welled in her eyes.

Sergei looked at his daughter. "Yes, my darling. More important, how are you?"

Chapter 42
1994
London

They had stayed in Harry's office overnight, chewing the fat and wondering how long they had to live.

"Well, kid, never a dull moment. Are you looking forward to seeing your father-in-law?"

"Very funny, Harry. Are you coming, or are you going to slip away?" Harry was busy snorting a line. "Is there a record for the longest line ever? Because if there is, you just broke it."

Harry wiped small tears from his eyes as the coke hurtled past them liked a speeding train to his cerebral cortex. "Now look, we've had this conversation before, musketeers, all for one and all that. Oh yes, I wouldn't miss this for the world. All's well that ends well. Or probably not in this case."

"How is the new hair growth potion coming on? What a shame it would be for you to have finally found one that works, and not have time to try it."

"You're sounding like Mickey. It's not a potion, and I'm not a witch. One thing I can tell you, there has never been a bald eunuch. The choice is clear, a penis or hair."

"Well by the end of the day, we might have neither."

"Yes, good point, well made," Harry replied.

1.45 p.m.

Anna sat playing with her hands at the table. "Mother, this feels like my first day at school." She heard the footsteps as her father approached. The door opened.

"So, my dear wife and daughter, what is this thing you want to tell me? I hope it will not displease me. You know, I had a bad day yesterday, so think very carefully about what you want to tell me."

Anna looked at her mother, who stumbled with her words. "Maybe we should leave this, Sergei. You are right, my love, your arm must be hurting, and we could have lost you."

Anna moved towards her father. "No, Mother, I must speak. Father, there's something I must tell you. I love you and I know this will hurt you."

He raised his hand. "My daughter, there is nothing you can tell me today, that will hurt me. You are too precious to me. I lost you once, I will not lose you again."

Anna's lips began to tremble. "There is, Father."

"Don't speak, Anna, there is something I want to show you, wait here." He nodded to Oleg, who followed him through the door.

1.52 p.m.

Sergei Levchenko walked through the door where Jason and Harry were waiting. "Jason, Harry, sit down. Yesterday was very interesting. It has been a long time since I have been so close to death. It's a very poor start to our business relationship when one of your men tries to kill me."

Harry grimaced. "Look, I know this has all got a bit messy, and your good countryman, are legendary for keeping things clean and simple, but I've been cheering myself up with the vague thought that if we were going to die, we would be dead already.

It's a small hope, but one that I have been holding onto with all of my might, through a very long and sleepless night."

Jason put his hand on Harry's knee and gestured for him to be quiet. "Mr Levchenko, what happened is because of me, not Harry, and if I'm to suffer, then that must be, but please, take Harry with you to Russia. He will be a great asset. None of what happened is because of him. He was a true and loyal friend to my father and will be the same to you. I loved your daughter from the moment I saw her and have not stopped loving her for one single second. I know you wouldn't choose me for your daughter, but we can't help who we fall in love with."

Sergei was smiling. "You talk a lot, young man, maybe you are talking yourself into trouble. My daughter has never spoken about you, except to say, she loved you, but it was a very short time together. You did not get to know each other in those few days."

"With respect, you're wrong, you can't know the feelings we have, and I know you met your wife and were married after less than two months together, for the very same reason, you loved each other."

Sergei smiled again. "You have done your homework well, but I am not here to play chess with you. You could have got us all killed."

"Can I ask, why such a clever man as yourself would put himself in the position you did?"

Sergei laughed. "That is a good question, young man, and one I have been asked a few times in the last twenty-four hours. Maybe, this is like a game of chess, which is my favourite game. Sometimes when people speak to me as you are, they do not see the next day. Arkady here, is very frustrated you are both not already dead. But I admire your bravery and the honesty of your words. Also, this is more complicated because of my daughter. As for Gregor, I do not like even to mention the name. You already know, his family died to pay for his crimes against my daughter. Do you not see, it's very dangerous to be with my daughter?"

"I think we can all agree on that, Mr Levchenko, but to compare me with him is wrong and an insult. I would never do anything to harm your daughter."

"I am not insulting you, what I am doing is making things very clear to you. As we have seen, misunderstandings can be very costly."

"If I ever gave you cause to kill me because of your daughter, I'd put the bullet in the gun for you."

"I might hold you to that." Sergei turned towards Harry. "Harry, you are very quiet, what do you make of the words of this young man?"

"In my opinion, he would make the finest of sons."

Sergei laughed out loud. "Harry, you are a very funny man. Wait here both of you," he said, leaving the room.

2.15 p.m.

Anna, Valentina and Dr Barinov looked at Sergei as the door swung open, all wondering what was going on. "Father, I must speak with you."

"Yes, it is time for us to speak, but it has been a very difficult few days as you know. The young man you met on the boat, Jason, his men tried to kill me yesterday. I was foolish to let you be alone with him, he could have killed you." He looked at his daughter and saw the shock in her eyes.

"No, Father, that cannot be, he would never have done such a thing."

"Anna, do you not see the evidence before you?" He indicated his bandaged shoulder. "Why do you defend this man, after such a short time together? What potion has he given you to make you say such things?

Anna had inherited her father's sharpness and was beginning to understand he knew much more than he was telling them. "Father, you know he was the Englishman in Spain, don't you?"

"Yes, I know it was him. Arkady is with him now."

"Father, please!"

The fear in her voice startled him. "Nothing will happen to him today. Why do you speak this way? Do you still have feelings for him?"

"I do, Father, I love him, I've never stopped loving him, from the moment I looked into his eyes. I could not believe it when I saw him the other day, I was happy again. Fate had returned love and meaning to my heart, and now fate is robbing me of it again. Father, please don't hurt him. If it means never seeing him again to save his life, then please let him live, and I promise you I will never see him again."

Sergei saw the tears in her eyes. "Anna, you would truly do that, such is your love for him?"

"Yes, I would. I don't believe he tried to kill you. He would not do that. Somehow, Father, you have this quite wrong."

"I did not say he tried to kill me, I said one of his men tried to kill me. He decided not to tell her it was Gregor. Olav, bring them in."

"What, he's here on the boat?" said Anna.

"Yes, and now I will see you together."

When Olav opened the door, all Jason could see was Anna. They walked slowly towards each other; no one tried to stop them.

"What are your intentions, young man?" Sergei's face was expressionless.

"I intend to marry your daughter, sir, with your permission." Anna looked at her father.

"I will think about it tonight when I get to know him a little better," said Sergei, looking at his daughter. "How beautiful you look today, Anna, I see the happiness in your eyes. Could it be this man you love does not know something very important to us?"

"No, Father, he doesn't." Anna grinned shyly at Jason.

Jason looked at her, confused. "What are you talking about?"

"Give me two minutes, and Father, please don't hurt him while I'm out of the room."

He laughed. "I will not."

Anna squeezed Jason's hand as she turned to leave. Sergei moved slowly towards Dr Barinov, but the movement caused him to wince as a sharp pain exploded in his shoulder. "Anthony, would you get me some more pain killers? And also bring the other thing we spoke about."

"Of course, but I think you will need an injection. That's causing you more pain than you're letting on." He too turned and walked through the open door.

"So many surprises, Harry, in a few short days. I shall be happier when life is quieter again and will be more careful about wishing for excitement in the future."

Harry grinned. "Yes, very wise words, Sergei."

At that, they all heard the sound of footsteps from the doorway and turned to see who had entered. Anna stepped into the room and closed the door behind her. By her side, holding her hand was a small blonde girl, whose, other hand, tightly clutched a teddy bear to her chest. Jason could not see her face, as it was buried deep in the folds of her mother's dress.

"This is Natasha," said Anna. "She is three years old; I'd like you to meet her. Jason, she is your daughter. Natasha, are you going to say hello to your daddy?"

Jason could think of nothing to say for a moment, then got down on one knee and gazed at the child. Slowly, sensing his presence, she turned and stared into his blue eyes. Her own were exactly the same colour.

There came a knock on the door and at the sound, Sergei spoke again. "So that is Anna's surprise for you, Jason. I hope it is a pleasant one. But it is perhaps not the biggest surprise for today. He turned towards the door. "Enter," he called softly.

The door slowly opened. There standing in front of them in a sharply pressed suit, looking as fit and well as Jason had ever seen him and wearing a broad grin on his face, was a man both he and Harry knew very well. A man they had been certain they would never see again. Mickey Warren.

"You didn't think I'd really done myself in did you?" said Mickey, laughing at his son's white face. "Come on you two, pick your jaws off the floor, you look as if you've seen a ghost. Now then, Sergei, where's that vodka you promised us?"